Shadows Over Dawnland

By James T. Powers

For information, or to order additional copies, please contact:

Beacon Publishing Group
P.O. Box 41573 Charleston, S.C. 29423
800.817.8480| beaconpublishinggroup.com

Publisher's catalog available by request.

ISBN-13: 978-1-949472-35-6

ISBN-10: 1-949472-35-6

Published in 2021. Printed in the USA.

First Edition. New York, NY 10001

Dedicated to the Quinnipiac People;

Past, Present, and Future.

Table of Contents

Chapter One

The flames formed a swirling column of red and orange as they towered upward, singeing the green leaves of the tree branches above and wrapping them in a gray cloak of smoke that merged with those of the other twelve burning weetous forming an undulating cloud above the village. That awful morning, the fires consumed the homes of my parents and others who had recently died from the horrific pestilence we were powerless to stop. The sound of the crackling flames was accompanied by the eerie, wailing cries of anguish from those of us who still lived. How could this be I had asked myself over and over as I stood numbed by shock, my eyes fixed upon the burning weetous I had shared with my mother, father, and sister until just a few days ago.

The fire eagerly ate away at the reed matts that had been the skin of the weetous, quickly exposing the frame of saplings that formed its skeleton. Everything my family had possessed except for a few of my personal belongings had been left inside for the fire to consume and through the smoke, bring them to my family's new home in the Spirit World where they would live happily with Keihtan, the Creator. They each had died, one after the other within three days; first my sister, then father, and finally mother. All suffered from fevers and were so weakened by pain they could not lift their heads from where they lay. Unable to swallow, they could not drink or eat. They died covered with bloody red spots and sores, the terrifying mark of the sickness. All I could do was sit by them, terrified by what was happening and the thought that I too might suffer their fate but even worse, be left alone.

Commossuck, our village shaman, tried valiantly to the point of exhaustion to remove the sickness that had found its way into them, using all his skill as a healer and conduit to the Spirit World. He had done the same for others from our band, the Mennunkatuck, but was only able to guide a few to overcome the sickness the strange men from across the sea called smallpox. Of that handful of survivors, one was my best friend Shambisqua, daughter of our sachem, the sunksquaw Shaumpishuh.

Little did I know that terrible day of the burning weetous, that it would be the start of my fifty year journey to follow in the footsteps of Commossuck in trying to help my people, the Quinnipiac, survive the flood of calamities that accompanied the arrival of the Awaunuy (English, "the coat wearers") to the shores of our Dawnland. I know now, from the perspective of time and age, that the dark shadows that formed under the smoke of those fires still have not disappeared and that my challenge, like that of

Commossuck, continues to be to guide the few survivors of the People through them to a place of light and life.

Through the hardened memories of my many years, it is easy for me to see how innocent we were. Trapped by a destiny forged by a collision of two worlds, how could we the People have known the heartbreak and suffering that would engulf our way of life? On the morning of the burning weetous, dark shadows began to descend and only thickened as the cycle of time spun on in its inevitable way. But as shaman of the People, I know the light of the past, much faded and obscured, still shines at the edge of the darkness; but is it too late to save our way of being? Though old and tired now, I still trust in Keihtan and will continue to search for a way around those shadows, or I will be forever haunted by them when I leave this life to dwell among the Spirits.

As Father Sun began his journey sinking into the sacred mountain tears formed in my eyes. This I knew would be my last summer solstice when the sun began its journey away, bringing the warmth of summer that would slowly fade into the cold of winter that slowly overwhelms all living things. Above the face of Hobomock, chiseled by his own hand into the stony side of the ridge, Father Sun formed a halo of light streaking brilliantly across the clouds to the west and behind the ridge that held the great healer. I began to cry.

How many times had I followed the line of sacred stones to this very spot from where the Quinnihticut met the sea—to appeal to Hobomock to heal the spirit of our people. Perhaps this time Hobomock might grant a sign showing a way to end the disasters that have overwhelmed the Quinnipiac and all others who dwell here in the Dawnland. Looking upon the face of Hobomock, I began to chant the sacred words passed down to me by Commossuck and generations beyond knowing.

As the Spirit Words urgently left my lips, the shadows of the setting sun mixed with the brilliant glow of its diminishing light danced around me confirming the presence of Manitou—the essence of all life and energy in the three Worlds. Here I was witnessing the great struggle between darkness and light that had engulfed the People. As the sun slid behind the ridge, I chanted the ancient words, appealing to Hobomock to come to our aid. While the clouds still held the glowing embers of burnt orange and red that played across the heavens, the shadows began to thicken into dusk and the face of Hobomock began to fade in the lessening light.

"What is the answer I seek?" at first I whispered, then found myself shouting so Hobomock could hear clearly. "What is the answer? Can the spirit and life of the People be healed?"

In the growing shadows, a warm breeze came suddenly from the southwest, the home of Keihtan the Creator, rising through the valley below that separated the western ridge line from the one on which I sat. With it came the smells of the forest which wrapped themselves around me like a familiar robe. Struggling to see the fading image of Hobomock, I suddenly understood. The stone face of Hobomock, as it always has, was turned to the north and it was then that I heard the voice I pleaded to hear as it moved in the wind. It simply said, "away".

Yes, away! But where? To the north with our brothers the Tunxis, along the river the Awaunuy call Farmington, to join the many who have already left? Awaunuy settlements on the river were already aggressively expanding and it would only be a temporary refuge. Farther north to join the Mahicans along the far reaches of the Housatonic? Even they are feeling the relentless, encroaching pressure from the land hungry Awaunuy farmers and their black-coated speakers of their book. Or should we seek refuge with our feared and untrustworthy enemy the Mohawk, beyond the great western river? No. I know we must find a way and a place where we can live our lives as Keihtan the Creator has always allowed us to live. So where, I continued to wonder, is away?

My plan was to spend the night on the ridge top facing Hobomock so I might wake in the morning to see the sun's first rays of light strike the face of the Great Healer. When that happened, I would know if the answer whispered in the wind was true, and in that I would know how to advise the People. While gathering dead branches and dried grass, a slight distance from the shear drop off of my perch, I recalled how after so many journeys here, that despite the hard surface of the stone that formed my viewing place, I was where I needed to be for the dawning. It was here I would sit as always, to watch, and listen for Hobomock. I took comfort that all around me were the sounds of this beautiful world; the slight breeze through the branches, our winged relations singing their evening songs, the insects and katydids saluting summer's warmth, and the familiar footsteps of the four-legged brothers and sisters.

While watching the last bit of day disappear to the west still defined by Hobomock's ridgeline, the air around me began to cool. Behind me to the east, through the stubby oaks and pines that surrounded me on the ridgetop, I could see the evening's first stars and I thanked them, the spirits of the ancestors.

"Yes" I said. "Ancestors, I need your help. The People look to me to ask for guidance." As I returned to chanting softly and rhythmically in the way

Commossuck taught me so long ago, the sky darkened and with it all around me. It was Commossuck who first noticed in me the gifts of a shaman, and the great powwow of our Mennunkatuck band of the Quinnipiac began to show me the ways of a dream walker and healer.

"Keihtan has chosen you for this and I see in you the qualities of a shaman if you dedicate yourself to that purpose and life," he had told me one evening as we sat on the great rocks that marked the sea's edge just to the south of our village. I remember how his dark eyes pierced my very soul at that moment to reinforce his words through the power of his spirit. With his great bear robe wrapped around him to ward off the winter chill, and his wild graying hair, he seemed to me Keihtan himself. Neither of us spoke for the longest time as together we watched the waves break against the rocks. When he rose to walk back to the village I did as well. Thus, began my journey into the mysteries of the Spirit World, and a life of traveling between the Sky World, the Earth World, and the Lower World for the benefit of the People.

It was during the winter of my twelfth snow after the loss of my parents and sister to the Awaunuy's smallpox, I was invited by Commossuck to live in his weetou. Commossuck had lost his wife and only son to the disease, which shook him to his very core and the People said he became withdrawn and sullen, that part of him had died with them. But the common bond of loss brought us together. Once taken in by him, Commossuck did not talk with me of becoming a powwow but looking back I realize how he had often tested me in ways that probed for the gifts that only Keihtan could give. As the months passed I watched and listened and began to understand how Commossuck had the ability to connect with the Spirit World. He strove to help the People maintain their spiritual and physical health as individuals and as a community, not just for our Mennunkatuck band, but for members of the other three bands at Mioonkhtuck, Totoket, and the Upper Quinnipiac. Even the Wangunk of Mattabasec on the Quinnihticut would call on Commossuck for his ability to prophesy and heal by the power of Manitou, the spiritual energy that pervaded all living and nonliving things within the universe and kept all in balance.

Exhausted yet energized after two days and a night of continuous climbing to reach the viewing platform, I continued to chant repeatedly the Spirit Words as I sat in the darkness. They would allow me to enter the Dream World where Hobomock might help me to see more clearly. Above me was the blanket of ancestors that formed the top of the Sky World, and below me the rock-hard surface of the Earth World. To my left was a great boulder taller than a man and as wide as a weetou. The boulder had split in half forming an opening to the Lower World. From which direction the vision might come only Hobomock knew. I had learned long ago to trust and allow it to happen in a sacred place such as this. I had intended to start a small fire but decided against it, instead finding comfort in the darkness and the sounds of nature, as well as the great silence the dark brought as it deepened. I hoped to achieve the trance state that would allow me to dream walk and see what needed to be known.

A wolf howled to the north and was quickly answered by another in the valley below my overlook. An owl appeared on the branch of a thick, twisted oak shaped low by countless winds. I knew my winged friend was curious to know who was visiting this sacred spot as she peered down at me in a way only her kind can. A rustling sound of a small, four-footed foraging for food behind me which caught the owl's attention and with a quick swoosh of her wings, she flew behind me to pounce on her meal only to be disappointed by her dinner's hasty retreat. As I continued my chanting I thought of how the owl and I had not eaten; the winged sister due to luck, and me due to the fast I began two days ago. It was part of the spiritual cleansing I performed as I climbed each of the ridges, following the line of sacred stones that brought me to this spot.

As the night thickened the air began to change as the breeze from the southwest grew stronger and warmer. It carried with it the smell of rain and the sound I often heard in my ears—a buzzing sound, that accompanied the trance state that preceded my entering the Dream World. Over and over, I repeated the spirit sounds that would help my mind, body, and spirit change, and bring with it my spirit helper, the red-tailed hawk. She was my guide on journeys into the Spirit World. Once there, transformed together, we might see a vision of the future I sought.

Just as Commossuck had helped me to see years ago how my dream soul could leave my body and walk, or in my case fly into the Spirit World, I began to see the top of the ridge where I sat chanting through the eyes of a hawk. Soon I was free and flying in the quickening breeze with my guide as the dark of night receded and the sun showed itself through clouds. Up the valley we flew past the face of Hobomock then turned back down it to the hunting camp of Nausup, the son of the Shaumpishuh. He had recently given over in a treaty with the Awaunuy of the town of Guilford, the last territory of the Mennunkatuck band that included the sacred face of Hobomock. At their camp by the lake called Quonnipaug, Nausup and his small party were busy with three deer they had recently taken. My guide and I did not linger but moved quickly through a blanket of fog that rose out of nowhere to arrive to visit the remnants of the Quinnipiac band at Mioonkhtuck on the eastern shore of the inlet they shared with the Awaunuy. I could see the weetous of the People in their village and the growing and filthy Awaunuy town called New Haven across the water.

While we circled Mioonkhtuck, the principal village of the People, I could see and feel the suffering and desperation that emanated from the place. I wanted to descend but I could not as my winged guide pulled me north and through another thick bank of fog-like clouds. We entered a valley I did not know. High, wooded hills framed a small village nestled along a stream and I recognized some of the people as ours. Before I could grasp where this valley was, the vision ended. A sudden loud popping noise brought me back to my body as the wind had increased and brought with it clouds and rain. My winged guide knew the danger of the storm and brought me back safely just as a branch, broken in the wind, fell a few feet behind where I sat. I woke with windblown rain against my face. Reaching for my robe made of deerskin and not of Awaunuy wool as so many of our people now used. I covered myself and slept.

I woke before dawn as the sky began to lighten. A soft, pleasant breeze from the north and a cloudless sky had swept away the storm and rain. I was surrounded by the sweet scent of the wet earth, stone, and leaves and I paused to thank Keihtan for the gift of another day in a place both sacred and beautiful. The face of Hobomock was still in shadow since it was too soon for the rising of Father Sun behind me to strike the image. I began to consider the vision seen in my journey and saw in each part, a significant message I would have to bring to the People. There was Nausup's hunting camp, the main village at Mioonkhtuck, and the unknown valley nestled in the high wooded mountains. Judging from the steepness of the hills and the types of trees, it must truly be to the north—perhaps beyond even the territory of the Mahicans.

If only I knew for sure I thought. Some of our people were mixed with others at the village in that valley. Does it mean we must band with others who also want to leave behind our ancient homelands to escape from the pressures and turmoil caused by the Awaunuy? These questions I must seek answers to. If only Commossuck was still alive to help me understand. But, this is my journey, as he once had his in his time.

My thoughts returned to my youth when Commossuck had begun to question his ability to help the People. We faced diseases he could not cure, as well as the overwhelming challenges brought by the Awaunuy; their strange ways, alluring trade goods, powerful weapons, and their insatiable thirst for more land to call their own. The sachems and their councils all tried fruitlessly to understand how to coexist with the increasing flood of these Puritans, as we heard some call them. The People constantly turned to Commossuck and the powwows of the other bands as they together struggled to find answers and restore a balance to the world.

Some of the People began to believe and whisper that Keihtan, Hobomock, and the entire Spirit World had abandoned us, but Commossuck did not believe it was so. He worked tirelessly despite his growing age to find answers; he knew the People had not been abandoned. In this work he guided me and since his death so many snows ago I have lived my life dedicated to finding the path. Have I finally found it?

Just then the first rays of Father Sun began to tickle the top of the cliff above Hobomock's face and I resumed my chanting looking for confirmation of what the vision had brought me. Slowly, the line of brightness descended, making the stone of the red-brown cliff come alive with color and fire. I continued to chant, louder and with more energy as the brightness on the rocky surface continued its downward path. Then, like the sudden brilliance of a firebrand first lit in the night, the full face, stern and strong in its ancient profile, a face as eternal and old as the Earth Mother herself, exploded in light. I paused my chanting to take in the message knowing for sure what I must do. At that moment, a lone cloud behind me shut off the light and the face of Hobomock faded into the side of the cliff. I turned solemnly to look behind me to see a great puffy cloud of white and gray pierced by streaking jets of amber and red from the rising Father behind and understood. This I must also tell the People.

A bit stunned and at first unwilling to move, I slowly turned back to look again at the dull face of Hobomock and knew it was time to return to the People. I would cross through the territory recently given by Nausup to the Awaunuy to my weetou in Totoket. There I would wait and make sure I understood the visions and the messages given to me before speaking to the sachems and their council at the Council Rock at Mioonkhtuck.

"First I must offer a sacrifice" I said out loud and I bent over to open my satchel made of fine otter fur, a gift given to me by Commossuck at the time of his leaving us. I carried many of the sacred plants I used for healing and dream walks in it as well as my pipe, held safe in the fur of one of Hobomock's water animals that was for many shamans a spirit helper like the powwow from the Paugassett to the west of the Quinnipiac. I took out my sacred pipe with the carved image of the Thunderbird, the powerful transformer of the Sky World and helper of Keihtan and filled it with the sacred leaves of tobacco. Striking my fire stones together to light some dry grass I lit some embers, then the tobacco, and offered the sacred smoke to Hobomock, Keihtan, and all the sacred spirits of Manitou.

Chapter Two

I began my descent from the sacred place with much on my mind but also much gratitude for the gifts I had been given. How many of my ancestors had gone to the edge of the ridge to look on the face of Hobomock with the hope of divining an omen that would help lead the People through a time of challenge? How many had followed the ancient spirit line of stone structures each with its powerful meaning, to witness the solstice? Making my way down the wooded slope, I hoped I would not be the last.

At the base of the ridge I looked across the valley through the trees at the face of Hobomock and hoped the great healer's message in the vision would help the People begin life anew. The cloud that rose to shadow Hobomock troubled me and I knew I would need more time and perhaps more dream walking to find the true meaning. Crossing a meadow I walked towards a path that led from Mennunkatuck on the shore to the great swamp called Coginchaug to the north where my people often hunted and met with our brothers and sisters the Wangunk who lived at the great bend of the Quinnihticut beyond. For all the people of the Dawnland, swamps were places of strong Manitou and in times of peril were often used as a place of refuge. But with the coming of the

Awaunuy these havens had failed many; the once mighty Pequot, the Narragansett on the great bay to the east, and even Metacom who had led the uprising ten snows ago in the futile attempt to drive the Awaunuy back into the sea where the power of Hobomock might crush them and restore the land to the People. I thought about the lengthy discussion at the Council Rock at Mioonkhtuck about Metacom and his uprising, and though most were sympathetic to his cause, the majority counselled against joining. Having lived with the Awaunuy so close across the harbor and at Totoket as well, the elders spoke of the futility in fighting them. Besides, the men from New Haven town lingered close to hear what was said and even warned of the dire consequences we would face if any sided with Metacom.

So, as a result we chose a different path along with most of the other surviving bands of people left in the Awaunuy Connecticut, their name for the great tidal river, Quinnihticut that cut through the territory they had traded for or simply taken over the years to make their place of refuge from their king across the sea. They said it was here they could serve their god found only in their holy black book and meeting houses. I had always thought it curious that this god did not live elsewhere, not in the sky, earth, the rest of world that surrounds us all, or even people. But this god had great power and the Awaunuy used it to crush Metacom and all who rose with him. In the end, so many of the others in Dawnland perished in Metacom's war that the survivors became the wretched pawns of the colony on the bay of the Massachusetts or the Mohegan Uncas. He had sided twice with the Awaunuy, first against his brothers the Pequot and then against Metacom. I did not trust the powerful Mohegan sachem but understood he had chosen his own path for his people becoming what the Awaunuy called ally and friend. In that way Uncas hoped to save his people and coexist with the Awaunuy. But his aggression towards others, including the Quinnipiac was distasteful to me.

Crossing the meadow, I came to a stream and stopped for a drink. As I cupped my hands to gather water a stag arrived a bit downstream. I could tell from the felt covered points of his growing antlers and his size that he had seen many snows like myself. "Good morning old man, I am thirsty as well," seeing in his age and size a great dignity. "Let us drink together and refresh ourselves before our journeys continue." The stag hesitated then dipped his head to drink though warily watching me as he did so. How odd it is that even the four-legged people are so careful around us now since the coming of the Awaunuy. Everything in nature, the Awaunuy have told us, is here for their benefit and taking including our fellow creatures of the world. They hunt with great disrespect to the animal spirits. We, the People, have always paid homage to the spirit of those we must kill for food; it is necessary to ensure their return so we might all live in harmony. In this way, they allow us to share through their life our own. But now, since the Awaunuy hunt indiscriminately and without the offering of respect and thanks, the four-legged ones are dwindling in number. Sadly, some of our people have taken up this form of hunting to trade meat with the Awaunuy for their goods they now believe they cannot live without.

"It is clear you know I mean you no harm, and that I admire your beauty and strength" I told my brother. In answer, the stag lifted his head and bowed to me, then he turned and moved silently into the forest. I waited quietly by the stream and ate the maize cake and dried rabbit I had brought with me when I first started my journey from the place the Awaunuy call Saybrook where standing stones of Manitou marked the start of the Spirit Line though it does exist across the water in the land of the Montaukett. There had once been a small village of the Niantic before the coming of the Awaunuy but they left their village after the second year of smallpox and moved to their villages on the east side of the river. It was near there the Awaunuy had built their fort just as the war with the Pequot began and had been the home of

Weequash, the Niantic who had married a woman from our Mennunkatuck band. I remember he had taken the side of the Awaunuy and had guided them to the great massacre of the Pequot at Mistick. He was said to have become the first of the People to become a Christian, as the Awaunuy call their religion, and some say he was killed for it. This I do not know for sure but suspect it was so.

Not having eaten for almost three days during my sacred walk along the Spirit Line, I sat by the stream and ate eagerly, after thanking Keihtan for the gift of nourishment. I thought of how the Spirit Line passed as straight as an arrow, shot by a great warrior, through territory in which the ancient ones had constructed the stone snakes, turtles, standing stones, chambers, and cairns too numerous to count. The line ultimately led to the face of Hobomock. I felt the tremendous power and energy of the line and its stone structures while I climbed up and down each ridge and crossed each valley. I tried to walk as straight as possible through the mix of jagged rocks, gullies, swamps, and forests, instinctively guided by the energy of the line. At each effigy or cairn made of piled stones, I would offer prayers of thanks. Each was a unique connection with the energy of Manitou through the Sky World, Earth World, or the Lower World.

To move along the line was to share in an ancient pilgrimage and ritual that countless generations of powwows experienced; they felt the same power and energy and I felt a strong link with them. My thoughts turned back to the first time Commossuck had brought me to see the solstice and the lighting of the face of Hobomock. Not only was it an important ritual to appeal to Hobomock during a time of trouble for the Quinnipiac, but it was a dramatic emotional event for me. It connected me through time and place to the ancestors who built the structures and first studied the heavens to understand the energy that the Line released and represented. "How many times?" I said aloud to the Spirits as I sat by the stream. I cannot even begin to imagine how many shamans in the past walked the Spirit Line seeking aid.

Thinking back to that first time, I remembered how Commossuck brought me to a great many of the stone monuments and how, over time, I came to understand how many there were; numbers as great as the stars in the sky. The large ones were usually found right on, or close to the Line itself; Others scattered on either side and often at a distance. Some were large and took advantage of the natural landscape, some were built in a place full of spiritual meaning. This, Commossuck had told me, was particularly important when it came to the undulating stone snakes. These were dedicated to Hobomock, whose spirit often manifested in this animal. They were creatures of both the Earth World and the Lower World, and were associated with stone outcrops, stones split with cracks and fissures in them, as well as caves. Hobomock used the serpents to guard these entrances to the Lower World; having dream walked enough in my life, I know this to be true.

Many powwows used the snake as their spirit guide, while others relied on other creatures associated with Hobomock such as the water-dwelling eels, shellfish, beaver, and otters. These were all creatures who though inhabitants of water, also had the ability to live outside it. This duality was a quality of Hobomock, who often brought problems and suffering to individuals or entire groups, but also, through ritual appeal, was the great healer of the problem and suffering. This was, I had learned early in my apprenticeship, what made Commossuck such a powerful and important shaman. He had mastered the ability to appeal to Hobomock through his snake and water spirits and because of this, his abilities went beyond those of most powwows.

This was also a major reason why Commossuck found himself struggling with the challenges the Awaunuy had brought and how frustrated he became given the powerful gifts he had received from the Spirit World. Try as he might, the powwow found it impossible to summon the Manitou of Hobomock to heal the traumas that afflicted the People. Commossuck knew he was not alone in his feelings, as all the shamans of the Dawnland shared his sense of impotence. This created a deep crisis of confidence for some in the understanding of how the Spirit World worked. For the People, this also led to a general questioning of how everything in our universe worked, and this caused many to lose hope.

Spotting a raven that had been circling above the stream, I spoke to the black feathered being as much as to myself. "You know my friend together we have found over time that although I became familiar with the spirit helpers of Hobomock and can harness their power, my strength developed through you and our other winged brothers and sisters, all spirit helpers of Keihtan" I said as the raven descended to sit on a low branch on the opposite side of the stream. "You and the red-tailed hawk bring me help and answers and this time I hope you might as well." The raven sat quietly cocking his head while watching me finish my meal. As I stood to renew my journey down the path that would lead me to Totoket, the raven called out to his family who I then realized had been sitting on the limb of a mighty chestnut tree behind me. Together, the three flew north in the opposite direction of my intended route, calling out as they did; I saw it to be a good omen for the future as I contemplated the direction. "Messengers of Keihtan," I thought, "and as representatives of light and life itself this gives me hope."

As a powwow, my thoughts again drifted back to the Spirit Line of stone figures and cairns and my first time walking it with Commossuck. It was the year after the smallpox had so decimated the People for a second time and he was helping me to see this world through the eyes of a shaman. I recalled when I first saw the great whale cairn, a beautifully constructed mound of stones and boulders made in the shape of the greatest of those who dwelt in the sea and a powerful spirit helper of Hobomock. As tall as a man and long like the whale itself, it sat on one of the rises and pointed towards the ridge that held the face of Hobomock.

"Ponaim," Commossuck had said to me, "this is the most powerful of all Hobomock's helpers and it is always important to appease and honor him. Do you recall the story of the Montaukett who mocked Hobomock for allowing the Awaunuy to come to their land? Shortly after showing their disrespect, a group of their warriors were in their great canoe on the way to meet with the Pequot when a powerful whale rose from the depths and tossed them all into the sea. Two out of twelve survived."

I nodded for the story had frightened me when I first heard my father tell it and for a time I was reluctant to venture far into the water. Commossuck reminded me that I had nothing to fear from the great water beast, but to always make sure to acknowledge his power and strength. Our people have always honored the whale. We rejoiced with ritual prayers and dances if the hunt from our canoes was successful. If one died and washed ashore we showed our thanks for the great offering of food for the people. I remember how shocked the People were to learn how the Awaunuy and Dutchmannuck hunted them, not for food, but to boil their flesh to make something they called oil. What that was used for I do not understand nor do I want to.

Another stone cairn that had a special presence on the line was the great turtle, the symbol of Earth Mother herself, home to all living beings we call Turtle Island. With its great head and front legs protruding from a giant shell made of stones, she seemed anchored to the earth, and thus a reminder of the stability and strength the People have always drawn from the land around us. She is also a creature of two worlds, and helper of Hobomock. Many of the People have revered the turtle for its slow, but steady, stabilizing presence in their lives.

I also thought of the great horned serpent and the many smaller serpents scattered along the line and how like the snakes, were built of curving rows of stones. I found the great one particularly frightening when I first encountered it. The length of a great tree that had fallen in a windstorm, it was the size of the boulders and stones together with the one that formed the massive head holding the naturally carved features of a serpent that I found unsettling. "Why is that Commossuck?" I had asked my mentor. "What is it about the horned serpent that makes me uncomfortable?"

"It is because it represents the evil side of our existence and the darkness that can befall each of us" the powwow said. "But the horned serpents also represent the power of regeneration, healing, and the energy of life. They, more than anything else symbolize what life in this world really is for we people and all creatures who dwell in it. They are here to remind us of all that is both frightening and harmful and all that is beautiful and meaningful. They along with Hobomock himself are the two sides of life, opposites yet together."

"I see the snakes and serpents are all on the highest points of the Spirit Line just prior to the viewing places" I said to my teacher.

"Yes, they point the way to Hobomock. There are also many near the prayer seats where we chanted the ancient words of appeal to Hobomock and the rest of the spirit guides and their world,"

Commossuck reminded me. "They mark all the places to pause and examine the true purpose of what we are doing with the hope that through fasting and chanting you will, with the help of the ancients who built them, prove worthy of their help." I remember how these words made me shudder, but also how I felt myself empowered with the hope that I might prove myself worthy of continuing the work of a shaman as gifted as Commossuck.

"Remember Ponaim, the power also of the split rock and its energy that leads to the Lower World for it is from there that great knowledge can come. One must not be afraid to approach them, for if your mind and heart are pure you will experience the energy of that world and can journey there when required. It is a place of tremendous strength that can help you to see the future, heal the sick, and guide those who will listen."

It was then that one of the most important moments in my learning the ways of the shaman took place. Commossuck had suggested I approach one particularly large and towering boulder as tall and wide as two weetous and that seemed to have been cleaved in two by a mighty war hatchet. I approached it with trepidation. But as I approached the large crevasse, I felt the surrounding air pull me forward, and it seemed my feet were lifted almost off the ground as I walked. I stopped short of the great fissure to admire the sheer size of the boulder and the force that must have cracked it, dividing it wide enough for a man to enter.

"Can you feel its spirit energy Ponaim?" asked Commossuck. "If you step into the space you may feel it even more" he said firmly yet with encouragement. Not wanting to disappoint him, I stepped into the fissure only to feel the warmth of the stone walls on each side having been warmed by the afternoon sun, bathing me with a sense of comfort and security. I looked up towards the top of the boulder and could see the moss clinging to one edge and the blue sky shaped by the two openings on either side. It was then that a raven suddenly flew overhead directly in line with the fissure and I knew it was a sign of my acceptance from the spirits of the Sky World in my quest to learn from Commossuck. I looked down to see a young copperhead snake, a child of that spring, curl quickly around my left foot and move down deeper into another crack in the stone and disappear. Taken by surprise, I jumped out of the fissure with startling speed only to tumble onto the leaf-covered forest floor as Commossuck laughed in delight seeing his protégé pop out so quickly.

"You were as the dried corn kernels we pop over the fire Ponaim" he exclaimed through tears of laughter. You shot up into the air as if going into the

Sky World only to land squarely on the Earth. In one moment, you experienced all three worlds, a great and powerful sign. The Spirit World is strong in you, you must continue to learn to harness and work with it."

When I told him about the raven and the copperhead, Commossuck immediately took a more serious tone and strongly grasped my hand to ask if I understood the power of the message, a moment I knew helped shape my entire life. "Yes, I think I do" I recall saying and from then on my life was never the same. Somehow that fissure in the boulder had moved me from a possible shaman to one who knew my destiny and the role I would play in this life.

Chapter Three

"Such changes I have seen in these many years that have brought me to this time of my life when my bones ache in the morning and I cannot walk or run for as long as I could in my youth," I thought as I began to cross the stream and the meadow filled with summer flowers and tall grass towards the path that would lead me down to Quonnipaug lake. Quonnipaug had always marked the more northerly reaches of our ancestral home; my family and others would often camp in the many small, wooded valleys formed by the ridges near the lake in winter. From there, access to hunting just to the north beyond Hobomock's cliff in the lands shared with the Wangunks was a shorter distance. As a boy, I enjoyed the winter camp protected from the cold, damp winds that blew off the waters of the sea. There I had learned much from my father and the other men; how to craft tools from stone, use the bow, and hunt the four-legged who provided the People with meat during the time of snow. They were happy and good times even though the influence of those from across the sea was already being felt. Dutchmannuck traders had started coming to the land of the Quinnipiac in the years before my birth and as rivals of the Awaunuy had established for a time a house among the Totoket. There was also the small settlement of Awaunuy in the land of the Wampanoag to the east and I remember my father and others talking of their fear of this group.

The fact was those people were different than the Dutchmannuck. The men discussed this over their council fire, citing that unlike the Dutchmannuck who came to trade and take wood from the forest, these people who called themselves "separatists" in their tongue had come with women and children and a stated purpose to stay and live on Turtle Island. What they wanted to separate from I never learned. My father had spoken about how they wanted others to join them from across the sea and what they desired was more land on which to live and call their own. Their ways were strange and their view of this world and that of the Spirit World was difficult to comprehend. "It still makes no sense to me" I said to myself with a tinge of anger. On top of that, those people seemed to the Quinnipiac to be aggressive and uncompromising. Our men all felt that Massasoit, the Wampanoag sachem, had made a mistake in welcoming them, thinking he could use them against his enemies the Narragansett, and expand his influence over other people of the Dawnland. All that seemed so long ago and now part of a dark dream. But it was true the arrival of that group of Awaunuy had begun this period of disaster and humiliation for the People and once again I felt the all too familiar sense of frustration and guilt that was my constant companion and guiding spirit as it had been for Commossuck.

"So much has changed since the Awaunuy arrived" I said aloud. "Even the forest and meadows are different now, overgrown and choked and not as they once were when the People kept them clean and open." I remember the excitement in my childhood of the fall and spring burning when the meadowlands and underbrush of the forest were burned off with the result that the trees grew to great towering heights and the meadows grew fresh grass that brought the deer so important to our way of life. I cannot even remember the last time there had been a burn, and now the woodlands are often tangled with undergrowth and brush making it hard to hunt. In addition ,like those Dutchmannuck at Totoket, the Awaunuy cut the trees and send what they call lumber back to their home across the sea. At times I have heard the forest and mighty trees weep.

As I walked I brushed both hands across the tall meadow grass, and I recalled doing this as a boy all those years ago in Mennunkatuck before the Whitfield people had come and our sunksquaw Shaumpishuh had agreed to let them settle where our village had been. Yes, I thought, so many changes and heartaches over these many years and while walking I suddenly felt the return of the pain I always carried when thoughts welled up in my spirit of the deaths of my parents, sister, and all those I had loved and known. As the years passed and countless others had joined them, the Quinnipiac had been reduced to a small number of survivors; this was still for reasons beyond understanding. Yes, there were the diseases that the Awaunuy and others had brought with them, the abandonment of our traditional way of life that caused stress and famine, the disappearance of our four-legged brothers, and of course the liquor that created confusion and a strange madness in our men.

Yet these were merely symptoms and signs of what many of the People felt was punishment for some unknown transgression on their part. It always came down to a simple question which I lived with constantly - what caused the Spirit World to abandon the People? "There has to be a cause," I mused as I paused and looked skyward to see in the billowing white clouds, the hand of Keihtan. Try as we all had however, I, like Commossuck and the rest of the powwows of Dawnland had been unable to under-stand what it was. For unknown reasons, the world of the spirits had deserted the People and brought the Awaunuy and others to these shores. Even though many had given up in despair, I was determined to find a way through the darkness that had descended upon us.

What had happened to my people and all those of Dawnland weighed heavy on my soul and mind and for a moment gloom permeated my very being. But then I thought of my vision and the signs given to me on the ridge overlooking the face of Hobomock, and I thought maybe I had the answer that would at least allow my people, if they so choose, to find a place of refuge and yes, salvation. I suddenly chuckled to myself when I thought of that word, salvation. Salvation seemed to form the very core of what the black robed god-talkers of the Awaunuy always seemed to focus on. Pearson, that annoying god-talker at Totoket for many years constantly used that word when he harangued the People and like others, I remember how I would laugh and point out to him in the language of the Quinnipiac, which Pearson claimed he understood, that we had no need for his salvation.

Having crossed the meadow and onto the trail I turned south and up over a slight hill that was framed by the ridgeline of Hobomock on the right, and a rock-strewn elevation to the left. It was then that I noticed the path had been rutted out by two parallel lines about a hand's width deep that snaked along it and I whispered to myself that the Awaunuy had taken their two-wheeled carts pulled by their beasts called oxen, repeatedly on the trail up into the Coginchaug and back again. "They certainly are quickly moving to claim what Nausup has given them," I thought. How soon will it be before they have carved up the rest of the land of our ancestors into their farms?

Nausup is a good and decent man who even though we at times had our disagreements, is trying to lead the People as best he can under extremely difficult conditions. I have watched him grow to manhood and now that he was the leader of the People following the death of Shaumpishuh, the sachem often confided in me and continued to have me sit around his council fire. Together with his sister Shambisqua and brother Keyhow, Nausup had realized that with the unrelenting pressure from the Awaunuy who were intent on claiming as much land as they could in Guilford, the name they have given to Mennunkatuck, they would eventually push us out of what was left of our ancestral home. The Guilford Awaunuy had wanted to finalize the northern boundary of their original purchase from Shaumpishuh when they first arrived on our shore. This led Nausup to negotiate with them as he had also done successfully in the past with the Awaunuy of New Haven on the other side of Mioonkhtuck at the mouth of the Quinnipiac.

If nothing else, Nausup is practical and understands that though he ceded to them valuable hunting land, they did put on their paper that the

People might continue to hunt and fish here. How long that would be possible was hard to tell, but the way the Awaunuy cut the trees and build their fences it will not be long. They do not take kindly to our presence on what they consider theirs and even will turn their dogs on us, some even calling us just "another pest" to be driven from the land. In council, Nausup has told me he wished to continue to bring the People together at Mioonkhtuck and Totoket in the hope that we might be able to stabilize ourselves and learn to live in the shadow of the Awaunuy. I, for one, said to him that was only a temporary arrangement and that as a people we would eventually lose ourselves to their ways. The fact was this had already been happening for many years. Nausup agreed, but also asked me what was the alternative? This I could not answer and thus my quest that brought me to the face of Hobomock.

I then thought of Shambisqua, who though a few years my junior, had been my best friend and confidant during my childhood, especially following the death of my parents and sister when I felt the most lost and alone in the world. We would take long walks and often sit together when our time came to guard the maize and chase the crows and blackbirds away as it grew and ripened in the summer sun. We talked, shared secrets, and she was my first and only love. I had determined at that young age that I would become a great hunter and warrior so I might win her hand and the consent of her mother and the rest of her powerful family. But Shambisqua was the daughter of sachems, and I was merely the son of a Wangunk father and Mennunkatuck mother and thus of a lesser lineage. Although my father was highly respected by the rest of the People for his skill as a hunter and provider for his family he had come to live with his wife as was our custom and thus had no relatives among the People. For the Quinnipiac and others, the family circle was a powerful and important part of the economic and social fabric of village life and though the entire Mennunkatuck band worked together as a unit to support one another it was the support of family, especially during the times of trouble and danger that often became a matter of survival.

When my family and so many others suffered and died at Mennunkatuck as well as at Totoket and Mioonkhtuck during the time of smallpox, the survivors turned to one another for help. Shambisqua, having somehow survived the pestilence, though for a while gravely ill the year it first came, had appealed to her mother to ask Commossuck to take me into his weetou.

She knew I needed a real home and the support of others if I was to live through those troubled times. The powwow having just suffered the loss of his wife and son and out of the frustration of being unable to cure them and the others who had died, had been away on a vision quest to ask the Spirit World and especially Hobomock to help those of us who still lived. He had journeyed far to the northwest following the Spirit Line beyond the face of Hobomock through many mountains and valleys and across the great western river to the high mountains that were the home of our enemy the Mohawk. There Commossuck knew there was a sacred place of great spiritual power and energy nestled against the base of a great cliff, a cave that was the entrance to the Lower World.

Commossuck had stayed for many days and nights, often in trance and performing rituals and sacrifices to Hobomock and calling on the entire Spirit World to give him the gifts to stop the suffering. When he did return, he explained that those who had survived the disease should perform a cleansing ritual that might allow them to heal and possibly prevent such a scourge from returning. This Shaumpishuh and the council agreed and under his direction the entire band began preparations.

It was then that it was suggested to the shaman that he take me in but at the time I was unaware of this until Shambisqua came to find me to tell me it was so. Commossuck did not approach me for many more days to bring me to his weetou. Only after he had led the People in the ritual dances and offerings did he send word that I should come.

The cleansing, healing ritual, and dancing began at dusk on the day Commossuck had determined would be most effective based upon the moon cycle and what his visions had shown him while at the sacred passage into the Lower World. For each of us who had somehow survived the pox this was an opportunity to help bring about through the energy of Manitou a connection with the Spirit World in order to re-establish a balance with the natural one that had been distorted and twisted, allowing the disease to devastate our band as well as the others of the People. Proud Montowese had brought his band from the Upper Quinnipiac and we were joined by many others from Totoket. Even Momauguin the Grand Sachem of the People had come from Mioonkhtuck along with survivors from that band to Mennunkatuck to take part. A great circular arbor had been erected in the center of the village creating the sacred space that would act as a threshold between this world and that of the spirits and in its center, the sacred fire had been built that once lit by Commossuck to the accompaniment of sacred chanting and drumming by those assembled, stayed lit for two days and nights.

After offering to Keihtan, Hobomock, and all those of the Spirit realm prayers with sacred smoke from tobacco, Commossuck began the rhythmic chanting, and was quickly joined by every voice present and drumming from those who had been given that gift through Manitou. Each of the men in turn began dancing. The first dancer was Nashump, the husband of Shaumpishuh. As he danced to the chanting, he was brought to a trance-like state by the sound of the drums and voices appealing to Manitou. He began, as was the tradition, to give away to those that had formed the dance circle what he had with him, and soon was stripped down to his breechcloth. He was then joined by another solitary dancer who took his place, and the same process continued over and over again throughout the night. The chorus sang until just before sunrise when Commossuck stepped forward to offer the sacred pipe to Manitou, the signal that the ritual had ended for the night. It would begin again the next evening.

I remember being exhausted from chanting and singing after two nights, yet I also felt strangely energized. I returned to the weetou of my parents to prepare for its ritual burning in the morning. This was our custom for the home of those who had died. The hardest part I soon realized, was our custom that after the weetou was burned, their names were never to be spoken again. I broke into tears knowing they were truly gone, but content to know that the ritual would help guide them to the southwest and the house of Kiehtan where their spirits would live forever in peaceful harmony without want. After all, we have always believed, as there is death, there is also regeneration for all life and time moves as a circle continuous and everlasting. This life is but one part of existence, and this never became clearer to me than during those nights of rituals led by Commossuck.

The calls of a flock of a dozen geese lowering to land on the lake caught my attention and brought me away from my memories and back to the beauty of the high summer day. I looked down from a gentle rise with a full view of Quonnipaug stretching like a fat finger southward, snuggling against a steep ridge to the right, and a gentler and rolling one that could be seen through the trees. The geese had noisily found their place on the sparkling water that reflected the sun in all its brightness. Insects buzzed and made their music all around me including one or two of those strange yellow and black striped ones the Awaunuy had brought with them to make honey – one Awaunuy addition to our world I had to admit I found delightful. My legs carried me down the hill along the path again rutted by cartwheels and I tried not to dwell on them as I stepped over to the right of them to avoid them entirely. This I thought, was just another example of how the Awaunuy think nothing of damaging the Earth Mother.

As I worked my way closer to the head of the pond where it was fed by a stream that came down from the high ridge, the trail led to a clearing. I sighted two young men of our people fishing with nets standing waist high in the water near the left-hand shore. One was the grandson of Shambisqua, a strong and athletic young man whose eager temperament sometimes prevailed over his spirit. That was acceptable, for it was a sign of his energetic mind and character which as he had grown became more measured, thoughtful, and less spontaneous. He and I got along well and I knew in time he might become an effective leader of the People.

"Hello Mequnhut" I shouted as I drew closer to the young man and his companion, Apoawein. "Don't let me disturb the seriousness of your work but I trust that you sacrificed to the trout and perch before you began so your efforts will be prosperous!"

"Manitou!" exclaimed Mequnhut, "it is a wonder to see you. We in Totoket had heard of your journey to the Spirit Line and the face of Hobomock though you had told no one."

"The People have no secrets!" laughed Apoawein. "We all had a strong suspicion what you were about with the arrival of the solstice." With that the pair stopped their fishing and waded back to the shore of Quonnipaug with a net holding five fluttering fish.

"You see uncle, you bring us the power and influence of your spirit and suddenly the net is full after many attempts had failed. You carry the light of Keihtan in you for sure."

Mequnhut had grown up with me as part of what he considered his extended family and from early childhood had called me uncle. For many of the People who respected but sometimes feared my shaman gifts from the world of Spirits, the close bond between the grandson of Shambisqua and myself, an elderly powwow, was recognized as something special. Although many powwows take a wife and have children as Commossuck had, I had not, believing that a family would become a distraction to my mission to bridge the worlds of men and spirit in order to help the People over these many years. Also, with so much death and suffering among the People, I felt in my heart that I might not be able to survive the loss of a wife, or especially, a child. Plus, the one who might have changed my mind had joined with another which I knew was for the best. For a powwow, wealth, power, and status were of no interest or use and a wife and children would have resulted in compromises for me in that regard. But I have always stayed close to Shambisqua and over time her family became like my own. None more so than Mequnhut.

"You had better return to your fishing" I teased the two "for five fish will not even feed this hungry old man! I will sit here by the shore and ask the helpers of Hobomock to make your net full." And with that I sat cross legged just up from the water and took from my pouch tobacco and my pipe. "I will make an offering to the finned spirit helpers."

With that the two young men solemnly paused to allow their prayers to join the smoke from the pipe as it ascended into the sky, wrapped in its crystal blue and the summer greens of the tree canopy behind me on the shore. Together with Mequnhut and Apoawein, I appealed to and asked for the help of those of the water world so the people might have fish to add to their winter stores. No sooner had we finished when the two felt a tug on the net they had made of lines of strong hemp fibers. Soon after casting it three or four more times, they had landed many more water brothers and sisters to fill their ash baskets. They had brought two with them in the hope of carrying their bounty back to the small camp they had made at the lower end of Quonnipaug.

"Thank you, uncle, for your help, you never fail to amaze me with your gifts. If only now you could bring back the deer and others who have fled our lands."

"You mean the lands of the Guilford Awaunuy and who knows who else," Apoawein said with a bitterness he made no effort to hide. "Nausup has promised us we will always be able to fish these waters, and he said he had it on that paper that was written. Old Sugcogisin who has learned to read and speak Awaunuy words has verified that he has seen it to be so."

"We must trust it to be true though sadly we have found over these many years while some Awaunuy say these things with all sincerity, others are all too willing to break the word and violate the agreement" claimed Mequnhut. "This is what angers so many of us young men who see the lands of our ancestors taken and destroyed and with it our ability to live as we choose."

I nodded in agreement and knew the anger of the young was born out of frustration as it was for their elders. I had seen it throughout my life and had also seen with my eyes the consequences of acting on those feelings. "I understand and share your anger and frustration and have carried it in me all my years, season after season. I have watched them take and sometimes cheat, and I have also seen them kill. The Awaunuy destroy all who stand against them with a ruthlessness that is unimaginable. Remember when you were young what happened to the Metacom and the Wampanoag as well as the mighty Narragansett? I also witnessed the fate of the Pequot when I was but a few years younger than you are now. No, we must find another way to survive."

"Is it worth surviving when we have no way to live and the shadows of the Awaunuy cover us wherever we go?" asked Mequnhut. "Soon the People will be no more."

As if in agreement with the gloom this talk had settled on their spirits, a bank of grey clouds had risen from the southwest and covered the sun, which led Apoawein to acknowledge "even Keihtan knows this to be true."

Chapter Four

As the two younger men gathered their catch and hefted the woven ash baskets to their backs, I gathered my thoughts and began to contemplate the fate of all the remaining young of the Quinnipiac. I saw in Mequnhut and Apoawein both the past and future, for here they were by the shores of Quonnipaug, taking fish to be dried and stored for the winter just as countless generations of ancestors had yet, as I watched them lift the baskets I knew they would probably be the last. "Perhaps not this summer, maybe the next," I heard myself say to the puzzled looks of my companions.

"What do you mean uncle by such curious words?" asked Mequnhut. He knew from experience that I often have conversations with unseen spirits while even amid others. His question was meant to ascertain whether my statement was meant for him and Apoawein, or others who were with me.

"My thoughts were of the future and would this be the last summer our people gather the bounty of this lake or not," I answered. "Our life's path is uncertain." The two young companions nodded and said little as we worked our way through the trees and up the slight rise where the trail wound its way along the eastern shore. The air had grown warm by mid-morning and the scent of the fish they carried was strong. It brought the turkey vultures that always prowled the sky above Quonnipaug up off the high ridge above the western edge of the water that was their sentinel post. The large black birds floated across the pond and began to circle languidly at differing heights above us as we joined the trail that led to their camp.

"Our friends smell their meal even before we have prepared it for them," said Apoawein as he gestured skyward. We all knew the buzzards would feast on the entrails of the fish once they had been gutted and prepared to be hung on racks, allowing the smoke of a slow burning fire to cure them. "Nothing goes to waste in a world that is balanced as you have taught us Ponaim. All that live have their role and place and this is what many of us find so disturbing about things as they are now."

"My friend, your words are true and have made me think of the Awaunuy. I cannot help but see them as a new and stronger breed of vulture who consume everything they come across as carrion" Mequnhut replied. "I have even heard it said by the Awaunuy at Totoket that their god has given the entire world to them to do with as they please. They certainly have shown us this in all their ways."

"In time they will clean us away as our feathered friends will clean these fish entrails. May they bring word to Keihtan for us" added Apoawein, "so we may not be as the fish."

With this my mind drifted back to a time when the vultures did feast on the dead of the villages throughout the Dawnland, and it seemed to be the end of time for the People as we believed none would survive. It was the year following the first appearance of the pox that brought an even a greater return of the scourge. Word of smallpox came first to the Quinnipiac from the Wangunk of Mattabasec shortly after a group of Awaunuy had set up a post for trade just north of their village along the Quinnihticut River at Pyquag. Like the Dutchmannuck who preceded them, these Awaunuy had come to trade with the people of the Dawnland for the pelts of the beaver, otter and other four leggeds they found less desirable but still hungered for. This trade had begun well before my birth and had placed considerable stress on the People. We along with other bands, competed with one another to take advantage of the trade or for some like the Pequot, to dominate it at the expense of all others. We all wanted their kettles and tools made of iron, their cloth made of wool, and countless other things they brought with them from across the sea. But most of all, the peoples of the Dawnland wanted their weapons for a warrior and hunter armed with one of their muskets was more powerful than one without.

When news of the return of the sickness came to Mennunkatuck, those who had just survived the previous onslaught of smallpox were mortified in their terror. I remember how Commossuck had immediately journeyed to Mattabasec to see for himself what was happening, while instructing me to begin gathering the herbs and plants of the meadows and forests he would need to help cure the sick if the pox did come to the People. Two days later Commossuck had returned and I will never forget the look of total dejection that covered his face and tempered his movements. Yet in his eyes burned a fierce determination and that fire gave his entire countenance an otherworldly appearance. He asked me of the herbs and plants he would need and went right to the bundles that I had strung from the ridge pole of the weetou, inspecting them to make sure all was ready. Then he told me he would immediately seek the aid of Hobomock and the rest of the Spirit World to protect the People. He left for the place he often went where there are hidden places of spiritual power and energy in the rocky outcrops to the west of our village off the path on the way to Totoket. He announced he would return in two days.

He had returned at night from Mattabasec so as not to draw attention to himself knowing his presence among the People would have caused all to want to hear of what he saw and learned there. I remember how I wanted to ask Commossuck what he had seen but knew not to ask. If the powwow wanted me to know he would have told me. So, I watched him walk out of the village and into the darkness towards his place of prayer with a tremendous sense of anxiety.

The next morning, as the village woke to another day that promised to be both warm and pleasant, all attention fell to the question of Commossuck and when would he return. Shaumpishuh had counselled all not to send any others to the River Bands until Commossuck returned adding to the level of tension. I was stricken with fear for I knew of his return and worried I might give his secret away. Inadvertently, I avoided eye contact with all I met which quickly raised suspicion amongst those who knew me best, especially Shambisqua. She as well as the others asked if I knew of Commossuck for it was clear my reactions to their questions were meant to deceive but I held tight to my silence. As Shambisqua and I walked to the maize fields that morning for our time to chase the black birds from picking at the ripening crop, she confronted and firmly probed me for news for she knew I was holding some.

"Why do you look down when I speak of news of Commossuck?" Shambisqua had questioned. I can see that you know of him yet will not speak."

I did not answer but instead bent down to gather stones to throw at the birds who thought our corn would make a delightful morning meal. This caused even more consternation in my friend and she quickly pursued the obvious.

"The news from Commossuck must not be good for you would tell me otherwise. You have your reasons and I will honor that. But there can be no secrets among friends such as we." She had a serious look on her face as she stared earnestly at me and at that moment a weakness engulfed me as I looked into her inquiring brown eyes. I felt the truth all but explode inside me and just as the words of what I did know were about to erupt they were diverted by a sudden and great commotion among the weetous. "Commossuck has returned!" Shambisqua proclaimed and ran immediately towards the village to see and hear what the powwow had to say.

I stood motionless near the field, my heart pounding and my mind racing as I watched Shambisqua run towards the crowd gathering in the center of the village. Had this been a test from Keihtan? I asked myself. Had he tested my resolve to honor my commitment to the wishes of Commossuck? I knew that the shaman would not return until he had journeyed to the world of the Spirits and had learned from them what needed to be done. But was I wrong?

But he had not returned. Instead it was Montowese and some men of his band that had come with news of what was happening among the Wangunk. The sachem strode proudly with resolution into the center of the village and as Shaumpishuh emerged from her weetou Montowese went quickly to her ignoring the voices that implored him for news. The two sachems greeted one another and Shaumpishuh gestured that they should enter her home where they might speak to one another. By then I remember I had awakened from my stupor and had run expectantly to the village to join the crowd that had gathered only to be ushered away from the weetou of Shaumpishuh by Nashump and other men who helped him do so. It was then we all turned our attention to the men who had accompanied Montowese only to have our entreaties to them turned away as well. But their faces revealed the gravity of the situation and some of the women began a ritual wailing that only added to the level of tension and fear that was engulfing the village. It was mid-afternoon before the two leaders emerged and Shaumpishuh called out that she would meet with her council at dusk.

As the afternoon waned and the rumors flew, many in the village began to gather some belongings thinking once they knew of the danger they would flee, either across the water to our friends on the far shore, or deep into the interior where they might save themselves and their families. A group of five men having been away on a hunt, arrived just before dusk settled into a great tumult as families were reunited amidst the growing sense of panic. They were greeted by Shaumpishuh and Montowese, but not before their leader, Wentubecum and others were speaking of what they had learned while hunting in the Coginchaug.

Two families from Mattabasec had sought refuge there and had described to them the horror of what had struck their village and others of the River Bands to their north. "What they told us of this pestilence is hard to imagine" stated Wentubecum as his comrades shook their heads in agreement. "We were told to flee for our lives and those of our children for this sickness will kill all as it has at Pyquag. They claimed it is worse than that of the past summer." As the anxious crowd surrounding the hunters began to shout in unison Shaumpishuh, being tall and powerfully built, used all the strength and presence her great size could muster, implored the hunting party to hold their tongues and immediately join the council by the central fire amid the weetous.

"We must all have time to listen and speak as is our custom and those of you with news of this sickness must share so we may learn of what has struck our relatives the Wangunk and prepare ourselves for what course we might take. We have all suffered greatly from the loss of so many the past year and this new threat to those of us who have survived is difficult to comprehend." After a pause, the sunksquaw asked with some frustration, "Is there no news of Commossuck?"

The sunksquaw looked directly at me, the stare with her one eye, having lost the other as a child, caused my knees to all but buckle as everyone turned to look at me expectantly. Somehow, I found the ability to blurt out "he is not yet returned to the village," to which the sachem nodded in acceptance and the attention of the People turned quickly back to the members of the council as they gathered together along with Montowese, Wentubecum, and the hunters. As they formed a circle around the fire and sat for the council in the failing light of the evening, an eerie silence fell across the village as even the birds fell quiet, stopping their evening songs in anticipation of what was to be heard and discussed. I remember Shambisqua making her way to me where I stood like a pillar of stone following my moment of tribulation, and yet triumph, as I had told the truth as Commossuck always said and yet had not given away his confidence. When she squeezed my hand, she broke the spell I was in and together we made our way to a gnarled and ancient oak near the fire that offered a perfect vantage point in its limbs from which to hear the council members speak.

"Montowese, would you do us the honor of lighting the pipe in the absence of Commossuck?" I remember Shaumpishuh asking and her fellow sachem took the pipe solemnly from her hands and thanked her for the honor for this meant he would be the first to speak. Montowese reached into the fire with a small stick and with the burning end carefully lit the pipe, inhaling slowly then exhaling the smoke so that the Spirit World would hear his words and know what he spoke was true.

"People, I have seen with my own eyes what has afflicted my relatives at Mattabasec. It is the return of a powerful spell from another world. They told me of how within days of falling ill nine out of ten of those at Pyquag had died and shortly after the people of Mattabasec began to become sick as well. It works it's evil much faster this time."

I will never forget the chilling sound of his words as those gathered around the council circle stood in absolute silence and I can still see their haunted faces, dimly reflected by the fire light as the growing darkness of evening settled into night around us. Like the others, I was stunned. All I could think was how could such a thing be happening again?

Montowese continued after once again inhaling the sacred tobacco and exhaling slowly. "The effect of the sickness on those who suffer is like before but more extreme. One moment those caught by it seem fine and the next they have developed a high fever which weakens them and they must take to their sleeping place. They suffer from a severe ache in their head and become so weak they cannot rise from their beds while complaining of a terrible pain throughout their entire person, especially in the back. Some begin to vomit uncontrollably and like last summer developed flat red spots the size of a thumbnail on their face, hands, and arms that eventually spread everywhere. The spots swell with pus and sometimes burst, but most dried slowly, and eventually fell off leaving deep pitted scars. Those same scars you may remember we had seen on the faces of some of the Dutchmannuck who came to Totoket many years ago and those of us who lived despite being sick last summer."

The sachem, his expression breaking into one of pain, caught his breath before continuing. His powerful shoulders slumped as he continued. "When some of those who were sick rose from their sleeping place, their skin tore off as if they were skinned alive. It is awful. Like before, some survive despite all this but most die within eight or nine days, many before." Hearing this those assembled began to mumble in disbelief mixed with fear realizing that this might be their fate. Montowese paused and inhaled from the pipe then exhaled once again as he looked to see how his words had impacted the People. "I do fear there may be no escape from this pestilence" he added as he gestured to Shaumpishuh that he had no more to say at that time.

Shaumpishuh took the pipe and rather than speak herself passed it to Wentubecum who accepted it with a bow of his head and slowly inhaled and exhaled from the pipe two times before speaking. "The two families we saw in the Coginchaug were very afraid; we could tell from the look in their eyes. They described to us what Montowese has said and told of how those that become sick also were covered with blood clots on the skin as well. They spoke of how many became delirious in their fever and had difficulty breathing as if they were drowning. Before the sick die, the Wangunk said it appeared that some demon bent on the destruction of all who were living, went to those who had cared for the ill and they soon develop a fever as well, the first sign of the disease." Wentubecum paused as everyone let out a collective moan wrapped around a sigh. He puffed on the pipe, exhaled, and continued. "They said the people of their band believed it to be a powerful and evil spirit that moves unseen from person to person and none know who might be struck next. This is why they fled their village."

Having said his part, Wentubecum noticed that Montowese had gestured that he once again wanted to speak and he passed the pipe to him. After again slowly exhaling the sacred smoke, Montowese added "some claim to have seen a dark specter clothed in the black robes of the Dutchmannuck and Awaunuy float from the sick to the healthy and that this has been brought by them and their god to our shores." With this those gathered around the council fire shouted loudly in anger mixed with dismay. The consensus was immediate that those from away had brought this to destroy the People and one man shouted out "as they tried last summer!" Shaumpishuh gestured to everyone for silence and following a few more moments of murmuring, angry words took the pipe from her fellow sachem.

"People" said Shaumpishuh as she rose from sitting, her large size lending a dignity and majesty to the moment. "I do not doubt the words of Montowese and Wentubecum and believe we must think of how we might be able to keep this black robed demon away. My thoughts are with those who are sick, those who have passed on to the house of Keihtan, and their loved ones. But as sunksquaw of Mennunkatuck I must look to you all for guidance as it is possible we can escape this if the Manitou of the Spirit

World will allow it." She inhaled then sent the smoke skyward. "We will seek the advice of Commossuck when he returns" standing quietly for a moment before passing the pipe to the gray haired elder of the band, Auqaihamch before sitting down.

"I have seen more snows than all of you and have had my share of sorrows including the death of my wife and three grandchildren from the pox last year" he said with a voice that quaked but was clear. "I remember like some of you who are a bit older may, the first time this disease, came to the Dawnland. The Massachusett, Wampanoag, and many others who dwell towards the rising sun were afflicted and word had reached us of their terrible suffering. Entire villages were wiped out within days as if some great wave had risen from the sea and swept them away. It was said that like at Pyquag, only a small remnant somehow survived. There were not enough living to bury the dead, and in many places their skeletons could be seen for many seasons later. Yet somehow that black robed demon, if that is what it is, never found its way here to the Quinnipiac. Maybe this time it will be the same for many of us can recall how Commossuck and all the shamans of the People were able to call on Hobomock and all the spirit helpers to keep us from harm."

When he was finished Shaumpishuh motioned for the pipe and asked if there were others sitting around the council fire who wanted to speak. Wentubecum made a motion with his hand and the pipe was passed once again to him. "I worry that perhaps the black robed demon may have followed we of the hunting party back unknown to us. A few of the children we met at Coginchaug appeared sick, were coughing, and seemed weak the entire time we spoke. Could it be that they were in the first stages of the disease and the black robe may have jumped from them to one of us?" With that, those gathered close to the fire to hear what was said seemed to step back in unison as they let out a spontaneous, collective groan. The hunter did not seem to notice before saying "perhaps those of us who met them should leave at once in case we too are afflicted."

Handing the sacred pipe back to Shaumpishuh, Wentubecum sat again and an eerie stillness suddenly enveloped the People and the atmosphere around the fire was heavy and solemn. Shaumpishuh having sat herself, stood again and silently took the pipe. She began to inhale and exhale a number of times, with each looking up towards the heavens in a gesture meant to call on Keihtan and the rest of the Spirit World. As we all watched expectantly, it was clear she was hoping to receive guidance and wisdom from the Sky World and Keihtan. After what seemed an eternity, Shaumpishuh stood to address the People as they anxiously leaned in towards the council fire forming a palisade of faces behind those seated around it.

"People, I do not yet know what course we should follow and though my thoughts lean towards waiting for the return of Commossuck, it does seem wise to follow the advice and wise words of caution that Wentubecum has spoken. But if the black robed demon has followed them, he may already be here and perhaps it is too late." As Shaumpishuh stood in the firelight, her countenance changed with the flickering flames as she looked steadily at each person there turning her head slowly to connect with each before adding " my brother sachem Montowese and his men may also have brought it with them unknowingly."

In the moments that followed, I was reminded of the powerful bonds that held the community together and was, despite this terrible threat, its greatest strength. In a clear, loud chorus every voice seemed to answer their sachem declaring that they were ready to face this unseen enemy together and that the hunters should stay for the unity of the People was what made us strong. The gray haired elder, Auqaihamch began chanting sacred sounds and was instantaneously joined by everyone else, the sound of which I can still recall to this day. Its strength and energy engulfed us in a ritual of unity that transcended time and gave real meaning to the very core

of who we were, had always been, and would hopefully always be. We were the People and would face
this together.

Chapter Five

It was a restless night in the village and the sense of unity only mildly tempered the anxiety felt by the People, which kept many from breaking the circle around the central fire even though the evening turned inevitably into the deep night sounds of summer. As families and friends clumped together to talk of their hopes and apprehensions, it was clear they were drawing from one another an inner strength and comfort they knew would be needed to face this latest onslaught of our world thrown out of balance. Shaumpishuh was present everywhere, moving like a beacon of reassurance from group to group as each came together, then broke apart only to form into another like waves broken by the shore only to be absorbed by those in their wake. I stayed alone to the side in the shadows, missing my family as I watched others clinging to each other in support and comfort. My loneliness became overwhelming, and I felt myself drifting quietly back from the fire circle and into the darkness.

I can still feel that overpowering sense of loss and even doom that enveloped me like a fog that rose from the sea when I think of that night. I remember thinking of the summer before when an indescribable terror and helplessness had engulfed me as I watched over three days first my sister, father, and then mother die from the pox. I sat in the far end of the weetou watching helplessly as Commossuck tried valiantly to save each, using his medicines and healing stones all the while chanting and making powerful spirit gestures in an attempt to draw out of each the sickness. In the end he had to surrender to the will of Hobomock and the Spirits who he pleaded with not to abandon the People.

I felt a deep darkness overwhelm me and remember thinking how could I, Shambisqua, and all the People ever survive this dark specter who brought this pox again? I remember my eyes filled with tears and I decided to run, run as fast as I could into the forest and away from certain doom, not so much for myself but for what was to soon befall the Mennunkatuck, my people.

As I ran through the fields of maize, squash, and beans; sister gifts from Keihtan that worked together to sustain the People and give us life, I thought of how I had once heard stories told by my father of the fields of the Wampanoag left unharvested when the sickness Auqaihamch had spoken of had decimated their villages. Would the same happen here I cried out through my tears as I stumbled and fell onto a mound of the sisters, breaking the tender maize stalk and bending it to the ground. Dejected and upset with myself, I sat for a moment hoping to gather myself only to fall into an even greater gloom that kept me there for some time before I forced myself to my feet and made my way quickly to the woods by the edge of the field. There I imagined, the trees might somehow protect me and I would feel safe. But once there, even though the smell of the night forest was strong with the fresh moistness of early summer that was familiar and normally a comfort to me, I felt terrifyingly alone. My eyes blurry with tears, I could hardly see through the trees the edge of the river that flowed to the sea from Quonnipaug lit by the moon. There, I assured myself, I will swim across to the other side and go to the ledges in the woods beyond where I can be safe and have time to think. But think of what? That you are a coward and have abandoned the People? Commossuck? Shambisqua?

I remember how I had walked making my way slowly and forlornly through the woods to the bank of the river where I sat trying to decide what to do, numb from my feelings of loss, fear, and confusion, imbued with a sadness that seemed beyond my ability to bear. I decided to rest for a while before swimming across and fell asleep in the tall grass there by the river. It was that night that Keihtan came to me in a dream walk for the first time, in the form of the mighty Thunderbird, and I recall being terrified by the mere presence of such a great and powerful creature, his feathers like flames of fire and his eyes like the sun. I felt my dream soul being drawn from my body by one tremendous swoosh of his wing as he hovered above me and to this day I can still see myself curled in sleep below as I was lifted by that wing to the sky and high above the village. He brought me to see the People and I saw them gathered in groups about the fire just as they had been when I left them and I felt the pull of a powerful emotional connection with them. Among them was Shambisqua who was with her mother, father, and brothers. She looked so small beside her mother. That was the last thing I remember for the next thing I knew it was the time just between night and day. As I opened my eyes there above me was the face of Commossuck whose expression was one of curiosity mixed with surprise.

"Boy, what brings you to the edge of this stream, away from the village and the warmth of the weetou? Has a calamity come to you and the People?"

Eyes foggy with sleep, I bolted up to a sitting position, not sure if what I was seeing was truly Commossuck or a spirit come to take me away having already died of the pox. But I soon regained my wits enough to stutter a few words.

"No," I said, "though a great fear has gripped the People. Montowese and Wentubecum came yesterday with news of how the disease has struck the

Wangunk and River Bands. Shaumpishuh held council and the People now wait for your return."

"And what brought you to the river so early that you fell asleep in the morning dew?"

"I became afraid of the pox and scared in the night of what we were told" I said with a bit of trepidation for my words made me sound foolish and a child. "It was the thought of so many dying so soon after the last time that led me to flee into the night but to where exactly I did not know. I stopped to rest and fell to sleep so here I am."

Commossuck nodded as he looked deep into me, into my very heart and soul. After a few moments that were more like hours the powwow said thoughtfully "there is something else I sense you have not told me."

Stunned, I was at first speechless yet felt myself all but forced despite my reluctance to look into the eyes of the shaman as if pulled by a rope made of sinew. I still remember hearing myself blurt out "yes there is, the Thunderbird of Keihtan came in the night and carried me to the village."

Commossuck nodded again and grunted in recognition of what I had told him before softly exclaiming "Manitou." Then, during what seemed an eternity, he simply stood looking at me with a studied expression before saying, "Come Ponaim, it is time to return to the village for we have both been on a quest and the Spirits have spoken." He reached down for my hand and helped me to my feet and then slipped silently into the trees to walk to the village as I followed.

As we traversed the woods and crossed through the fields of the Sisters, the sweet fragrances of summer began to rise as the sky began lightening in the east and it seemed all that had happened the day and night before were but a dream. How could Keihtan really bring such doom to the People when all seemed so calm and peaceful I thought as I tried to keep up with the powwow, whose pace was one of earnest determination. From his gait and sense of purpose, it was obvious that Commossuck had returned from his vision quest armed with what I hoped would keep the dark demon from the village. I knew we would all have to trust in the great powers and gifts granted to him by Hobomock. I suddenly felt reassured that the People might be protected from this latest test brought by the Awaunuy.

As we entered the circle of weetous smoke from the central fire that still smoldered drifted towards us and two of the dogs near the home of Auqaihamch barked in recognition until Commossuck motioned with his hand for their silence. Like many great shamans, he had the ability to talk with or without words to all creatures, a gift he later helped me cultivate. As the dogs approached wagging their tails, he motioned that they should be still and lay down as we passed.

Our weetou was on the far edge of the village under a great oak tree that provided shade when the afternoon sun rose high to the west; as we circled to the right of the central fire a few people, just rising for the day shouted out "Manitou" at the sight of Commossuck and in an instant we were surrounded by a number of anxious villagers.

"Commossuck has returned shouted first one, then another, then another." Yet out of respect for the powwow, they did not harangue him with questions or implore him to tell them what he knew or had seen. As their number grew, some spoke softly to one another as they moved like a stream on either side and behind us as we made our way to our weetou. When we were but a few yards from our home of saplings covered with woven river reeds mats, a raven of enormous size came to land on the dome-like roof and uncharacteristically stood silently staring at the growing gathering before him, cocking his head from side to side as if sizing up the growing crowd. A gasp went up from some in recognition of his presence as Commossuck stopped abruptly and raised his right arm in salutation. The raven, a messenger from Keihtan, cawed and croaked out his acknowledgement and Commossuck bent down to enter the low entrance to the weetou, pulling up the deer skin flap as he did. Because he did not indicate I should follow, I was left outside with the others equally enraptured by the omen sent to us in our hour of danger from the world of Spirits. The raven showed no intent of flying off and remained at his post upon the weetou staring down upon the curious villagers which as the morning proceeded slowly began to melt away. All the while I remained sitting just to the left of the door of the weetou unsure of what to do or where to go.

Keihtan's messenger remained on the roof, a sentinel sent to assure us all that the Spirit World was indeed present. Small groups, of men, women, and children would occasionally wander over and approach within twenty feet or so to look upon the raven and then drift away to be replaced by another; always silent in reverence of what they were witnessing. None spoke to me or acknowledged my presence; it was the raven and the man inside the weetou that mattered.

As Father Sun reached his highest point and the summer heat was strongest, Shaumpishuh and Montowese approached, having stayed back by the council fire since earlier in the morning, just watching before walking out of the village towards the shore accompanied by a small group of elders. Now as they came within ten feet of the weetou, the raven for only the second time since his arrival cawed in a chortling way to acknowledge the two sachems then rose up to his full height and flapped his wings as if to say, "do not come closer." Understanding the message, the sachems bowed and backed away slowly then turned to walk west about fifty yards where they proceeded to sit silently under the huge spreading red oak that since the time of our ancestors was a sacred site of prayer and council. There they remained, patiently waiting.

It was only then that I realized how hungry and thirsty I was for the sun was hot and I had not eaten or had water since well before the council meeting the evening before. But somehow I knew it was my role to stay by the entrance and wait for word from Commossuck who had been quiet all that time and this gave me a strong feeling of being needed in a way I had not experienced since the death of my parents the year before. It was important that I remain and as that idea grew stronger I remember that strangely the heat of the sun, pangs of hunger, and dryness of thirst began to diminish. When Shambisqua held up a gourd full of water and motioned from a distance that she would bring it to me I remember shaking my head to say no for I was finding strength in my new sense of purpose and responsibility. Maybe it was the raven, maybe it was the energy emitted by Commossuck inside the weetou behind me, or maybe it was my fate. Which it was to this day

I have never been sure of but I sat and waited, energized, and empowered by my sense of purpose.

When Commossuck finally did emerge late in the afternoon, his face and body were painted half red and half black and though he wore only a breech-cloth his head was crowned with a great black head-dress made from the head of a bear and on his back was a cloak made from the fur lined skin of the same brother that fell nearly to the ground behind him. I remember jumping up as if bit by a snake only to be awed by the sight of the shaman as he simply nodded and handed me a bundle wrapped in the fur of the otter.

When Commossuck had come through the opening and stood before the weetou, the raven called out loudly and instantly darted towards the grandmother oak where the two sachems waited. Shaumpishuh and Montowese rose to their feet at the sight of the powwow as Keihtan's messenger flew to a branch above them and called out as he landed. In answer to his call two companions quickly flew in from the trees to the southwest beyond the edge of the village to join him on his perch, landing in silence. Commossuck paused briefly as they flew in low above the village and once they had landed began to walk straight towards the sachems who waited silently while he crossed the ground between them. It was then I remember all I could see was the powwow as he moved and everything else became blurred as if wrapped in a foggy mist. Time itself seemed frozen in that moment of supreme and universal magic as he seemed to float instead of walk. Later, when I asked Shambisqua and others what they had seen it became clear I had seen a vision for what they saw was the shaman simply walk towards the sachems. This vision I did not share with others including Commossuck until much later only because of my uncertainty and fear of what might be happening to me following the visit by the Thunderbird the night before. Was I really up to what the Spirits were beginning to call me to?

Just as Commossuck was about to reach the Grandmother tree, I found myself able to focus my vision and realized I was still standing by the weetou door frozen in place holding the bundle given me by the powwow. Knowing that he had given it to me for a reason I summoned my courage and quickly crossed the fifty yards and stopped about the length of a man behind him and to his right. Once there I sat not wanting to call attention to myself just as Shaumpishuh greeted Commossuck .

"Commossuck we need your counsel in determining the extent of the danger we face from the return of the pox and how we might keep it from us. Momauguin and the elders from Mioonkhtuck and

Totoket have been sent for and will be here soon. We must face this together."

Montowese added "I have summoned the shaman of our band, Pawquash, for I know the two of you have worked together in the past to help us understand what Hobomock wants and how we might appease him."

Commossuck raised his arms as if embracing the mighty tree before him and looked beyond and above the sachems as he began to chant spirit words that called to the ancestors. The sachems stood silently in recognition of his call. The three ravens launched themselves from their perch and began circling the tree in a counterclockwise manner not making a sound. By then the People had gathered behind us facing the tree and their voices soon joined that of their powwow. When the chants began, I had risen to my feet and was swept up by the emotion and spirit of the moment. In the power and energy of the chanting joined by drumming, I felt assured that Hobomock, Keihtan, and our ancestors would respond for how could they not hear the prayers of the People?

The shaman and the People continued their chanting for quite some time and all the while the ravens circled. The voice of Commossuck, with arms still raised, sounded like thunder above the sound of the rest and he continued the chant until the three messengers, having circled one last time, flew off to the southwest towards the home of Keihtan, disappearing beyond the trees. As he fell silent and his arms dropped to his side, the People fell quiet as well and all stood expectantly waiting for what would come next. Still facing the sachems and the mighty oak, the shaman made a motion towards me, half turning his body to the right but never removing his eyes from the great spread of branches. Moving quickly, but still in a bit of a foggy trance from the chanting, I hurried to his side holding out the otter fur bundle. I was terrified I would drop it and almost tripped over a half-buried root that spread from the Grandmother as I approached him. I held out the bundle in my hands and the powwow unwrapped it and removed his sacred pipe with its long wooden stem carved into the body of a snake and soapstone bowl holding the image of the Great Horned Serpent, servant, and helper of Hobomock.

For the first time Commossuck spoke. "We will wait for the arrival of others and then council under this tree of our ancestors for Hobomock has told me this is the place of power that we must use to protect the People from the evil demon I have seen with my own eyes in both vision and among the Wangunk. This, our grandmother, who is rooted in the Lower World, lives in this world, and reaches into the Sky World where our appeals and prayers must journey. It is the gateway and path through which our ancestors have always sought guidance and we too must do the same. Here we shall wait." Not waiting for a reply from the sachems, Commossuck walked past the two and sat cross-legged at the base of the great gray trunk, the sacred pipe across his lap, and closed his eyes.

Chapter Six

In mid-afternoon, Momauguin along with his uncle Qussuckquansh, arrived with twelve men each in two great dugout canoes. Tall like his sister but lean, the Grand Sachem of the People wore a simple red smock made of Dutchmannuck cloth and deerskin leggings. His head, shaved, but for a strip four inches high and two wide that extended from the top of his forehead to his neck, was adorned with four eagle feathers each symbolizing one of the four bands of the Quinnipiac people. On his chest was a mantle of the finest wampum, blue and white beads made from quahog and whelk shells that spoke of his lineage. His bearing though regal, was not haughty and he smiled glowingly at the sight of his sister and her husband. Not waiting to be greeted, he quickly embraced the sunksquaw as their uncle proclaimed "Manitou! It is the will of the spirits and ancestors that brings us together again so soon following the planting festival. May they look upon us with favor in this time of peril."

"Uncle, your words in council are always wise. May they lead us to overcome this new threat brought to our villages," said Shaumpishuh as she turned to hug her uncle. "Totoket has known these people from across the sea longer than any of us and though the Dutchmannuck have since abandoned their fort near your village, your people know their ways more than others. Is this pox of their doing?"

"Word from our Dutchmannuck friends is it came with the Awaunuy on the Quinnihticut near Pyquag. They had warned us that they were not to be trusted but our brothers in the River Bands after losing their fight with the Pequot a number of years past invited them to come and settle among them. They see the Awaunuy from the Massachusett and Wampanoag lands as protection from further humiliation at the hands of their foe. They also think they can break the stranglehold the Pequot have on the trade of fur for the goods we all are wanting from these people from across the sea."

"It is known that the Dutchmannuck from the island of Manhattan have favored the Pequot making this a dangerous game they all play" added Momauguin with a tone of disgust. "And now it is we the People who may pay the price for such folly."

Shaumpishuh nodded in agreement before saying "Come, let us sit under the Grandmother oak, Commossuck waits for us there. He has been in a dream-state since emerging from his weetou following his return early this morning. He had been among the Wangunk and saw the effect of this pox. Montowese has as well. He was restless waiting so went to the cove beyond the village to fish. I will send for him at once."

As the sachems walked through the village towards the Grandmother, people emerged from their weetous or came in from the fields and woods surrounding the village to welcome them with cries of "ho" and whoops of welcome . Yet it was impossible to miss the expressions of anticipation and even desperation on many as they began to crowd the three as if somehow getting closer would bring some relief. Having remained sitting a short distance from Commossuck since he fell into his dream-state, I anxiously leapt to my feet as the sachems approached yet tried to make myself as inconspicuous as standing exposed would allow. It was then that Momauguin acknowledged me and said "Ponaim, I know of your family's return to the home of Keihtan, we all have lost so many loved ones this past year. Be brave, we need you."

"Thank you sachem," I replied mustering in myself a semblance of maturity that I hoped hid my growing nervousness. "This is a hard time for us all."

The sachems having made their way to the Grandmother, gathered close to the sitting Commossuck who at first gave no sign that he was aware of their presence until he abruptly stood and shook his head in the manner of a bear waking from its hibernation; the black furred headdress of the beast adding to the likeness. Adjusting his focus to take in the sachems, the powwow greeted them with a sweeping gesture of his right arm as if welcoming them into his home as they moved unspeaking to a shaded spot tucked up against the southeast side of the sacred oak. At the same time, those who had followed the sachems parted like water flowing around a rock as Montowese, followed by the five warriors who had accompanied him the day before, approached, exclaiming his greetings to the new arrivals.

"Manitou, it is a good day," proclaimed the sachem from the Upper Quinnipiac. "It gladdens me to see you all are well and I hope it is the will of the Spirits that we will all remain so." He grasped the left hand of the Grand Sachem with his right pulling him close in an embrace before doing the same for his mother's cousin, Qussuckquansh. "I am hoping that Pawquash will arrive soon for his counsel together with that of Commossuck may help us protect the People from this demon that has been let loose to prey upon us."

Just then Wentubecum approached from the left beyond the edge of the village clearing with a small frail looking man with a headdress made from a deer skull complete with a set of three pointed antlers, the lower half of his face painted black and leggings made of skin. Around his shoulders was a long blue blanket of Dutchmannuck wool despite the day's warmth, which gave him the appearance of floating instead of walking. As he drew closer, it was obvious that despite his age he had a spritely manner. Montowese called out in welcome. Pawquash raised his right hand that was holding a rattle made from a turtle shell and shook it four times, once for each of the sachems.

I for one was enthralled by the site and knowing that Commossuck and he had a long friendship having both become shamans in their youth through the guidance of the same powwow at Mioonkhtuck. There had always been, according to my father, a bit of a rivalry between them despite their sincere friendship. But on seeing Pawquash, Commossuck became almost gleeful as he threw back his head in a gesture towards the sky for he knew that this new threat was going to take all the gifts and power the two could bring about from and within the Spirit World so that Hobomock might take notice and protect the People.

As Wentubecum and the powwow arrived at the Grandmother, after an exchange of greetings, Momauguin suggested the sachems and shamans sit and together review what was being said of the pox, what had been seen by Commossuck and Montowese, and what information the Dutchmannuck traders who had stopped at Totoket and Mioonkhtuck the day before had shared. They had recently left their trading house they called the House of Hope just to north of Pyquag fleeing the pox leaving only a handful of men to keep the operation going.

Montowese wasted no time describing what he had seen in his father's village at Pyquag. "There were more people sick than not, most in various stages of the illness and a number had already died. Their shaman was so sick he could not rise from his bed. Sowheage, my father, warned me to move my band west to escape what he called certain death. When I returned to my village, many were already preparing to leave. I gave them my blessing, not wanting any to remain against their wishes. But this sickness coming at a time when the Sisters need tending, and fish and game need to be brought in and dried for the winter will bring hunger if the People flee."

"I agree Montowese, we may be facing hunger this snow if our people move away, but if we stay will there be any of us left?" Momauguin responded. "It may be best to trust in the Spirit World and our shamans to protect us while remaining in our villages."

"We cannot force families to stay" added Shaumpishuh agreeing with her cousin after a few pregnant moments of silence. "That is not our way. This pox coming a year after it last came may be more than the People can stand or even survive. I for one will not ask any to stay against their wishes."

Commossuck had been listening intently as was his way before standing and stating emphatically that before any fled the home of their ancestors a ritual should be held at each village to call the Spirit World to protect the People. Pawquash agreed by shaking his rattle and exclaiming loudly "ho!" glancing quickly at each sachem before settling back on Commossuck.

"It must be done" he said.

Qussuckquansh agreed but cautioned that they must make sure the People of each band understand the danger involved and that their wishes would be honored. "How can we do otherwise?"

With that, the council ended and they immediately found themselves surrounded by the anxious villagers; young, old, female, and male. All were survivors of the first outbreak who now faced this sickness again. The People had heard what was said and to a person they appeared ready to participate in a ritual that might save them. As Shaumpishuh and Nashump escorted Momauguin, Qussuckquansh, Montowese, and their warriors to the central longhouse for a chance to eat and rest, Pawquash and Commossuck drifted quietly towards the powwow's weetou to prepare for the ritual that was to follow the next morning at sunrise. I followed.

Once at the weetou I paused not knowing whether to enter or wait to be invited. They might already be planning the ritual I thought, "if so I certainly do not want to disturb them." My wait was not long however for within minutes Pawquash called from inside "come boy."

I pulled up the deerskin flap to see the two sitting by the small fire in the center of the weetou preparing some dried fish and leeks they had just begun to boil and once they saw me Commossuck gestured that I should sit with them and eat. Commossuck had just started the fire and the smoke from it gave the air inside of the weetou a slightly foggy quality adding to the Spirit World appearance of the powwows. I moved quickly to the fire and sat on a mat made of rushes to the left of Commossuck and began to eagerly eat some strawberries, dandelion greens, and maize cake for until that moment I had not noticed the extent of my hunger.

"In the morning Ponaim, the ritual will be held on Tuxis Point where the peninsula looks to the sun as it rises from the sea and we need you to prepare a pit for offerings from the People. This is a great honor and responsibility Ponaim, one we both think you are ready to perform" Commossuck said in a reverent tone.

I was surprised by their request yet proud at the same time. Although Commossuck in the past would occasionally speak about certain aspects of ritual and the Spirit World he had never asked me to actively participate other than assisting him by holding objects he might need or gathering plants required for healing or ceremonies. Perhaps my vision of the Thunderbird made him think I was ready. It felt good that he had confidence in me as I began to imagine that this was my true calling. "Yes, thank you for your trust in me Commossuck, I will go right away" was my eager response.

"Not so fast Ponaim, first finish your food for you will need your strength today. Plus, we need to talk with you about how to prepare the offering pit for Hobomock. He is very particular and we have no room for error" Pawquash added. "The pit must be dug in front of the large stone that Mashup the giant dropped many years ago. You know the one, right?"

"Yes Pawquash" I replied.

"Make sure it is to the depth of your waist and as wide as your arm from shoulder to wrist. Line the bottom with sweet grass and prepare cedar boughs to cover it after the offerings have been made," said the powwow whose eyes glowed with an intensity that I found a bit unnerving.

"After all the People have placed an item of sacrifice into the pit, Pawquash and I will then light the pit on fire so make sure that there is a good quantity of sweetgrass on the bottom so the embers will catch and our sacrifices will ride the smoke up to Ho-bomock the healer and Keihtan the creator" instructed Commossuck.

"But before you go, you must be painted for the spirits must see that you go about their work and not that of man. You must choose so we can prepare you for your paint which must cover your chest, back, arms, and face" said Pawquash.

My mind raced in a thousand directions as I struggled to think of what my paint would be when it came clearly to me: the Thunderbird of course. "Shamans, the Thunderbird came to me last night, it seems right to choose her."

"Your dream flight confirms that the spirits have called you Ponaim" said Commossuck with nodding agreement of Pawquash. "It is a sign and a great gift.."

"I choose to be painted white with a red Thunderbird on my chest and back" I proclaimed with a confidence that startled me. "White for purification and red for the fire that will burn our sacrifices."

"Manitou! You have spoken the truth about the boy Commossuck" said Pawquash in a joyfully excited way. "You should know Ponaim that Keihtan does not choose many. It is a great honor. We will prepare your paints."

While I ravenously finished eating my meal, Pawquash made up the white paint by creating a paste of shell that had been crushed to a powder, clay, and water while Commossuck ground red ochre and mixed it with red clay and bear grease to make the red. When I was finished, Pawquash applied the white paint and then Commossuck created the image of the Thunderbird, first on my back and then my chest all the while chanting. My long black hair was tied back and each placed a raven feather in the knot in recognition of the messenger Keihtan had sent earlier that day. Then Commossuck lit a twisted braid of sweetgrass while Pawquash lit one of sage and they silently and slowly moved them around my head and body in a solemn smudging ceremony to purify me and my intent.

"You are ready Ponaim" said Commossuck. "But are you?"

An intense wave of emotion overcame me at that moment and I could feel my strength increase as the spirits of my parents and all the ancestors seemed to swirl into me and I felt a confidence and purpose that I had not felt before. "Yes" I said. "I am."

When I emerged from the weetou having followed the powwows out and began to walk in the direction of Tuxis through the village, most stopped what they were doing and simply stared while some called out "Manitou!" Shaumpishuh and the other sachems stood and nodded as I passed the longhouse and Nashump quickly went back in and returned with one of the iron tipped digging tools the Dutchmannuck call a shovel for he understood what I was tasked to do. As I reached the edge of the village clearing and entered the path through the woods that would lead me around the saltmarsh Shambisqua caught up to me by cutting through the trees. She asked no questions and did not speak, just proceeded to follow a few steps behind. I could feel my heart racing as I wanted to speak and say so much but knew that it might somehow contaminate the mission the spirits had called me to do. I had to remain focused. So, we walked silently along the trail to Tuxis.

By the time we arrived at the rock as Pawquash had instructed, I felt energized by my part in the ritual that might protect us all and I immediately began to dig with the tool Nashump had given me. It had an odd feel to it at first but as I moved the sandy soil I began to realize how much easier and faster it was to work with than our stone or shell scrapers. As I dug, the deeper I got the more energy I seemed to have as my arms seemed to move feverishly on their own. In what seemed no time at all, the pit was dug and I jumped out feeling strangely gleeful yet solemn at the same time. Pleased with my work I began to gather the sweetgrass needed to line the bottom while Shambisqua sat nearby watching silently enthralled by the transformation that was taking place in her friend.

I did not have far to go, just to the flat area a little to the north of the rock, to find the grass and I began cutting it with my knife and gathering it in bundles in my arms. Though scratchy against my arms and chest, the smell of the fresh spring growth was sweet and almost intoxicating and I thanked Earth Mother for sharing her bounty with me. I cut enough to fill the pit up to the height of my knees and then set about getting the cedar boughs that would be needed to cover the pit once the offerings had filled it, placing them in a pile off to the side so as to be ready to be used.

When I was done, I was aware for the first time of the streaks of sweat that had smeared the paint on my face, chest, and arms and a sudden feeling of fatigue. But the tiredness did not last long for as I stood looking towards the ocean in the direction where the sun would rise in the morning, a rush of elation embraced me as I again realized that the world of the Spirits, nature, and man would be my path. I turned to see Shambisqua coming towards me with a bladder of water she had brought with her and she handed it to me. I drank from it with gusto then handed it back to her with a nod of thanks and picked up the Dutchmannuck shovel. Together we walked silently back to the village in the warmth of the late afternoon.

Chapter Seven

As Shambisqua and I entered the village as dusk began to fall, there were immediate shouts of welcome and support from all those who gathered around us as they knew I had been about the work of Keihtan and Hobomock. Worry was hard to hide for many as it was evident in their faces and in the way some warmly embraced me. This gave rise to a feeling of self-consciousness in me because since the death of my family most in the village despite their own losses and heartbreak, had looked upon me with pity knowing that at a young age circumstance had set me adrift in the world as a lone pup even though I had been taken in by Commossuck. Suddenly I was being welcomed as a symbol of hope and that change left me honored but uncomfortable because this was unfamiliar to me.

Here I was a skinny young boy with my paint smeared from sweat and dirt, an orphan suddenly the symbol of hope for the People. I began to think of how strange it was that the spirits had led me to this moment and as I continued to walk towards the weetou that was now my home and Commossuck, a growing sense of purpose and responsibility rose in my heart. I had become part of something greater than myself; I now had a role in the preservation and protection of the People, a role I would perform for the rest of my days. Though exhausted and a bit confused by it all, I felt the strength of this new empowerment and responsibility that also brought with it a sense of pride, dignity, and purpose which I knew I had to carry into whatever the future might hold.

Pawquash greeted me as I neared the weetou, took my hand, and led me inside. There Commossuck stoically sat, holding his sacred pipe, and staring it seemed, blankly at the matted wall. He said nothing as Pawquash ushered me to sit across from him with the low burning fire between us. "This boy is your place of honor for the task you have performed for the People, our ancestors, and the Spirits. It is imperative that together we do all we can to bring about a return of balance to the universe. About this we must now speak."

"Of course, Pawquash" was my reply as I sat, my eyes transfixed upon my mentor who continued to sit silently as if no other was in his presence. His paint remained on his face and body from earlier in the day though his bear cap and robe had been put to the side. Besides the pipe, his hands held a bundle of sacred items wrapped in the skin of a seal, another servant of Hobomock, and he wore only his breechcloth.

"We have seen through the eyes of our helpers that you have done well Ponaim" said

Commossuck turning to look at me after we had sat in quiet for a while. "It is important to speak now of what we do tomorrow so that the spirit energy given to you by Keihtan may help us deliver our message to the Spirits."

With that, Pawquash, who had been standing by the weetou door, sat down to Commossuck's left and the two shamans closed their eyes and seemed to drift away. I watched intently for I had seen Commossuck in such a state many times this past year, but this was different. The air in the weetou began to take on a different quality, seeming to swirl and causing the walls to pulsate. All the while the powwows sat silently, their eyes closed in a state of rest, their backs straight, their faces expressionless. I remained sitting motionless and closed my eyes as I felt the space around me continue to spin and swirl creating a sense that I was disconnecting from this world and moving into another realm of existence; somewhere between here and elsewhere. It brought me into a state of trance that was both exhilarating and frightening for I felt I was no longer in control of who I was or where I was.

I do not know how long we sat in such a state, but during that time I felt myself enter a dreamworld, one that Commossuck had often described to me, and suddenly my dream soul ventured beyond this existence and I could see the ritual tomorrow already happening. I saw myself, the two shamans, the four sachems, and the people of Mennunkatuck gathered before the sacrificial pit and the rock of Mashup while I floated above it all. All was in motion, fluid and misty as if I were viewing what was happening through one of those wavy but cloudy containers the Dutchmannuck call glass. The offerings had been made and they had been set alight and in the east Father Sun had begun to brighten the sky. But dark clouds descended upon the horizon shading the sun and keeping its light in shadow as a wind began to howl from the northeast whipping the flames in the pit and blowing sparks onto the People who began to scatter. My heart felt their fear and my eyes filled with tears. Startled by my vision, I opened my eyes to see the shamans looking at me intensely.

"You saw it too" said Commossuck. "The clouds, the wind, the sparks of the fire."

"Yes" I replied. "It frightened and saddened me so I opened my eyes."

"Ponaim, the gift given to you by Keihtan brought you forward to see the future. It is a powerful but fearful tool we shamans can use to help protect and guide the People. But this vision, which we saw too, is one we must not speak of for if we were to, the People might lose hope and if that happens, much more will be lost than what we fear is going to happen" the powwow said.

"It is a dark omen" Pawquash added. "But there was some hope in what we saw. Did you see it Ponaim?"

"The People scattered before the embers but were not burned. Could this be a sign of our survival?" I asked.

"It may very well be, but a scattered people is a broken people. My hope is that those who survive may come together in the future after this pestilence subsides as we did last year. But a greater concern is this vision may not be about the pox, but of a darker future beyond this moment," Commossuck said as he lifted his hand to his forehead in a motion that embodied his deep worry and consternation.

Anxiously I pointed out that even though the sun did not rise through the clouds, the sky did brighten behind them. "Does that mean hope for the future? For where there is light is there not always hope?"

"You are wise beyond your time in this world" said Pawquash. "It is true that though covered in clouds the sun did brighten the sky in a sign that Keihtan was aware of the suffering of the People and that there might still be a future for us. Tomorrow we must keep our vision to ourselves as well as when we go to the other bands. If we can help the People have hope and faith that the Spirits will favor them perhaps the magnitude of our vision will not come to pass."

We remained quiet for a time, each absorbed in our thoughts about what we had seen. The silence was broken when Pawquash said "It is said that a dark demon dressed in the black of the Awaunuy god-talkers moves silently from person to person inflicting this pox upon them. The people of Pyquag are sure of it as are the Wangunk of Mattabasec. If so, we will have to journey into the Spirit World to confront it and drive it from us."

"There may be a sorcerer among the Awaunuy who has unleashed this demon to rid the Dawnland of its People" added Commossuck. "After all, it is said that since their arrival many from the Spirit World who have always interacted with us and helped the People have gone away. Even the giant Mashup who so often helped our ancestors and left the great rock where we will sacrifice in the morning has not been seen by any since the Awaunuy arrival fourteen years ago, the year of your birth Ponaim. I am afraid these people from across the sea carry with them a powerful supernatural ability that did not at first seem apparent."

"If the dream souls of our people are going to be captured by this sorcerer, then we will have to journey to wherever that sorcerer may bring them to retrieve as many as possible before the sickness can kill them. But I do, Commossuck, fear this demon or sorcerer may dwell in a Spirit World unfamiliar to us, maybe even back across the waters where the Awaunuy come from" said Pawquash.

Again we drifted into silence until I was compelled to say, "I remember the stories of Mashup. "My mother would tell them to my sister and me before we went to sleep when we were small. I always hoped that someday I would see the great giant. Shambisqua and I would sometimes sneak away from the village and climb the very rock we will sacrifice in front of tomorrow in the hopes the giant would come and we would see him. The thought of such a being has always excited me."

Pawquash smiled as he thought of my story and the benevolent giant and said "Ponaim, you know that the fog that comes off the ocean is really from his smoking pipe. He is believed to live on an island beyond our shores where the Dutchmannuck, Awaunuy and others cannot reach him. Some say he will return someday."

"And chase these people from our shores," I proclaimed to the affirming grunts of the shamans.

The two powwows then took on a more solemn and serious demeanor as the conversation shifted to the ritual that would take place before and during the sunrise the next morning. They began by reviewing each of the steps that would be taken culminating in the lighting of the offerings the band members would place in the pit. Each family or individual would bring forward one of their most cherished and valuable possessions as an offering to let Hobomock and the rest of the Spirit World know that the Quinnipiac were really nothing without them and in doing so were making an offering and appeal to them for protection from the smallpox now striking others in the Dawnland. I listened intently to what they planned, knowing that our focus tomorrow would be crucial. Beside the offerings, the prayers, drumming, and singing would send a sincere and powerful message since in them would reside the true heartfelt intentions of the People.

When the plans had been discussed and my role in the ritual was explained, the shamans both returned to silence wrapped deeply in the blanket of their thoughts. By then it was well into the night and Mennunkatuck, which had been buzzing with activity in preparation for the morning ritual, had grown calm and still. I imagined each person was turning inward and examining what role they may have played to bring about the twin calamities that threatened our very existence; first the pox of a year ago and now its looming return. Every Quinnipiac knew from childhood that the community's health and well-being was only as strong as the collective character of its members. Disease, famine, war, and other negative conditions were usually the result of the group turning away from their basic moral practices and the right way of living that had been ordained by and given to the People by Keihtan. The result was a breakdown of the vital physical and spiritual energies and forces that maintain a balanced and interconnected universe. With the arrival of smallpox, this appeared to be what has happened and all in Mennunkatuck knew that this crisis was a collective fault and not that of any one individual. They had to as a community take responsibility and make amends through the willing confession of their turning from the true path as they make their offerings to Keihtan and Hobomock.

Commossuck had taught me that evil exists in many forms and dwells among the People in this world with permission from Keihtan, Hobomock, and the rest of the Spirit World. It takes advantage of every opportunity so when the People turned from the traditional ways and being close to Keihtan, it had an opportunity to inflict great harm. It was made clear to me that night that the People, in order to save themselves would have to return to the ways of being of our ancestors as given to us by Keihtan. Had the desire to obtain the many goods brought by the Awaunuy and Dutchmannuck become so important that the People were willing to abandon and even forget the old ways that had maintained the world balance?

Since the arrival of these people from across the sea to trade a few decades before my birth, increasing numbers of the Quinnipiac of all bands had given up the seasonal way of life that had sustained us for generations to live more permanently in their shore villages so as to be able to trade more effectively and easily with first the Dutchmannuck and more recently the Awaunuy. Many of the People had already become dependent on those goods brought to the Dawnland and were unwilling to give them up. Some even made fun of those who advocated a traditional life and I remember my father having had strong words with some here in Mennunkatuck who soon after left us for Totoket so as to obtain the metal, cloth, and glass beads of the Dutchmannuck more easily. A growing number were even succumbing to the burning water that turned men into fools.

Well before the first evidence of light began to brighten the eastern horizon, Commossuck woke me in order that along with Pawquash, we might ritually cleanse ourselves in the river beyond the village. I had spent a restless night in anticipation of the morning thinking about whether or not our vision would actually come about knowing that according to the shamans, what is sometimes seen in a vision is a metaphor of future developments and not an actual event. Still I could not help worrying about how I as well as the People might react if the ritual really unfolded as the vision revealed. I also could not keep my mind from wandering into what the future might hold for us all for it was obvious that the return of smallpox was something so terrible it might even mean the end of the all the Quinnipiac. I told myself I had to trust in the vision because if the People were not burned but scattered then perhaps as terrible as the impact of the disease might be some of us might survive. Both those outcomes frightened me so I decided to cling to the hope that our ritual might somehow prevent the demon who brings the pox from coming to Mennunkatuck or any of the other bands.

As the three of us made our way to the river, the sounds of the night surrounded us and made me feel comfortable and at ease knowing that Earth Mother was blessing us with a reminder that despite the current circumstances she was still here sharing the beauty of Keihtan's creation with us. The gentle sound of the leaves rustling in the soft breeze, the katydids and crickets calling for mates, came together in an eternal song of summer. We walked slowly and purposely to the river, shed what clothing we had, and slipped quietly into the water to ritually wash the contamination of this life from our bodies. The water was cool but refreshing in its brackish way, the smell and taste of salt from the sea mixed with those of the fresh water coming down from Quonnipaug. An otter, curious to see two-leggeds in the water this time of night, paused as it swam by to ascertain why we were there, his head bobbing up and down in the moonlight as he studied our purpose in being there before turning and swimming upriver to his journey's end.

"Look, a helper of Hobomock" said Pawquash softly as he slowly rinsed his left arm with the river water. "Perhaps he was sent by him to verify our intentions."

"Otters are usually creatures of the night, especially since the Dutchmannuck came to trade for their pelts and that of their brother the beaver. It is rare now with so many being trapped during the last twenty years that we might even see one. It makes my heart glad" said Commossuck.

I could hear frogs calling in the marshes beyond the river and a few ducks speaking to one another in the distance and while the breeze continued to work its way through the trees I could not help but look upon my two companions and feel a strange and powerful connection to both. I had seen what they had seen, I reminded myself, and they had welcomed me into their world, one that few are called to and even fewer tread. I was convinced if I do manage to survive this pox, it would be with their help. I ducked my head under the waste deep water of the river, bending my knees to do so, and felt its coolness completely surround me. Raising myself up, I could feel a powerful new energy; trepidation was gone and a surging sense of purpose replaced any foreboding I might have felt. I felt as if I was born again.

The subdued warmth of the night air greeted us as we emerged from the river and made our way back to the village. The cloudless sky held a canopy of the lights of our ancestors and as we arrived among the weetous we could hear stirrings in some as the sleepless had begun their preparations for the day. By the time we ducked through the entrance the wetness of the river was gone from us except for our hair and Pawquash and Commossuck began quickly to prepare the paints we would wear for the ritual. "You know Ponaim, the paint we wear is a representation of our connection to the Spirit realm and it symbolically aids in the transformation we must make while conducting rituals or in healing and curing. Like us, you have chosen yours through the gift given you by Keihtan."

"You must apply as much of it yourself as you can starting with your face and working your way down the rest of your body, as much and where determined by the Spirits and the circumstance of the ceremony to be performed. It is vital to be recognized by the Spirits from the Sky World, Earth World, and

Lower World for it is they who will accept or deny our appeals and offerings" Pawquash said with reverence.

The white paint that had been made for me the day before was in a gourd bowl and Commossuck handed it to me. "But what of the Thunderbird" I asked, "I cannot paint it myself on my back."

"For that today we will help you but in the future you must seek instructions from him on how to represent it in a manner more symbolic than realistic. You can find that answer in a dream walk but as for now, time is upon us" answered Commossuck. I nodded as I took the gourd and began covering my face starting with my forehead, then cheeks, nose, chin, and neck. It felt greasy but cool as I continued to paint my arms, chest, legs, and as much of my sides and back as I could reach. Pawquash then made the red image of the Thunderbird on my chest and back while Commossuck applied his black and red paint to his own face and body. When Pawquash had finished the red Thunderbird on my back, he then turned to his own paint which was a deep vermillion that covered his face, arms, and hands with black dots in a horizontal row across his forehead and on each cheek just below the eye. Both powwows then placed their headdresses upon their heads and Commossuck donned his bear robe. Commossuck and I wore only our breech cloths, moccasins, and paint while Pawquash had put on his deerskin leggings as well and his woolen blanket which he wrapped around his shoulders. The hair of each of us had been left loose and untended lending a wild look to the two elderly shamans while a single raven feather was secured upon my own with a strip of sinew tied around my forehead and knotted behind.

Commossuck and Pawquash each picked up their sacred bundles that held their pipes, tobacco, and herbs. I was asked to take the seal skin that held the sage, sweetgrass, and cedar that would be burned to create the smoke to smudge each person taking part in the ceremony, and a sack made from a beaver pelt that held the shells that would hold them. Together we left the weetou and walked quietly into the night towards Tuxis and the site of the ritual that would take place. I remember the stillness that had descended as we walked through the trees disturbed only by the rhythmic sound of breaking waves against the shore as we came out of the woods and into the openness of the peninsula. The nearly full moon lit the trail as we walked lending a mystical quality to the marsh grasses to our left and the sandy beach to our right accented by the moonlit foam of the waves as they ended their journey against the sand.

Mashup's rock was easily seen in the moonlight and as we approached it with the offering pit before it Commossuck asked me to make a small fire off a bit to the side and out of the breeze that came gently off the water to the south. I quickly sprang to my task after gently placing my two bundles on a bed of leaves under an old windblown oak, and in no time I had a fire started within a ring of beach stones I had collected the day before. Meanwhile, the powwows stood in front of the offering pit softly chanting the sound songs that would alert the Spirits of our arrival and intent, their arms raised towards the heavens in supplication. Each sound was not a word but a cosmic sound that was more hummed than sung in a repetitive manner. As they chanted, I could see a faint brightening on the eastern horizon and though still worried about the omen in last night's vision, felt relieved in the sight of the cloudless star filled sky.

While the shamans continued their chanting, out of the darkness, a stream of the People emerged from the tree line led by the four sachems, winding their way along the trail to pool into a cluster behind the powwows. Each carried what was to be their offering by individual or family to Keihtan. I vividly remember how quiet they were, not even their footsteps could be heard. The sachems, led by Momauguin, moved silently to the front of the rest, he and Shaumpishuh to the right of Commossuck and Montowese and Qussuckquansh to the left of Pawquash. Once they were in place, the shamans stopped chanting and Commossuck motioned to me to bring the shells and sacred plants that would create the smoke that would purify the People as they made their offerings.

My job, as had been explained to me, was to fill for each powwow two shells and light the mixture with a burning pine twig full of summer sap so each would hold the smoldering plants and if one needed to be refilled or lit, I was to do so. In each shell I placed a mix of sage and cedar twisted together with sweetgrass. Then I lit them with the burning end of the twig, so the smoldering and smoky plants might purify each person as they made their offerings.

Commossuck began by smudging the head and body of Momauguin, gently waving a wand of three eagle feathers to guide the smoke. The Grand Sachem then stepped forward and placed an ornately carved and decorated war club, a gift from his grand-father, into the trench, bowing as he backed away. Commossuck then turned to Shaumpishuh, who after being smudged, placed an intricate belt of white and blue wampum beads as an offering. Pawquash did the same for Qussuckquansh and Montowese as each person of the band then stepped forward one at a time to make their offering. As the plants in each shell burned away, I handed each powwow the second while refilling the first as quickly as I could. Just before Father Sun began to start his journey above the rim of the world, the offerings had filled the pit and Commossuck asked me to bring two burning brands from the fire, one for him and one for Pawquash.

As I hurried to fulfill his request, I looked expectantly towards the eastern horizon expecting to see a bank of clouds crowd out the rising sun as in our vision. To my relief and surprise, the sky remained clear and there was no hint of a northeast wind. I grasped the pine sticks that became torches, each burning with an intensity created by the pitch within them and brought them quickly to the pow-wows who had begun chanting again, joined in their rhythmic and repetitive song by all present, accompanied by handheld drums whose sound is sacred to Keihtan. Commossuck approached the trench towards the right side while Pawquash did so on the left and together they lit the sweetgrass at the bottom, then placed their torches in the center and the entire pit with its offerings was quickly in flames. Our chanting continued as the flames leaped high and I imagined each person to be in a place of spiritual reconciliation and confession in hopes that Keihtan and Hobomock would hear their prayers. I too joined in the chants and sincere appeal to the Spirits while asking them to forgive my sometimes selfish and self-absorbed actions and thoughts that I at times wallowed in since the death of my family. As I watched the flames reflected off the rock of Mashup, I was overwhelmed by the urge to ask Keihtan for the strength, courage, and guidance I knew I would need to follow the path of a shaman.

The flames began to die down and Commossuck motioned to me, while continuing to chant, to bring the cedar branches I had gathered and together with he and Pawquash, placed them over the pit. They ignited quickly and the sparks began to fly up into the air above the height of the rock. It was at that moment I feared the vision for if the People were to be burned, it was would be then. But a northeast wind did not rise and as we sang our chant, the flames slowly died until Father Sun had fully risen and what was left of the offerings were charred and turned to ash.

Chapter Eight

Unlike most rituals and ceremonies that were rather loud and raucous affairs with individuals and groups dancing, singing, and drumming, to beseech the Spirits in a joyous and frenzied manner, the ceremony at Mashup's Rock that morning was a solemn and subdued one, unusual in that quality and one I often remember for that reason as well for what followed. It was clear to me in retrospect that we were all in an unknown place yet aware that the balance that had preserved our world to that point had been drastically disrupted. These new and frightening threats to our very existence and understanding of the way the universe had always created an atmosphere of severe trauma and questioning amongst the People that grew more extreme in the days and weeks that followed.

I remember vividly that when Father Sun had risen over the horizon to become the familiar life giving disk bestowing his brilliant light as he had always done, the People, including Commossuck, Pawquash, and the sachems, stood frozen and silent staring at him and the smoldering pit that held our offerings. None wanted or dared to move for that would bring on the reality of what we all knew we would need to face but not ready to confront. Would

Keihtan and the spirits, especially Hobomock accept our offerings and save us from the black robed demon? To return to Mennunkatuck would open us to the possibility that we may not be so fortunate. So there we all remained, clinging to the desperate hope that our reluctance to leave might somehow delay the inevitable and we would be spared.

In the silence accompanied only by the sound of the waves and the morning songs of our winged brothers and sisters, I recall Momauguin, quietly, was the first to move, gesturing to the other sachems that it was time to leave the place of offerings. He looked to Shaumpishuh who stood gazing towards the horizon before gathering herself together enough to speak.

"People, we have done what we can, let us hope our offerings and sincere appeals to Keihtan will protect us from the threat of the return of this disease brought to our land." The sunksquaw then turned to look upon the people of Mennunkatuck who still stood frozen behind her. She smiled and raised her arms as if embracing them while saying "We can only do now what we must to help one another in the days to come and stay pure of heart and mind for that is what Kiehtan would expect of his people, the Quinnipiac. Let us return to the village and live according to the ways of our ancestors."

At that moment, I remember turning to see Commossuck, in his red and black paint, wrapped in his bear cloak and headdress, lean towards the trench that held the smoldering offerings and fall to his knees in a gesture of reverence and humility. Pawquash had moved to the left of the pit and had begun to sing as he motioned with upraised hands towards Father Sun. At that instant I felt myself suddenly pulled towards Mashup's Rock as if a rope had caught me. Before I was even aware, I leapt into the offering pit and could feel the warm ash envelop my moccasins and begin to burn my ankles and shins. But I felt no pain, only the urge to lie down in the trench to find rest and restore my sense of being, wrapped in the pure joy of being one with the Spirits. I remember hearing the cries of those who saw me jump and the fuzzy dream quality of seeing Commossuck lean towards me and grab me by the armpits to haul me up and out. What followed was a moment and sensation I will always remember; one of warmth, serenity, and a strange lightness as I was both in my body and outside it, a duality of existence in which I was acutely aware of my dream soul and body soul being separate yet one as the powwow lifted me from the trench. I felt absolutely free and overwhelmed with happiness.

As Commossuck lay me on the ground near the offering pit and Pawquash and others rushed to my side I remember looking up at the cloudless blue sky while feeling the warm sandy soil against my back. Three ravens floated high above us all, gently flapping their wings as they leisurely circled. I could hear cries of "Manitou!" as everyone pressed forward to see what they were sure were severe burns from the hot ash and charred remains of the offerings in the pit. To the surprise of all, there were none on my feet, legs, back, or arms. "Manitou!" again was the collective cry as my people acknowledged the powerful sign that this represented and Montowese proclaimed what had happened was surely a sign of the Keihtan's favor towards me and a good omen for the days ahead.

Nashump and Wentubecum stepped forward and lifted me gently to my feet as Pawquash began a song of celebration that everyone soon joined. As a group, led by Shaumpishuh and Momauguin, we moved down the trail and back to the village to the rhythmic and repetitive songs and drumming.

I can still remember the sound of the songs and cries mixed with appeals to Keihtan who the People were sure had seen and heard their offerings. They continued to praise the Spirits for sending a message through me that they had indeed been given a sign of redemption from their fear of the pox that was ravaging our neighbors and as they did so they looked to the heavens. I was carried by Nashump,

Wentubecum, and two others who would not allow me to walk and that was probably wise based upon the hazy state of betweenness I was still experiencing.

Commossuck walked before us and Pawquash behind as we wound our way along the trail that led from the beach and marshes into the woods and under the green leaves of summer that formed the canopy above us intermittently broken to reveal the brilliant blue of the morning sky. As we entered the village I was brought to the weetou of Commossuck; the ravens who had followed us lazily flying from tree to tree, found a perch on the old oak beside our weetou.

I remember looking up to see them just as I was brought to the door as the chanting, singing, and drumming continued mixed with shouts and whoops. We had followed Commossuck in and he gestured to those carrying me to place me on my sleeping bench to the right of the door where he began to smudge me with a mixture of sacred tobacco and sage. I felt my eyes close and remember drifting into sleep to the smell of the smudge and the sounds of the People's singing and chants only to wake in the evening to the sight of the two powwows sitting across the fire circle in the center of the weetou staring at me. Their paint had been removed and their hair pulled back and as usual Pawquash had the blanket of

Dutchmannuck cloth wrapped around him while Commossuck wore deerskin leggings and a necklace of bear claws draped across his bare chest.

Seeing me awake, Pawquash shook his turtle shell rattle three times and smiled while Commossuck nodded in a sign of pleasure. "Ponaim, are you feeling alright?" the powwow asked. "You have been brought to a special place by the Spirit World. It is a sign of their favor."

I sat up and remember feeling at ease and rested as I looked once again at my feet and legs, wondering if I had in fact been burned by the ashes or whether it had all been simply a dream. There were no signs of burns as I rubbed my ankles, shins, and thighs making sure I was in fact unharmed while Commossuck continued to speak.

"We must all begin to prepare for what Hobomock will bring in the days to come for we will know whether our offerings will replace the vision we have seen or whether in fact the pox will arrive and scatter the People in its wake. But for now we must eat and rest then tomorrow gather the medicines we may need."

Looking back now I remember how the next few weeks had a dreamy quality as first along with Pawquash and Commossuck, I traveled to Totoket to repeat the offering ritual to ask the Spirits and ancestors to protect the People from the dark demon.

Following the ceremony, some at Totoket felt it wise to destroy what was left of the old Dutchmannuck fort and trading post that sat on a bluff just to the east of the summer place of their weetous on the neck of land they had shared for many years. Qussuckquansh suggested that a council should take place to determine the right course to take so as not to offend the Dutchmannuck while others saw the fort as a gateway by which the demon might enter the village. Then there was the problem of the three Awaunuy men who lived across the river who had been workers for the Dutchmannuck and had remained following the closing of the fort. They often used the ramshackle outpost for their own purposes, usually storing goods. How might they react?

The council, held the day following the offering ritual, was heated as the People were clearly divided by the choice. Since the shaman at Totoket had died from the pox the year before, the council turned to Commossuck and Pawquash for advice as to the best course to take and the two powwows agreed to seek guidance from Hobomock and return with what they could determine. Together, the three of us left Totoket for the place of sacred stones, outcrops, and cliffs in the forest between that village and Mennunkatuck. While I made a fire and tended to our camp tucked against an east facing, stone chiseled ridge, the shamans climbed to the top of the ridge and entered the dream state to gleam from Keihtan and Hobomock the best course for the people of Totoket to take.

As darkness began to wrap itself around us Pawquash and Commossuck had not moved from their perches on the ridge top about twenty feet above and it became obvious that they might very well remain in their meditative state well into the night if not beyond until the reawakening of the Earth Mother in the morning. The sounds of the night became louder as the shroud of darkness grew stronger and soon the only light was that of the rising moon and the small fire I maintained. I could no longer see either of the shamans in the dark though each was only twenty feet above the camp for Mother Moon did not touch them with her light. As I readied a meal for myself of parched maize a rustling among the low bushes and scrubby growth on the ridge behind the powwows became louder and from the soft grunting sounds, it was clear that a bear had begun her nocturnal search for food.

Picking up a broken pine branch full of pitch that I had placed in the fire, I quickly lifting it up towards the ridgetop above me only to see in the dim light a black bear with its nose an arm's length behind Commossuck who, if he was aware of her presence, did not move from his crossed legged sitting position. Sniffing, the bear moved a bit to the powwow's left and then right as if ascertaining his reason for being on the ledge. Then with a low grunt, she turned and moved along the ridgeline to the north and into the darkness. During her visit, neither Commossuck nor Pawquash ever moved, both seemingly oblivious to her and it was then I recalled that the black bear was a power animal and spiritual guide for Commossuck, and that she may have carried a message to him. I returned my torch to the fire and sat to finish my meal.

By then Mother Moon had risen to her full height and her light brought a different feel to the cloudless night. The blanket of ancestors above also looked brightly down upon us and I felt a feeling of peace and calm in my spirit as I knew that somehow the efforts of the powwows would protect us. The balance of the world will be brought back I assured myself as I pondered the circumstances that had led to this moment. Perhaps I thought, I too should try to enter the dream world in order to see or learn what I might find out that could help. So I banked the fire to allow it to remain burning slowly and moved to the base of the cliff roughly between where I knew Commossuck and Pawquash were above me. I sat with my back against the stone face and began to softly chant the sacred sounds I had often heard Commossuck chant while closing my eyes in the hope that I might be given the gift of vision by Keihtan.

I am not sure how long I sat chanting but it was that evening that for the first time I came to know my spirit guide, the red tailed hawk. At one point while I chanted I saw her coming toward me in my mind's eye while my eyes remained closed and I was focused on my chanting. Her powerful wings carried her swiftly as she came from the southwest and over the back of the ridge where I sat and as she came closer she brought with her the light of day as if she were pulling a blanket. Straight as an arrow she came until she was almost upon me when suddenly I felt myself or rather my dream soul lift up toward her, much as I had felt the night the Thunderbird came. Together we began to move through the air though it was unclear to me whether we were the same or separate as we did.

Surrounded in the sunlight she brought with her, we flew over the top of the ridge where I saw the powwows sitting in meditation and then instantly we were at Totoket where I could see Qussuckquansh and others standing near the old fort and among them the three Awaunuy and the one called Molinar was gesturing angrily. He was angry as he raised his fist in a threatening way while men from the village stood near the fort gate with torches, clearly ready to enter and burn the old fort. The two other Awaunuy were holding their firearms and seemed ready to shoot at the sachem while the men of Totoket held spears, war clubs, and bows ready for their arrows.

Then, just as suddenly as my guide had brought me to Totoket, we were back to the ridge where the shamans were and the next thing I remember I woke to hazy morning sunlight while still sitting by the base of the ridge. Pawquash and Commossuck descended to my left a short distance away. I rubbed my eyes to make sure I was in fact awake and as the powwows came towards me I was suddenly consumed by an overwhelming sense of danger.

"Ponaim," said Commossuck, " we must leave right away for Totoket. We will eat and talk as we walk."

"Yes Commossuck," I said as I stood up and moved quickly to our little camp to join the shamans as we began to pick up the few things we had brought with us. Clouds had begun to come from the southwest and were thickening and would soon swallow the sun bringing the scent of rain with them. A dampness could also be felt coming from the sea a short distance to our left as we moved to the trail that led to the village.

Once we had entered the path after a short walk through and around a series of jagged, craggy cliffs and hills full of tumbled boulders and rocks, Commossuck began to speak. "Pawquash and I in our visions have seen a great darkness descend upon the People confirming our worst fears. Within that darkness we have both seen the sorcerer who seems of the Awaunuy for his face was pale and his eyes were blue like winter ice. His face was fierce and the air that surrounded him cold like that during the Wolf Moon when the snow comes and the frozen trees crack in the wind. When we approached him we were instantly thrown back by a powerful wind. We tried four times, each time from one of the Four Sacred Directions; East, South, West, and North. But nothing worked. His power is strong and of a type we have not seen before. The worst thing was this sorcerer was gathering the dream souls of the People and others here in the Dawnland, making a pile of them before him. He dwelled in a tunnel like a cave with fire behind him despite the cold and we could not see a way around him." The shaman paused for a moment to collect his thoughts then said, "We must find a way to confront him and take back the souls he will capture for it is certain he will come."

"Or prevent him from taking them" added Pawquash. "We do not have much time."

A chill ran down my spine as I grappled with the gravity of their vision and the frightening image of the sorcerer as they described him and I began to shake a bit nervously as we walked. Here I was, a boy of fourteen winters - how could I help confront such a spirit clearly set on destroying us all? Then I remembered my own vision and knew I had to gather myself and tell the powwows of my journey with the red tailed hawk and the confrontation at the fort.

"Shamans" I began after we had walked a bit in silence. "I had a vision as well last night when a red tailed hawk came to me and brought me to Totoket where I witnessed a confrontation between the three Awaunuy who stay across the river and Qussuckquansh and some of the men of Totoket. The Awaunuy were threatening the sachem while our warriors stood by with torches ready to burn the Dutchmannuck fort. I did not see the outcome because we flew back to the ridge and our camp but it seemed there would be violence unless the People left the fort to the Awaunuy."

"We must look to this vision right away" said Commossuck, to bring about a fight with the Awaunuy or Dutchmannuck would not be wise for the People at this time and the deaths of those three would certainly bring that about. We must counsel Qussuckquansh on this matter right away."

When we arrived at Totoket, the village was like an ant hill disturbed by a stick as a state of agitation had set in for the three Awaunuy were coming down the river having left their dwelling place on the other side a short distance upstream. They were clearly armed which was unusual for them since an amicable but at times tense relationship had always existed at Totoket since the early days of the Dutch-mannuck. Both the Awaunuy and the People had pretty much always gone about their own way only to trade and occasionally share the fire water that made Molinar in particular unpredictable.

We found Qussuckquansh standing by the shore of the river where the Awaunuy would land and with him were a number of the men of the village already armed with weapons in anticipation of a confrontation. One of the Awaunuy by the name of Lord, shouted to Qussuckquansh as they drew within an arrow shot.

"Sachem" he started in broken Quirpi, "do you intend to do the palisade and us harm? You are many and we are few. We know these are uncertain times and danger lurks now for us all."

Qussuckquansh motioned for the three to land while stating "we mean you no harm yet you bring your weapons upon us. We are to hold council today to speak of what we the People should do to confront the pox that is coming. You are free to come and join us for our concern is not you but some here fear the fort is a doorway for the demon who carries the sickness. We know you know of it because it comes from your world. We are waiting for the Spirits and Kiehtan to help us decide what to do about the fort among other things."

Molinar shouted out words which the other, Lord tried to translate as their boat drifted to a stop and was being held by their oars from coming to shore or drifting in the gentle current of the river.

"He says we will only land with our weapons at the ready" translated Lord. "For you are many and we are three."

"Then you shall not come ashore Awaunuy I fear it will lead to violence" was Qussuckquansh's reply. We will council and tell you of our decision."

Molinar stood in the boat and shook his fist as he shouted an answer to the sachem, visibly angry. Lord did his best to translate and yelled out the main thrust of his leader's rant. "There can be only one choice for you to make. The post must stand. If it does not then there will be a reckoning!" With that the Awaunuy turned their small wooden vessel around and with their oars, moved it slowly back up the river the short distance to the place where they lived and sawed the great trees of the forest into pieces to send away in Dutchmannuck ships when they came three or four times a year.

Commossuck, Pawquash, and I had stopped a short way behind the gathered warriors of the village as the exchange had taken place and once the Awaunuy had turned away, Commossuck approached the sachem.

"Ah, powwow, Manitou! It is good that you have arrived for this issue must be resolved for the good of the People. Let us move to the council tree on the hill that forms the heart of our village. From there we can look down upon the Dutchmannuck fort and not be in its shadow."

Nodding his agreement, Commossuck, and the rest of us walked up from the shore and through the village to shouts of welcome as we worked our way to the council tree. As we formed in a circle, with Qussuckquansh near the base of the ancient, storm worn oak and the elders, the powwows, and the head of each family forming an inner circle and the rest of Totoket an outer one, the talking began.

Qussuckquansh took out his sacred pipe, handed down to him by his father from fathers before, and placed sacred tobacco in the bowl. Holding it up before him, his arms raised high with the pipe at eye level, the sachem began. "With this sacred pipe, I beseech the spirits of my ancestors, of all our ancestors, and Keihtan himself to come and aid us in this moment of decision. For to destroy the fort of the Dutchmannuck may bring a confrontation with the Awaunuy. We will truly be forced to kill Molinar and his men. But if we let the post stand - will we bring the pox to our people?" With that he lit the pipe, inhaled deeply, then exhaled the smoke upward to the heavens.

The sachem turned to the shamans who sat to his left and as he motioned towards them, Pawquash stood and accepted the pipe and slowly took in the sacred smoke before exhaling as Qussuckquansh sat. "Keihtan and Hobomock have given us sight in the woodlands near the stony creek where the stones and ridges are heavy with Spirit. The demon that brings the sickness will come, we have seen it" the shaman paused to murmurs and cries of distress. He will come regardless of whether the Dutchmannuck fort is destroyed or not."

"Manitou!" was shouted as all of Totoket reacted to what the old shaman had said, some in disbelief, others in dismay. Auquansh, a respected band elder motioned to Pawquash for the pipe and as he slowly drew in the sacred smoke all eyes fell upon him. He was respected as a man of great wisdom who had been a great warrior and hunter in his youth.

"People, I have lived long enough to remember a time before the Dutchmannuck and Awaunuy came to our land. When I was a young man some of these people from away would come in their ships to trade for food and furs, but they never stayed and they were few and their visits were rare. I also remember when our sachems, even those from Mioonkhtuck, gave the Dutchmannuck permission to build their post and fort among us here in Totoket for we knew we could gain from them the metal and cloth they brought and they might protect us from our enemies the Mohawk and the Pequot."

"It was, we all now know, the beginning of the times of trouble that have plagued us these many years since. And what has it gained for us besides trinkets, metal, and cloth all the people of the Dawnland trade for? Has it protected us from our enemy the Mohawk or helped us break the power of the Pequot over us?" Auquansh paused and slowly looked at all gathered, hanging on his words, and anticipating what he would say next.

"It is time we must stand for we are the People. The fort is a symbol of all that has harmed us these years and I for one am tired of the insolent Molinar who to me is but an insect to be squashed" he said to shouts and cries of agreement and support. "If we are to die from this sickness as so many of our loved ones did last summer, then let us die as men and women of the People and resist those who have come to destroy our world and us in the process!"

Shouts and cries of agreement continued as Auquansh handed the pipe to his sachem who then turned to Commossuck for his counsel. I had been watching the shaman all the while and as others spoke he had a look of far away that seemed to carry him to a different place. But then, as Qussuckquansh offered the sacred pipe to him, he stood and held the pipe high, offering his words to the Spirits in the hope they would help the People decide what they must do. Then he began.

"Pawquash speaks the truth of what we saw in our visions, the pox will come and that many will suffer and die. There is a fierce sorcerer from the world of the Awaunuy that has come to gather the dream souls of the People and others here in the Dawnland and we must all resist to the best of our abilities. Pawquash and I have seen him and we will do everything we can to confront him." He closed his eyes and drew a long draught from the pipe and then blew the smoke solemnly towards the heavens. The people of Totoket stood in quiet awe as they waited to hear what the great powwow would say next.

"The Spirits and Keihtan himself have spoken to another on this matter as well - the boy Ponaim." With that, all turned towards me as I sat among the people of the village. I felt my heart racing as he motioned towards me with the pipe and as I stood trembling, those around me parted so I could move towards the inner circle as Commossuck motioned I do. When I reached where Commossuck stood he gave me the pipe and sat. I looked at him and he motioned that I should draw in the sacred smoke and exhale it as a prayer to the Spirits and a sign to the People that what I was to say was the truth.

As I breathed in the strong taste of the smoke neither burned my mouth nor did it make me cough as I had anticipated and I closed my eyes to find my thoughts. As I let the smoke out the words that needed to be said came to me. I felt slightly dizzy as I spoke of where the red tailed hawk had brought me and what I had seen here at Totoket. It was clear I said, that Keihtan wanted me to know that if there was a confrontation over the Dutchmannuck Fort, there would be bloodshed and to what end?" I asked.

As I stood there unsure what to do next to shouts of "Manitou!" and "He is the boy that was not burned at Mennunkatuck!", Qussuckquansh came to me and reached out for the pipe freeing me for the moment and I was unsure if I should remain standing, sit, or return to the outer circle. Commossuck saved me by gently touching the top of my shoulder and ushered me to a sitting position. All I could do was sit and look at the ground, I was terrified to make eye contact with anyone despite their calls of encouragement and agreement.

The sachem again held the pipe high before drawing more smoke and when he did so all quieted to hear what he would say. "People, we can destroy the fort, kill the three Awaunuy, and bring the wrath of those Awaunuy among the Massachusetts and Wampanoag lands upon us. Maybe even the Dutchmannuck. Where will it lead? If the pox is coming regardless as the powwows have spoken, why make a situation that is already perilous worse? I say we leave the Dutchmannuck Fort in place. What do you say?"

I remember from my vantage point seated next to Commossuck seeing the faces of the people of Totoket who looked as anguished and uncertain as those faced with difficult and potentially devastating choice could only appear. Yet slowly, one by one they began to proclaim their choice and by the time they were done, all but a few led by Auquansh, had disagreed with their sachem. The fort would stand. Qussuckquansh asked for three men to take a canoe to inform Molinar and his men and Auquansh stepped forward along with two others who had sided with their sachem.

Chapter Nine

An uneasy peace descended over Totoket as Molinar and his men had returned to their side of the river and Auquansh and the others had reported back that the vile Awaunuy had accepted the results of the council yet still made threats against future attempts to destroy the ramshackle old fort. Villagers began to go about their daily routines the season dictated as the women returned to their round of chores; some scraping hides, sewing clothing, making baskets, or tending to the Sisters who were reaching the stage when they would begin to bear fruit. The men however, gathered in small groups to discuss what had taken place and speculated on what the near future may hold for Totoket. Some spoke of leaving in canoes and crossing the water to the long island on the other side while others said maybe inland and away from the coast. Individually and in small groups they came to the shamans all afternoon to seek advice and more information about the pox. They asked about what had been seen in their visions and what had happened in Mennunkatuck just days before. Commossuck and Pawquash did their best to answer truthfully but in a way that was not overly alarmist. The truth had to be told; what was to be could not and would not be hidden from those who must confront it Commossuck later told me.

So that is how we passed much of the rest of the day on the edge of the red sand dune that marked the highpoint on the neck of land that the village shared with the old fort, looking out onto the sea and listening to the concerns and questions of those who came to talk. It was a strange afternoon; the gloom of the atmosphere was magnified by the low clouds and damp air that drifted up from the surf as it worked unceasingly against the base of the dune. I remember watching two harbor seals make their way towards the shore stopping short to stare curiously at the three of us perched above the beach as Pawquash called out to them in their own words. They would raise their doglike heads and tilt them towards us as they bobbed up and down in the waves trying to take in his meaning before ducking suddenly beneath the waves only to pop up again a short distance away. "I've asked them to bring a message to Hobomock which I hope they will do" the old powwow remarked after the two brothers of the sea turned away and swam towards deeper water.

In the evening, we were welcomed by Qussuckquansh to eat in his weetou which we gladly did and the talk naturally drifted towards what would be next. Commossuck explained that we three were to go on to Mioonkhtuck to assist Tispaquin the powwow there in a ceremony at the great Council Stone to help prevent the arrival of the sickness and it was suggested by Pawquash that we afterwards journey to the mountain to the north where Hobomock himself lay like a sleeping giant to further ask for his intervention and help. Qussuckquansh, the oldest and wisest of the sachems, spoke of his worry for the people of Totoket and all the Quinnipiac and how he would suggest crossing the water to seek refuge with the Setucket until the pox had passed and would make that suggestion to his band in the morning. He worried though about the maize, squash, and beans that needed to be tended and harvested later in the summer because they would depend upon them for food during the winter and spring. He would stay and hoped some would stay as well if only to make sure there would be a harvest later. But, as was the way of the People, each man and family could decide whether to stay, join another band, flee across the water, or move inland. It came to a simple matter what each thought best.

"And what of the Pequot?" asked Commossuck. "They will surely come to collect tribute, especially now that they have battled the Dutchmannuck over the killing of their sachem Tatobem since the Awaunuy have come to the Quinnihticut."

"They come for the furs we trap for them and the wampum beads we make from the shells that come from our place of shells. We all know they use them for trade with the Awaunuy and the Dutchman-nuck despite their recent fight with them and will expect the amount they have demanded from us. I will ask those who make the wampum beads to continue whether they leave or not for the wrath and retribution of the Pequot will be hard if they do not receive what they have demanded" answered the sachem.

"If the demon comes upon them then perhaps the tribute will not be asked" said Pawquash knowing full well that the Pequot, who were stronger in numbers than all the Quinnipiac Bands together, would still demand payment if they can. To this Qussuckquansh merely shrugged his shoulders.

Looking back to that time, I can still see the look of worry and concern on the old sachem's face though his head was held high despite all the uncertainty that rested upon him. Little did I know then how that summer would be when our world really began to unravel. Along with the powwows, I had seen in the visions what would befall us but thinking about it now I remember how hard it was to grasp the magnitude of the powerful forces both physical and spiritual about to be unleashed upon us.

It was growing late in the afternoon as I sat in the camp of the young fishermen when I realized I had journeyed in my mind to the past and was revisiting what had been the summer the black robed demon came to all the bands of the People and scattered us as the vision at Mashup's Rock had foretold. Mequnhut and Apoawein had gutted their catch and had placed it on drying racks above a smoky fire to dry the fish and were both sitting in the shade of a tree knapping and hammering at pieces of bronze broken off a trade kettle to make points for their arrows. I was curiously proud that despite their young age, the two had forsworn the use of the firearms most of our people had adopted and instead valued traditional weapons.

"The two of you remind me of my father and uncle making points when I was just a boy" I said nostalgically. "I fear it will soon be a lost art. I even remember those who worked the white quartz we found locally and the chert and jasper we traded for from the Rampano and others to the west."

Hearing me speak and realizing I was now with them, Mequnhut responded. "Uncle, I am happy you have joined us again as you have been away for most of the afternoon. I am sure it was a safe journey?" he asked with a bit of a wry smile and a wink. "We are camping here for the night since we must tend to the fish before we can take it back to Totoket. Besides, we both crave the fresh, clean air away from the stink of that Awaunuy town that straddles our village and smothers us on all sides. The young man stood for a moment looking out towards the lake gathering his thoughts before he turned back to me and said "before long the shadows will appear and it will be too late for you to continue your journey to Totoket. Will you stay with us?"

"Perhaps Ponaim, you will tell us of your wanderings while we sit by the fire" suggested Apoawein. "Your stories have always given us insight into the world of the Spirits and how we once were as a people."

"I was in a dream world remembering the time the smallpox returned the year following its first visit that had sent my family to Keihtan" I said with a hint of sadness. "It was a terrible time and one the People and all others in the Dawnland have never recovered from. It was the beginning of these times of trouble and despair that have gripped us all."

"We have often heard of it; no Quinnipiac has lived outside its shadow since" said Apoawein. "My grandmother still chants sacred prayers to Keihtan whenever it is mentioned."

"It was a time of dark shadows and to this day I know that if it was not for the efforts of Commossuck and Pawquash perhaps none of us would have survived" I began to explain. "When the pox returned to the People, it came quickly and with the ferociousness of a storm that blows in from the sea bringing winds that topple trees and rains that flood the rivers and streams. All the powwows who had survived the pox the season before worked tirelessly to try and heal the sick and rescue the dream souls that were gathered by the black robed sorcerer."

"We have always heard the stories of such a powerful sorcerer - was he indeed human or a spirit?" Apoawein asked. My grandfather would tell me the stories of him when I was little, which always made me afraid."

"I never saw him but knew well of him because Commossuck and Pawquash often journeyed into the Spirit World to confront him. As far as I knew at the time this terrible sorcerer was from the Awaunuy world of Spirits and not ours; one they brought with them."

"Of course Uncle, that makes perfect sense since all they have done since coming to our shores is work to destroy us and our way of life. What greater weapon than to kill with sickness" Mequnhut said in a spiteful tone.

"It was so, yet we survive."

"Yes Ponaim, but to what life do we survive to?" asked Apoawein bitterly.

"I hope a life where we may still live the life Keihtan has always allowed our ancestors to live. Despite everything, I still believe he has not abandoned us" I replied in a hopeful tone.

The three of us sat silently for a time deep in our own thoughts as memories rushed into mine like a flooded stream in early spring. Looking up into the late afternoon sky with its billowing white clouds that randomly drifted above, I contemplated those horrible days for a while before asking, "do you want to hear of the time the pox returned?"

"Yes Uncle, if we are to walk with the People into the future we must know the past" answered Mequnhut to the nodding agreement of Apoawein.

"It is so Mequnhut, I will tell you of that painful time." And so began my telling of the events that took place when the black robed demon descended upon the People and when it was over, all but a few of us had been spared through the intervention of Commossuck, Pawquash, and the Spirits.

It was the morning after the council's decision not to destroy the Dutchmannuck fort that word came to Totoket of the arrival of the pox among the Quinnipiac. A runner came from Montowese telling of a small number of his band falling ill which immediately stirred Pawquash to want to return to his home. As he prepared to leave Commossuck and he talked of what they would do to see what might be effective; what plant medicines would possibly counteract the effects of the sickness and what curing rituals might work best. They agreed to stay in contact and work together as best they could to battle the demon and save as many of the People as they could.

As Commossuck watched his old friend leave the village and start off on the trail that would bring him northwest towards the Upper Quinnipiac and his home, I could sense in the shaman an air of concern and worry. "So it begins Ponaim" he said turning to me. "We are all in a battle we must win if the People are to survive. We have much to do. I am sorry to pull you, so young, into this struggle. If this is not what you want I will understand. But if you do want to assist me, there may be no turning back."

Surprised and a bit frightened by his words, at first I could not muster a reply. Instead I simply shook my head in acceptance as he put his arm around my shoulder and said, "you are a brave young man Ponaim and I am glad you will be with me." We turned to walk back into the village to prepare to leave for Mioonkhtuck and the village of Momauguin just as Qussuckquansh and some village elders approach us.

"I have sent word to Momauguin of the news from Montowese and I am sure that he has also sent word" Qussuckquansh said. "The elders and I want to seek your counsel and that of the Keihtan so we might best guide the village. But word has spread like fire before the wind and everyone is tending to their plans in the face of this. The reality I fear, is there will be no place that will be safe."

"You speak wise words and I agree with a heavy heart." The powwow paused for a moment before continuing. "There will be no safety - but if the People can sincerely turn to Keihtan and Hobomock and search through their souls and minds for what is right perhaps we may not suffer as we did last summer" Commossuck added to the hopeful agreement of the elders in whose faces I could see only worry. "Taboos have been broken and we must all return to the basic morality, beliefs, and ways that have always sustained the People."

By the time we had walked the short distance back to the weetous, the men and women of Totoket had gathered in the center of the village to talk of what to do; many had already prepared to leave; some across the water and others to seek refuge inland among the isolated upland valleys found there. It was best they said, to stay away from others in the hope that the sickness would not find them. Some of the families, however, along with many who had lost loved ones to the pox the previous summer and some who were alone as I was, decided to stay at Totoket, thinking that no place was safe and that they would rather face the sickness together in the home of the ancestors. Here they agreed, they would maintain and harvest the Sisters when they ripened, continue to hunt, fish, and provide food for the winter for it would be needed if they were to survive. They agreed with Qussuckquansh that famine would hunt them otherwise.

By late that afternoon, some began their trek inland to the hugs and farewells of those they were leaving behind with the hope that the black robed demon would not find them in the valleys nestled between the hills that had been used for generations for the winter camps. Many at Totoket had not moved so in the winter for many years, some even since the arrival of the Dutchmannuck. Like many of the Quinnipiac and others of the Dawnland, they had abandoned that practice to stay along the coast to trade with those from across the water. Others decided to leave the next morning, while those who planned to cross to Setucket, led by Auquansh, worked to load their canoes and wait for the morning as swells in the sea were high from a wind that had risen from the southeast. "The wind comes from the sea and Hobomock" Commossuck noted "a sign that they should not leave today or maybe at all."

I can still remember how warm that wind sent by Hobomock was that summer afternoon and how it seemed to speak to Commossuck as he stood on the crest of the dune looking out onto the water. He had asked me to gather the few items we had brought with us from Mennunkatuck; the sacred bundle that held his pipe, tobacco, and medicines along with the two other satchels that held our tools, fire stone, and a bit of food. The shaman said the wind had told him it was time to return to Mennunkatuck instead of going on to Mioonkhtuck and we were needed there. Qussuckquansh said he understood and would send word to Momauguin. As we left the village and passed under the shadow of the old Dutchmannuck fort, Commossuck sent a black curse to it, the first time I had ever heard or seen him do so.

As the evening spread and the light faded along the path leading to our village, the wind continued to come with us and as it did so, the pace set by the shaman quickened. He did not speak but carried an urgency and as the moon came to guide us with her light and the sounds of the night sang to us, we moved quickly and silently. With every step, however, I felt a rising anxiety and fear in me since I could feel the energy that was driving us toward the unknown tomorrow and did not know how I might face it or master my fear. I felt lost in both this world and that of the Spirits, small and insignificant in the face of everything despite and because of what I had experienced those past few weeks. "How might I understand all that was happening around me?" I asked Keihtan as I worked hard to keep up with the pace set by the powwow.

It was the deep part of the night when we entered Mennunkatuck to the barking of a few of the village dogs who customarily kept watch as sentinels and it was not long before two men approached us to find out what their watch had discovered. They greeted us in an excited yet subdued manner when they recognized Commossuck and spoke anxiously of what had happened in our absence. They talked of news from the Upper Quinnipiac and how many in the village were planning in the morning to seek safety either inland or across the water like those at Totoket. They also had more startling news: Wentubecum and one of the hunters who had been with him in the Coginchaug, Meishunk, were not feeling well and had set themselves in an isolated spot just to the east of the village across the Kuttawo river in case the demon had struck them. Shaumpishuh was hoping for the shaman's return so as to help them fight off the demon and they were planning the next day to build a sweat lodge that they might purify themselves for the battle they knew they were face.

Thanking them, Commossuck and I walked to our weetou where exhausted, I was ready to sleep. The shaman on the other hand spent some time gathering many of the herbs he would need to aid him in the purification ceremony he had decided to assist the hunters with. But before I could rest, the powwow asked if I was comfortable helping with the ceremony for he would be in the sweat lodge with the two men and needed a fire keeper outside who could heat the stones needed to create the steam and also pass the water to him to pour onto the stones. Drowsy but attentive, I agreed despite my selfish fear the demon might leave the two hunters and focus on me. The last thing I remember was Commossuck sitting by the fire, softly chanting, the glow of the fire casting a dim light of a different world upon him.

Commossuck woke me before the sun returned and we hurriedly ate some maize cakes, greens, and dried fish. He gathered his hatchet with the head of Dutchmannuck iron, a gift from the father of Shaumpishuh, his knife, pipe, and medicine bag and asked me to carry two seal bladders to use to gather water. We left the village for the Kuttawo and the two men on the other side. In the pre-dawn light, Mother Moon looked down on us through the trees lighting our way to the river where we found a canoe at the crossing place. We quickly paddled the short distance across and saw the fire the hunters had already lit for they had begun preparing to construct the Spirit Lodge.

Surprised to see us, Wentubecum shouted out a greeting that was followed quickly by a warning not to come close for he feared the demon had entered him and Meishunk. "We do not want you and the boy to bring the dark one back to the village

Commossuck" he said. "We will build the Spirit Lodge and will each take turns inside. Meishunk and I have gone into the home of the Spirits many times with you and know the chants and ritual."

Commossuck never hesitated and with me in tow within the time it takes for a deer to flick its tail three times, we were standing with Wentubecum and Meishunk before their fire.

"Send the boy back to the other side of the Kuttawo Commossuck, we do not want to send him to see his parents in the home of Keihtan" implored Meishunk.

Suddenly I heard my voice say " I am here to help fight the demon and I have already survived the pox once so Keihtan must be protecting me" surprising the three men with the tone of my outburst. Commossuck hearing me speak, turned to look at me and then with a nod of affirmation, turned back to the hunters.

"Ponaim will tend the fire, heat the stones, and pass the water" he explained. "It is time he learned the ways of the Spirit Lodge and his life, like ours, is in the hands of Hobomock and Keihtan."

"Manitou!" exclaimed Wentubecum. "We are grateful you are here to help for our heads have begun to ache and a strange weakness has already crept upon us while we slept. We are beginning to fear the worst. After a pause and realizing that the shaman meant to stay, Wentubecum added "so we welcome your help Commossuck. Meishunk and I have already cut the saplings for the frame and we brought grass mats for the covering as well as the skins of six deer and even a Dutchmannuck blanket."

"The blanket we cannot use for it will poison the ceremony with its connection to the Dutchmannuck world of Spirits. For the ritual, all must be pure" the powwow explained. "Ponaim, go to the marsh just past that turn in the river and cut long strands of marsh grass to tie the saplings of the frame together while we start building it."

I quickly left for the marsh, a bit relieved to be away from the fire and the three men. I walked the short distance to the grasses feeling conflicted as fear and the remembrance of the suffering of my mother, father and sister began to come at me like the waves of the sea. Here I was, thrust into a series of situations since their deaths that were hard for me to comprehend. I began to wonder how I or any of the People would survive this collision of worlds that had brought all this about. But as I bent down to begin cutting the tall strands of grass, a feeling of purpose erased my fears, as I worked I thanked Keihtan for giving me a role to play in this battle for survival. Besides, I reminded myself, if the pox did take me, I would be with my mother, father, and sister in the house of Keihtan.

I gathered up the grasses and quickly returned to the site where the sweat lodge was beginning to take shape. Commossuck had found a spot that was partly hidden by a large rock and behind a stand of young hemlocks that shielded it from the river. The rock also had a large crack in it that extended below ground and I knew he had chosen the place for that doorway to the Lower World of Hobomock. Wentubecum and Meishunk had gathered Grandfather Stones from the river the day before and they quickly dug the fire circle that would hold them which would be connected to the Spirit Lodge by a Spirit Path. Commossuck explained to me how I was to bring the stones once they were heated and the ceremony had started, each about the size of an infant's head, to the sacred lodge one at a time carrying them in a sling made from thick bear skin with the fur side out to protect my hands and arms. The shaman demonstrated to me how I should place the Grandfather in the bear skin as I walk the Spirit Path from the fire to the door. We then placed twenty eight Grandfathers in the bottom of the fire pit, four for each of the Sacred Directions, and constructed a cone shaped stack of wood above them leaving an opening to the east, south, west, and north for the Spirits to enter the stones and for me to retrieve them with two forked deer antlers to scoop the Grandfathers out.

Commossuck had me practice so I felt confident I could retrieve them and carry them safely.

Once I felt ready, Commossuck asked me to light the sacred fire and handed me the fire stones. He explained that I should light the kindling through each of the four openings starting with the one to the east and moving then to the south, west, and north. At first I found striking the fire stones together within the opening difficult but after a number of attempts sparks ignited the kindling and from there I moved quickly to the other openings. Soon, the blaze began to build and the powwow reminded me to tend to it with a keen sense of commitment while acknowledging the Grandfather stones inside.

While I was left to tend the fire, he, Wentubecum, and Meishunk began to build the sacred Sprit Lodge by placing the ends of the saplings in the ground, bending them down into a curved shape that formed a dome and then tied other saplings horizontally across the structure with the grasses I had gathered. This formed the sturdy domed frame which would be able to hold the mats and skins. Commossuck explained that there were seven horizontal rows of saplings, each representing the Seven Sacred Directions; East which represented truth, South which represented kindness, West - sharing, North - Caring, Sky - Strength, Earth - Respect, and Kiehtan - humility.

In the center of the lodge, Wentubecum dug a shallow, circular pit that would receive the heated Grandfathers. Just as Father Sun began to rise higher in the eastern sky, they had finished securing the mats to the frame and covered the entire dome it formed with the deer skins. It was completely dark inside for no light, Commossuck said, must enter once the small doorway was covered with another mat and skin. The darkness represented the womb of Earth Mother, the source of all life from which we all came. The door faced eastward towards the rising sun, the source of light and life, the direction from which the Spirits would come to bless and aid the participants. Leading from the doorway was the Spirit Path which the ancestors and Spirits would follow into the lodge and beyond that a small Spirit Mound was created from the earth dug from the pit inside the lodge and the one that held the fire that heated the Grandfather stones. On the Spirit Mound, Wentubecum and Meishunk placed sacred objects before they entered the lodge that they had brought as offerings.

Meishunk had brought a large clay cooking pot that was to be placed next to the fire and I was instructed to fill it with water once the fire was well underway. Commossuck gave me a small pouch he had brought and opened it. "Ponaim," he instructed, "when the water begins to boil you must place these two medicines into the pot. Put all of both because they are the medicine that will speak to the Spirits through the steam produced. When I call for you, scoop out some spirit water with one of the smaller pots and bring it to the door so we can sprinkle the sacred medicine onto the Grandfathers. The sage will take away all negative energy and protect us from it and help us to be humble before the Spirits and ancestors. The cedar will remind us to be kind and truthful for our hearts must be pure if we want the Spirits to help us. We will also place fresh cedar and sage on the hot Grandfathers rocks so the Spirits and ancestors can breathe in our offerings.

"I understand Commossuck and will do as you say," I said with a mixture of nervousness and pride in having such an important role to play in the ceremony.

"You must understand Ponaim, that what you are being asked to do is usually performed by one who has experienced the blessings of the Spirit Lodge many times. But Keihtan has chosen you for his purposes and I know he will be with you in this."

The powwow put his hand on my shoulder in a gesture of confidence which helped to calm my nervousness a bit. As he did so I looked up to see high on a branch behind him in a straight line along the Spirit Path and the Sacred Lodge, a red tailed hawk—a sign from Keihtan. I smiled.

152

Chapter Ten

It was early afternoon by the time all the preparations for the ceremony had been completed and the fire had burned enough to properly heat the Grandfathers. The men who were to enter the lodge fussed a bit with last minute details while I went to the river with the seal bladders to gather water to fill the pot that would hold the medicine to be used once the ceremony began. I walked to the edge of the Kuttawo that beautiful summer morning with the sunlight reflecting off the water and the freshness of the breeze as it moved in gentle waves towards me feeling grateful to Keihtan for the gift of that day. I found myself fully aware of the beauty around me; the sparkling, slow moving river, the smells of the forest on both her shores that were canopied by magnificent trees, and the chorus of song from the dozens of winged ones present. At that moment I felt as freely connected to the Manitou of the universe around me as I have ever been. As I knelt to fill the bladders, I thanked Keihtan aloud for allowing me the honor of living within his creation.

Returning to the sacred fire, I filled the clay pot and once I had done so Commossuck, Wentubecum, and Meishunk walked to the Kuttawo to ritually bathe in preparation for the ceremony. When they returned, each dressed in a breechcloth, they circled the fire three times then sat down in a semicircle by the fire on its western side so as to keep it to the east and the direction that the Spirits would come. Commossuck asked me to retrieve his otter skin bundle that held his sacred pipe and the mix of tobacco, sweetgrass, and healing herbs. Motioning to his right, he said "Ponaim, sit with us for we are to partake of the tobacco as an offering to the Spirits. You will be first as is the right of the fire keeper." Taking up a cedar twig, Commossuck placed an end in the fire which quickly ignited with a bit of a snap from the sap within. "A good omen" he said "for the cedar has spoken to us and acknowledged our request for healing" to the agreement of Meishunk and Wentubecum who exclaimed "Manitou" simultaneously. The powwow continued. "Ponaim, since this is only your second time drawing in the sacred smoke, remember not to inhale it but hold it in your mouth for a moment, then exhale slowly to release it as sacred breath towards the heavens. It will carry with it your prayers and your spirit. Then take a second puff and when you release the smoke that time, move it around your body with your hand as a way of purifying your physical nature. In this way both your spirit and your body will be ready to participate in the ceremony. Once done, pass it to your left."

Commossuck handed me the pipe and I felt the smooth long wooden stem and the sight of the sacred tobacco burning red hot in the bowl he had carved from soapstone he had gathered far to the north in the land of the Agawam in his youth. As I drew in the sacred smoke, I expected it to burn but instead it felt surprisingly warm and soothing and I worked hard not to swallow it despite my urge to cough. Letting it out slowly, I tilted my head towards the Sky World and as I did so, again the red tailed hawk returned to my sight, this time drifting at twice the height of the trees and almost directly above us, catching the rising heat generated by the fire to glide in a lazy circle. It was hard for me to take my eyes off who I now know has been my spirit guide and companion all these years yet I knew I had to and lowered my gaze so as to take the second draw on the pipe. Holding the sacred smoke in my mouth, which was much easier than the first time at Totoket, I re-leased it. As I did so, I held the pipe in my right hand and with my left guided the grey cloud in front of me across and down from my head to my legs which were folded cross legged like the others. Moving the pipe to my left hand, I passed it to Commossuck.

By the time the others had taken their turn with the pipe, the water in the clay pot had begun to boil and the shaman signaled to me that I should add the sage and cedar from the pouch he had given me.

The wood stacked on the fire had burned down significantly and some of the Grandfathers could be seen through the openings. Commossuck said to me that they were going to enter the Spirit Lodge and that when he called for me, I was to bring seven stones, one at a time to the door which he would in sequence take from me and place in the center pit. Meanwhile, I was to ready the four smaller clay vessels in order to fill them with the medicine water and bring each when called at the start of each stage of the ceremony. He and the others would sprinkle the medicine water in turn on the hot stones, creating the steam that would purify the men inside and bring the Spirits to them.

With an affirming nod, Commossuck smiled at me, his dark eyes flashing with intensity while he turned quickly toward the others, his long gray hair cascading loosely down his back. Wentubecum helped Meishunk, who was clearly growing weak, to his feet and led by Commossuck, all three walked down the sacred path towards the opening of the lodge. After circling the lodge seven times, once for each of the directions and Keihtan, they entered one at a time; Wentubecum followed by Meishunk and then the shaman. I realized, I was alone and for a moment fear entered me as I worried I would somehow fail in what I needed to do. But I reassured myself with a confidence that surprised me and just in time because within a few moments, Commossuck called for the Grandfathers. The shaman had told me to take one first from the east, then south, west, and north in sequence and carry each in the bear hide sling to carry it to the door. Using the two deer antlers, it was quite easy to pick up the first one though it glowed red from the heat. I carried it quickly down the sacred path to the door and exclaimed the sacred words "all my relations" when I arrived as I had been instructed. This let him know I was there but more importantly acknowledged the spirits of our ancestors as embodied in the Grandfather Stones.

The shaman opened the door flap ever so slightly and took the bundle from me, deposited the hot stone in the pit and handed me the sling back. I moved as fast as I could back to the fire and picked up a clay pot, and dipped it into the medicine water, filling it to the top. I quickly returned to the lodge where I announced my arrival once again. Commossuck took the pot and I could hear the steam created by the medicine as he sprinkled some on the first Grandfather, chanting as he did so. I turned and returned to the fire to retrieve a second, then third Grandfather, each time repeating the process until seven had been brought. During this first stage, each of the men took turns pouring the medicine water on the glowing red stones while introducing themselves to the Spirits, ancestors, and spirit animals that began to arrive, drawn by the prayers chanted and steam created. They also thanked Keihtan for the sacred elements, the darkness of the sweat lodge, the connection with Earth Mother, the rocks, the fire, the water, and the steam. The three also thanked their grandfathers and grandmothers across time for bringing them life.

At the end of the first stage, Commossuck opened the flap of the door so as to allow some fresh air to come in from the east and within a short time called for the second round of the Grandfathers to be brought to the lodge. First however, he asked me to bring the second pot of sacred water which I did. With each stone, the process was repeated and soon there were fourteen hot stones creating a hot steaming atmosphere within the dark lodge. During this stage, the three prayed for all things of this world, the People, their families, and all two legged beings as well as the four legged ones, those with wings, and those with fins. They prayed for all that sustained the life of the People including the rains and snow, Father Sun, Mother Moon, the Three Sisters, and the medicines that have always healed the People. At the conclusion of this round, the door flap was once again briefly opened and by then I knew it was time to prepare for the third stage.

A third pot of medicine was brought to the door followed by seven more Grandfathers in sequence bringing the total to twenty one. As the medicine was poured on each added to the earlier ones, the intensity of the heat and steam within the sacred lodge intensified and when Commossuck did open the door flap to accept each stone, the steamy heat escaping felt like it would burn my face, arms, and body. I could not imagine what it must have been like inside the Spirit Lodge and have to admit I was content not to be inside. Later of course, as I grew older and participated in and ran the ceremonies myself I laughed at my innocence for after this first time witnessing the ceremony, I understood its power and potential to heal both spirit and body.

The third stage was an important part of the ritual for it was during it that the participants, knowing that the Spirits and ancestors were present, asked their help in healing specific people, places, and situations. The focus Wentubecum later told me, was asking them to aid in the struggle with the pox brought by the black robed demon and somehow preventing the way in which the Awaunuy in particular were threatening the land and way of life of the People. They prayed for all those who were suffering and threatened by the callous actions of others.

By the time, the fourth and last stage had begun, it was late afternoon and I was exhausted more from the intensity of the situation and my role than the actual physical part. Like the other three times, it started with the medicine water and then the last seven Grandfathers bringing the total to twenty eight and I remember wondering how the three men could survive in there, especially Meishunk who had entered already visibly weak. This Commossuck told me later, was the healing round and in it the Spirits were asked to assist the participants in renewal, personal strength, and change that will allow them to overcome their weaknesses, shortcomings, and troubles. This included ailments and problems both physical and spiritual. During this stage, the men remained in the lodge until the steam and heat slowly dissipated and as the door opened and fresh air eventually won out, they continued to chant, pray, and sing sacred words and sounds. As the evening shadows began to creep in, they each slowly emerged from the lodge; first Commossuck, then Wentubecum, and finally Meishunk. As I stood by the Grandfather's fire, I was surprised and overjoyed to see each bound out as if fresh from a good night's rest; each endowed with a renewed energy and purpose that flowed through and out of them. Even Meishunk showed no sign of his earlier weakness and without saying a word, all three walked to the Kuttawo for another ritual bath.

As was the custom of the younger when an elder spoke, Mequnhut and Apoawein did not interrupt while I was speaking but when I finally did pause in the telling of the story, they both sensed an opportunity to ask questions. "Uncle" Mequnhut asked, "I do remember my father telling the story of the healing that took place that day and how later when the pox did strike the Mennunkatuck it did not affect Wentubecum or Meishunk and they were able to help those afflicted as well as provide food for the sick and the well throughout that summer."

"I have always heard it was so and that it was Commossuck and the time in the Spirit Lodge that not only healed them both but made them resistant to the sickness around them. I do remember Meishunk would say that he and Wentubecum had been given a Spirit Shield that day that protected them" added Apoawein. "Was it so?"

"It was true. The Spirits, ancestors, and Keihtan had given them protection and as time went on I came to understand that it was a sign from Keihtan that somehow some of the People would survive. Why else would two who were sick be cured?" I paused for a bit before adding "Commossuck told me a few days later that he had seen the robed demon float above the Spirit Lodge during the third stage and that the spirits of the ancestors had chased him screaming away from the lodge with a mighty flash of light. But he also said that it had also come about because the two afflicted were truly pure of heart and committed to a return to the ways of the path Keihtan had always set for the People."

"I do remember they were among those who struggled to avoid the ways of and contact with the Awaunuy and they were both known for keeping the old ways. Is that why Meishunk eventually left Totoket years later even though he was older in years?" asked Mequnhut.

"Yes, even when he lost his eyesight and could no longer see Meishunk continued to follow the path of the ancestors and it is said when he did die some saw them come for him in the night and carry him to Keihtan. A great honor that is given but a few."

"So uncle, what happened after the Spirit Lodge ceremony and when did the smallpox come?"

"It was literally the next day. We may have angered the black robed demon by driving him away from the Spirit Lodge for he struck with a vengeance intent on gathering as many dream souls as he could."

The evening shadows had turned slowly to darkness by then and the sounds of the night creatures sang loudly accompanied by the frogs and loons on the lake. Mequnhut suggested we eat some of the fish that was partially smoked and the three of us did but not before thanking our finned brothers and sisters for their offerings to us. When we were done and had built a campfire separate from the smoky one that dried and cured the fish, the two asked me to continue the story.

The night of the Spirit Lodge ceremony we all stayed near the fire and I remember sitting among the three amazed at the vitality and energy that had returned to Wentubecum and Meishunk. Only Commossuck seemed a bit tired, no doubt from the draining experience of conducting the ritual. While they spoke quietly and intermittently into the night, Commossuck remained relatively quiet. I for one had many questions to ask him but it did not seem the proper time. I believe by then he had already seen what was to take place.

The four of us spent the night by the fire that had once held the Grandfathers and in the morning we dismantled the sweat lodge and dug a pit where it had been and buried all the parts including the clay pots as an offering to Hobomock before returning to our village. While we worked, clouds had gathered from the west and brought with them the smell of rain and by the time we entered the village a mist had begun to fall in the heavy air. Despite the rain, Mennunkatuck was busy with activity as on the surface it seemed most in the village were attending to the daily activities that summer always brought. We soon found out that was not the case. Shambisqua and Wentubecum's daughter were first to spot us from their perch on the platform above the field of the Sisters armed with stones used to fend off the blackbirds. They shouted out their greetings as they climbed down and ran to us. "Father! Manitou! You are well!" shouted the hunter's daughter as he scooped her up into his arms. "I was so afraid you had the pox like some others now do!"

"I have been healed and so has Meishunk" said Wentubecum. "But what is this of others falling sick?"

Shambisqua jumped at the question while all the while looking at me. "Although some of our people had left for across the water yesterday, others were planning on leaving today. But by the time the light of the day was ending word began to spread that some in the weetous were feeling sick, it started with two who had been in the Coginchaug with you" she said to Wentubecum as she turned to look at him. "This morning it seems even more were not feeling well."

"So we were indeed the ones who brought the demon to our people as we worried when we both began to feel ill" Meishunk said to Wentubecum. "We must do what we can to help those who will become sick for we both have our Spirit Shields. I do fear for my family and all the others."

"Meishunk, your wife and children seemed fine when I saw them earlier though they spoke anxiously about you" said Shambisqua. She paused for a moment before turning to me. "Ponaim, I was worried for you. Have you brought a Spirit Shield too?"

"I am well Shambisqua" I replied as we all hurried towards the weetous. "I do not think I have one" I replied as I looked to Commossuck for confirmation. I realized from the distant look on the shaman's face he did not hear my question for his mind and spirit were already engaged in what he knew he would have to do.

As we neared the weetous, the families of Meishunk and Wentubecum ran to them and we were all greeted by Nashump who asked about our health and was relieved to hear we were all fine, especially the two who had left a few days before visibly unwell. He warmly welcomed Commossuck and asked if there was anything he might need knowing that his daughter would have already told of the arrival of the pox. Shaumpishuh he said, had gone to Mioonkhtuck by canoe to talk with the other sachems at dawn and was to return later today. She had brought six of the young men of the village with her so that they could go and return quickly but with the rain falling and the wind beginning to increase they might have to wait for the sea was not a safe place in a storm.

"I will need to know who has become sick Nashump so that I can try to protect their dream souls from the Awaunuy demon. Ponaim and I will eat and then we will begin to do what we can."

"I have asked each family to let me know who is not feeling well and asked those who were planning to leave the village to reconsider only because they might unknowingly bring the disease to others. To stay here is best for we can tend to one another" said Nashump with a grave look of concern.

"That is best Nashump. I have seen there is no longer a safe place to go" the powwow replied. "Once we have eaten I am going to send Ponaim to the woods to gather more of the root and plant medicine we will need. He could use some help."

"I will help father" said Shambisqua who had continued to follow us. "Ponaim can show me what to gather and I do remember what Commossuck used when I was sick with the pox last summer."

"Yes, the two will be able to get the work done faster" said the shaman while Nashump agreed.

It had been many days since we had been to our weetou and the air inside was stale and close from the summer heat. "We must eat Ponaim because we will need our strength for what lies ahead. Light the fire and we will have some of the dried deer meat we have once we warm and soften it over the heat."

Just then the voice of a woman elder was heard outside the weetou accompanied by those of two others.

"Commossuck, we have brought you and the boy food. We want you to know how grateful we are for your return" said the first echoed quickly by the others. Commossuck stepped out of the weetou and into the mist to accept their offering. We ate with relish.

Chapter Eleven

It was growing late and the evening's warmth had settled into a comfortable, soft night. An owl called out from across the lake and up on the ridge that rose above it and another quickly answered from the trees behind us. Their calls brought me momentarily to a pause in the story and my two companions sat patiently while I gathered my thoughts and retraced in my memory those days of trauma brought by that second visit of smallpox for the People.

"Uncle" said Mequnhut as he broke the silence of the moment. "I know some of the next part of the tale for my grandmother has always felt proud to have helped you gather the roots and plants that she believes to this day saved some of the People including my great-grandfather, Nashump." He poked at the fire with a stick prompting a brighter flame to flare up and casting a warm yellow glow on his and Apoawein's expectant faces. "She has often told how she helped you gather two large bundles of roots and plants; some just the leaves and others the entire plant that went into the medicine that Commossuck prepared. In helping you she felt she was doing what she could to help save others."

"Yes Mequnhut, in no time at all we had gathered enough to bring to Commossuck who had filled a large clay pot with water that was already boiling. He showed both of us how to cut up each different root or plant and exactly how much to blend together. I was surprised he let your grandmother stay and watch but later he explained that more than one person in the village should know in case we both were no longer able to make the medicine. Your grandmother was excited but scared she later confided knowing she had witnessed something of great spiritual power."

"She never included the scared part in her telling" laughed Mequnhut. "Only her feeling of importance."

"While we were out gathering, your great-grandfather had told Commossuck who was sick and the condition they were in. So by the time the medicine was ready, the shaman had decided which weetou he would visit first. At that point he asked Shambisqua to leave because he needed to discuss with me what would happen next, even though I had a good idea having witnessed his efforts to save my family the year before. Because so many needed his help, he did not think he had time to go into a dream walk to fight with the black robed demon over each patient. That he thought would take too long and that he needed instead to work quickly and steadily. He also said he would treat the less sick first since he thought they would heal more quickly and he could then spend a longer amount of time with those who were in greater distress. In this work he had asked Hobomock for guidance and was told to use the healing stones. I had seen him use them with my family and your grandmother had been healed with them the year before. My role was to beat the drum as he directed and assist in various ways as he required."

"After filling a gourd with the medicine we left for the first weetou, that of the hunter Malpua, one of those who had been in Coginchaug and was quite ill. Commossuck told him he would give him some medicine to drink but was here first to treat his two sons and wife. Malpua gladly agreed with a feverish shaking of his head while his wife sat across from him holding the youngest of their two boys. About two years old, his face was blotchy and streaked from tears but he bravely drank the medicine with his mother's encouragement. The pow-wow then turned to his older brother who was about ten and sitting on the other end of the sleeping platform. With an air of dignity beyond his years, he accepted the gourd and thanked Commossuck for coming on behalf of his family. As he did so he looked at me as one of his longest friends; he seemed to be acknowledging what had happened to my family and was determined to put on a brave show of face. Sadly, of the four, only the youngest boy survived and the last I heard of him many years ago he had gone to live among the Narragansett."

"Before we left our weetou, Commossuck had explained to me how important it was to allow the stones to speak to him so that he could then use a hollow piece of a deer leg bone to draw out the disease by sucking it up spiritually into his mouth. If he were successful he told me, he would spit it into another gourd bowl we had brought that was half filled with beach sand with a lid of wood. The lid needed to be placed immediately in order to force the disease into the sand where it would be trapped. The sickness if sucked out might take the form of a small spirit dart or insect sent by the sorcerer and Commossuck explained that he would have to be careful not to swallow it as had happened to some shamans a year ago. That would mean he would also become ill and most likely die."

"The powwow explained that the disease could be sometimes drawn out if the patient had been true to Kiehtan but it really came down to the individual's strength and ability to fight off the demon. He wanted me to make sure I understood that Keihtan could not control who might die and in the end it was each person's path that determined what would happen. Keihtan's role was only to give him the strength and gifts to try and help those who were sick."

"Commossuck had brought four healing stones that were spherical and smooth, having been shaped by the sea. Each was of a different material and color; they would tell him which of them would work best on each patient by speaking to him in spirit language. Besides helping the patient fight the illness, the medicine would allow the stones to be able to locate the sickness since both were of the Earth Mother and the spirit within each would show the way. Each stone fit into the palm of his hand and once the right one revealed itself, he would rub the stone gently over the patient's body. While doing so, Commossuck sang his stone healing song as I beat the drum to the rhythm he explained to me. But before he used the stone, Commossuck sang his healing song while passing the eagle feather wand over the patient's entire body from head to toe four times, calling to the medicine to aid the healing stone in finding the location of the illness. Once it had been found, Commossuck would attempt to suck it out using the hollow bone. If he were unable to remove it, he knew the patient would probably die or have to be able to heal themselves through their personal spiritual connection to the Spirit World."

"Commossuck, does Keihtan or Hobomock speak to you through the stones?" I asked just as we were leaving our weetou.

"If they know I am sincere Ponaim, in my desire to help those who are afflicted, they will allow me to hear what the stones will tell me. It is a great tool and a special gift from them. I hope you will learn it so you can help the People in the future."

"Where does the sacred stone song come from? Do you dream walk to find it or does it come to you when you are ready?" I asked. He was ready to leave the weetou but patiently stopped to answer me.

"Mine came in a vision; others dream walk to find it. For them, the song is waiting for them. We need to go now Ponaim. Bring my drum, the sand gourd, and the eagle feathers and I will bring the stones and the medicine."

With that we began our attempt to help those who the black robed demon had struck. As we walked to the weetou of Malpua I could not help but ask one more question, one that I knew I had to ask. "Commossuck, when will you know it is time to try and retrieve the dream souls of the sick from the Awaunuy demon?"

The shaman stopped and looked directly into my eyes. "Ponaim, that is done when the patient or patients cannot be cured by me with the aid of the spirit stones. That means their dream souls have already been gathered and I must try to retrieve them.

This may be difficult for this sorcerer from away is very powerful."

"I am afraid Commossuck" I said, my voice a bit shaky.

"You should be Ponaim - that is why you will make a great powwow someday."

So many memories began to flood into my mind at that moment and I paused for a while deep in thought, trying to sort out those terrible days as I followed Commossuck from weetou to weetou trying to help those who had fallen ill. Some families and individuals did flee with the hope of saving themselves but in the end that was of no use and not being with a shaman most often sealed their fate. Mequnhut and Apoawein waited patiently hoping I would begin again and after a time Apoawein could wait no longer.

"Shaman, I have seen you use the four stones and the hollow bone many times. Are they those of Commossuck?"

His question brought me back and I quickly answered "yes they are. When he knew he was about to leave this world some years after the Awaunuy had come to settle across the water from Mioonkhtuck and then at Mennunkatuck, he gave them to me. It was then and still is a great honor. I always think of him when I use them."

"You said uncle that Malpua and most of his family did not survive?"

"That is right, only the young boy lived. Commossuck was able to suck the sickness from him but the others he could not. Sadly, that was the way things went as the black robed demon had his way with our village and all the others of the People. By the time autumn came, there were very few of us left. It was difficult for us to bury all those who had died with a proper ceremony because each day brought more deaths. We did our best to do so and most weetous in the village were burned because so many died. To this day I am not sure why some were chosen to die while others such as myself were not."

My thoughts went back to how hard Commossuck worked to save as many as he could and though discouraged he never gave up or complained. I was exhausted after the first three days as we travelled among the weetous but when the powwow was able to save someone he became energized which gave him the strength to continue. I remembered he did not sleep the first few days or nights though he insisted I did. I need you to be strong he would say.

"Uncle, I have seen you work with the sacred stones many times and as you do so you sing your stone song. Was it also given to you by Commossuck?"

"No we must each find our own but his will forever live in my memory. Since he is no longer with us but in Keihtan's weetou he gave me permission from the world of Spirits to sing it. Would you like to hear it? It always gives me strength and as an old one I sometimes need that now."

"We would be honored Ponaim if you shared it" said Apoawein, it would be good for us to learn it so we might pass on the healing stone song of the great Commossuck to the People so they will remember it in future years."

I closed my eyes and began to quietly chant spirit words to let the Spirit World know I was to share the song of the powwow and after I had been given permission to do so I began:

"He ho he
You cannot hide
The spirit stones will find you
We are looking for you
And will find you
The stone will find the sickness
And will show the cause
The stone is the eye of Keihtan
The eye of Hobomock is here
The stone will tell me
You will soon be gone"

"We will remember this uncle. I have seen you work with the stones while you have sung your stone song which is similar. You have said in the past that following your song, the stone moves itself to find the location of the disease. Is this true?"

"That is true, while I am barely touching it, the healing stone shows me the way and then hopefully I can remove the sickness. Like Commossuck, I have often been successful and often not."

"My great-grandfather Nashump had told me he was cured even though the healing stone and hollow bone did not work for him. Was that true shaman?"

"It is. The dream soul of your great grandfather was one that Commossuck and Pawquash were able to retrieve from the black robed sorcerer in their many journeys to confront him. They were able to bring back some but Commossuck always talked with sadness of those they were unable to bring back and how few they were."

Apoawein played with the fire again as all three sat quietly for some moments before he said "Ponaim, can I ask how the powwows were able to bring the dream souls of some back? I have always been curious and I know you have done so as well over these many years. It is well known you have saved many of the People though not always from the black robed demon who we have always been told never came to visit with such strong intent again."

"That is true Apoawein, that one never really came back much to my relief these many years. But since that time so many other diseases both of the body and spirit have struck the People. I have been able to bring back some, but not all."

"It is late but I will tell you what Commossuck told me about their struggles against the black robed demon" I said with a slight feeling of discomfort just thinking about it. I stared into the fire for a time before I began to describe what the Commossuck and Pawquash told me they saw and how they were able to eventually confront the demon who was sickening the People and gather back some dream souls.

"This sorcerer was not of this Spirit World but from that of the Awaunuy. That was certain for his face was as white as a new snow and his eyes were blue like the ice which is thick in mid-winter. He wore the dark robe of the Awaunuy god-talkers and his face was drawn and thin, his hair straggly and black as charcoals left by a fire. Compared to us, he was not very tall and seemed almost sickly and weak to the shamans. But that was not the case; he was strong and powerful despite his size. He dwelled in a tunnel of rock as wide and tall as a weetou that seemed to go on far beyond him with no end and even though there was a blazing fire close behind him, the air around him and inside the tunnel was freezing cold. When the powwows first saw him they knew why he was gathering up the dream souls of the People; he was tossing them into the fire behind him sometimes one at a time, sometimes by the armful."

"This reminds me of what the Awaunuy god-talkers are always saying to us uncle, that because we do not accept their god and become like them our souls will go to what they call the fiery pit of hell where their devil lives. Was this sorcerer that evil one they speak of?"

"Of that I am not sure Mequnhut, but that the demon dressed as an Awaunuy did not come to the Dawnland until they arrived. So it may be that he is the same one but I do not know. Commossuck was convinced he came from their world and not ours."

"How were Pawquash and Commossuck able to battle him and bring back some of the dream souls of the People?" asked Apoawein. " I know they had to do this in the Spirit World."

"That is what the powwows had to learn how to do because their first efforts were not successful. The sorcerer threw them back every time they approached. His power and strength despite his size was extraordinarily strong. He threw them through the air without ever touching them."

"Poor Pawquash, I understand he was quite old by then and frail. Some say it was these battles with the black robed demon that in the end weakened him and he died shortly after. Is that true Ponaim?" asked Mequnhut.

"Sadly yes, but not before he and Commossuck discovered a way to retrieve some souls and bring them back" I continued. "They discovered that the demon despite his strength and power could not see when they were to his right, his eye must have been bad. So their plan was rather simple. They would take turns approaching from his left, yelling, singing spirit songs, and generally distracting him. The one to distract would shape-shift into their spirit animal in doing so to give them more spiritual strength and power. Pawquash was the stag and Commossuck the bear when they did so. This gave them some spirit protection because the power animal they became drew its strength from the Spirit realm. When the demon reacted and turned towards him the other with a satchel made of three otter skins, would run up on the blind side and gather souls and put them into the bag as quickly as he could. Of course the black robed demon would turn and throw the gathering powwow back but when that happened they would always hold the satchel tight and it turned out the demon could not penetrate it for it was made from the skins of the otter, the spirit helper of Hobomock."

"So this became a game of life and death" said Apoawein.

"It was, and after confronting him enough times to fill the satchel, the powwows would leave exhausted. But in this way they saved some of the People, but sadly not enough. The two could only confront the demon so many times for it was completely draining and they would then have to rest and spend time restoring their spiritual and physical strength while still tending to the sick in their villages. But thanks to them many survived like Nashump."

"Did they inform the shamans of the Quinnipiac, Wangunk, Paugassett and others what they were doing to gain their help?" asked Mequnhut. "If others had helped maybe more could have been saved."

"They did Mequnhut, but by then many were sick themselves or did not have the gifts and powers to do so. Tispaquin from Mioonkhtuck did however and sometimes the three would journey into the tunnel together. One time Tispaquin snuck too close to the demon while gathering souls and was touched on his right arm by the demon's icy hand when he turned. Until the day he went to the home of Kiehtan, he could not move or use it."

We all sat in silence for a while as the reassuring sounds of the deep night made all what was told seem hard to imagine. Yet I knew my two companions understood and that they would keep the story alive for the People when I was gone. After some time, Mequnhut spoke again.

"Uncle, My mother and father have always told me that this was the greatest disaster to strike the People. So many died that very few were left. Our population had dropped to a small number in each village including here in Mennunkatuck."

"That is true, in some villages among the People and throughout the Dawnland as many as three out of four people died, families were wiped out, none were spared. Those of us who did survive could hardly consider ourselves lucky. So many were gone, so many" I said as just the thought made my eyes begin to water with tears.

"I remember my grandmother saying how her mother, the sunksquaw, never became ill despite working hard to help those who were but two of her younger brothers died."

"And we have always been told the story of Wentubecum and Meishunk and how with their Spirit Shields they were able to help many and provide food for the village so that the People could eat and there would be meat and fish for the winter. "It is said that both lost their families to the pox, was that true?"

"They did, and it broke their hearts to be spared while those they loved were not" I replied.

Apoawein poked at the fire again and then stated bitterly "I have also always been told that this sickness so weakened the People and others in the Dawnland that when the Pequot War came we were few and the defeat of the Pequot then allowed the Awaunuy to come in many ships to our land as they still come to this day. We could not stop them and by the time Metacom tried it was too late. Now their towns and farms surround and choke us."

"Yes Apoawein, we were then as today so few and each year their numbers grew and still do. They offered us peace and protection from our enemies in return for the right to settle among us. But by then who were left to be called our enemies? The Pequot had been destroyed and their survivors scattered in the wind. Uncas and the Mohegan? He cared only for himself and his people. The broken River Bands or the Paugassett and others to our west and the setting sun? They were as we were. Yes, the smallpox that year was the start of these times of dark shadows."

Chapter Twelve

With the first hint of light in the morning I quickly pulled my sleeping robe and few belongings together and hoping not to wake my companions, went to the lake to wash and cleanse myself both physically and spiritually before continuing on my return to Toto-ket. The water felt cool on my skin and the air already warm but dry. I thanked Keihtan for this day and prayed that all the People would be safe and happy as they wake on such a beautiful morning. The air hummed with the sounds of the insect world and a dragonfly circled around me before lighting upon my right shoulder. "Hello friend, what news do you bring me this morning?" I asked her as she slowly raised and lowered her wings two times. "Ah, you bring me a message, thank you. You and your family are the ones who often bring word that a change or new per-spective is needed and it would be wise to heed what you have to say. Change; that certainly follows the recent messages from Hobomock. Is it he who sent you? Being a creature of his two realms; water when young and the sky when an adult, he often sends you to those who will listen."

The dragonfly sat motionless for a short time and I did not move for fear of disturbing her. If there was a message, I wanted to know. Again, she raised her wings twice, paused, then rising from my shoulder flew quickly south in the direction of our former village where the Awaunuy town of Guilford now was. Twice she has told me two times, I must think about this for a while, as a nymph in the water the dragonfly lives for two years and if she manages to survive and become an adult she will rise into the sky as a creature of light because the translucent quality of her wings always captures the rays of the sun. As a messenger of change, she was quite insistent. She raised her wings twice; two times. Suddenly the meaning came to me. Two years - that has been how long we the People have been talking at Totoket and Mioonkhtuck of leaving. Is it time? Two times. But does this mean there are two paths?

Of course, two paths. The message makes sense for the debate among the People was of two directions; one to stay in the land of our ancestors and live with the Awaunuy and the other to leave and find refuge away from them and return to the ways of our ancestors. Which would the People choose? I will tell them these messages from Hobomock and then the People can decide as one or as individuals which path to follow.

As I left the water and returned to the fishing camp Mequnhut was tending to the fire and Apoawein was busy examining the fish that had been drying overnight in the smoke. "They need more time Mequnhut before they are ready," he said to his friend. "I am anxious to return to the village but it seems we must stay for at least the morning. I will go to the lake and catch us breakfast." As he turned to walk to the lake with the net for fishing Apoawein saw me coming up from the water to the camp. "Good morning Ponaim" he said. "We knew you had not left us for your sleeping robe and satchel are still here. I am going to catch us some breakfast, you will join us of course."

"Thank you Apoawein, but I have a strong urge to begin my walk back to Totoket right away. I have been given a message to go to Guilford village on my way but the reason was not given."

"I understand shaman, you must go where the Spirits guide you. I will see you back at Totoket and look forward to hearing more of the stories about the past" the young man responded with a smile. "We must remain with the fish since they are not quite ready to take from the smoke." He turned and started the short distance to the lake and I found myself smiling with the thought that maybe those among the People like he and Mequnhut might somehow find a way to carry on the traditional ways.

"Good morning uncle, how are you this gift of a day?" Mequnhut asked as I returned to the camp. "Will you eat with us?"

"No, I am anxious and ready to return to Totoket, but have been given a sign to first go to the Awaunuy town where our village once was. One of Hobomock's messengers greeted me this morning at the lake so I am curious to know why. She pointed that I was to go that way."

"I understand uncle but be careful for there are some who do not remember the early days when the People welcomed Whitfield and the others and helped them to survive those first years. It seems all they care about now is to take more of Earth Mother to cut with their plows while claiming we are the children of their devil who must be driven away. You in particular are suspect, your powers and gifts are well known among them and some fear you because of them."

"There are still some who I have known for many years and despite the differences in our ways of talk welcome me and are curious about our ways" I replied. Because I walk with the Spirits and our ancestors I have no fear of the Awaunuy."

"That is true uncle, but if you wait until the sun is high Apoawein and I can travel with you."

"No it is best I go alone for an old man crossing their fields is not seen as a threat or a problem. I will follow the river that flows from Quonnipaug, that trail is open and wide."

"May Hobomock walk with you uncle and we will see you soon at Totoket" said Mequnhut as he tenderly placed a hand on my shoulder. "We all have much to learn from you still so journey with the spirit of the fox who is always alert and careful."

I smiled at his advice and nodded my agreement in appreciation of his expression of care and at that moment he reminded me of his grandmother and how she had often said those exact words to me often over the years. The spirits of the ancestors live in him I thought as I picked up my bundle and walked toward the well-worn trail that led from the foot of the lake.

The morning was brilliant in its beauty, the sky cloudless and blue amidst the breaks in the green canopy of leaves that formed above the path. How many times had I walked this trail in my many years I thought. Yet somehow this time felt different; like so many other things in this rapidly changing world, would this be my last?

Alert to the sounds and smells of the woods around me, I was momentarily lulled into a place in my mind from long ago when my father and uncle first brought me to hunt among these trees for deer and how proud I was to be considered no longer a child. I remember how I tried not to be nervous and walk carefully in silence so as to not alert our prey. Now here I am, an old shaman - following the advice of the young warning me how I should avoid falling victim to those who might do me harm.

Leaving the lake, the ground along the river flattened out to the west and though the trail led along the eastern bank which snuggled up against a long, low rocky ridge, I decided to cross the quickly flowing stream to walk instead through the woods and fields of tall grass on the other side. I always feel more comfortable in Earth Mother's home I thought than on our ancestral trail now scarred by Awaunuy cartwheels as I waded across the thigh deep water which felt cool as it swirled around me. Climbing up a low part of the bank that had been cut and smoothed by the river's relentless journey to the sea I could not help but think about what might lie ahead for me in the Awaunuy village. I had not walked through it for a number of months and even my travel from Totoket to the start of the Spirit Line had been through these woods to its north where I was more comfortable and the land was still mostly the realm of the Earth Mother. How odd I thought, that these Awaunuy seem to also love the land and hunger deeply for it , but not for what it can provide, but what it can produce for them. In doing so they reshape and scar it and take pride and are satisfied in what they do. It saddens me.

The grasses on the west side of the river had already grown close to the height of my knees as I turned to walk towards the south following the course of the river. "How sweet the grasses smell" I thought as I moved slowly through it, the voices of our insect brothers and sisters greeting me as I did so. In the distance a bit to my right, a line of trees stood as sentinels along the edge of the meadow just as they always have. But behind them and hidden from my view beyond the gently rising hills I knew was a trail the Awaunuy had cut through the forest to clear the land of trees in order to sell the wood and ready the ground for their planting. I decided to cross the meadow and walk through the trees to see what changes they had wrought.

Entering the woods, I heard in the distance up the crest of the second hill the cries of an Awaunuy who I could eventually see through the trees as he prodded and spoke gruffly to his two horned beasts as they were being put to a task. "Ah yes, oxen" I said to myself. As I approached the edge of the tree line I could see that they had been busy gathering the trees they had cut in the winter and the beasts were laboring to pull two of them stripped of their branches towards the Awaunuy path that led south to their village. As I watched the beasts labor with their burden the second Awaunuy to their right noticed me and called out to the one with the oxen.

"Hold Benjamin, we have company. It is the old devil from Totoket himself peering at us through the timber. It is he it is said who we are always warned can cast a spell on those who are not faithful. May the Lord protect us. Perhaps a few stones will chase him off."

"No Isaiah, perhaps it is best to leave him alone for was it not you who fell asleep during the Reverend's sermon this Sunday past? You may put you soul in jeopardy if you have not repented!" Isaiah teased with a lighthearted laugh. "Besides, my uncle William, as you know can speak some of their tongue and often says he finds him of interest to speak with and says he will not harm those of a good heart."

As the two young men stood watching me, I moved out of the woods and walked directly towards them softly chanting a prayer for the spirits of the trees they were collecting. This caused a reaction in the young Awaunuy who had first called out and he picked up an axe that was near him and began to raise it in a threatening manner. His companion quickly said something to him and he lowered the tool to his side while eyeing me cautiously. I looked straight at him and said softly and assuredly " he had nothing to fear and that my chanting was for the trees."

"What do you want old man and why do you sing?" asked the one with the axe. "Are you casting your devil's spell upon us?"

"Isaiah; I do not believe he is threatening us at all but speaking to the timber. See how he is looking to them as he sings" Benjamin remarked just as I reached out to touch one of the forest sisters.

"How sad it is that you harm the tree people" I said to the young men which elicited an anxious look from one while the other seemed relaxed. "I often hear their tears in the winter when you cut them while they sleep."

"He is mad Benjamin. I think we would be wise to chase the demon away. Besides, did not their sachem sell this land to us? So why is he here?"

"Isaiah, he is old and probably set in the past. Let us sit for a short period and I am sure he will be on his way."

As the two Awaunuy spoke, I decided to circle around the two trees as well as the beasts that stood calmly waiting to pull them. As I did so, I spoke again to the two young men and let them know I meant them no harm. "I just want to appeal to the Spirits to protect those who still stand and thank those who you have killed. You have done enough harm already."

As I passed to the front of the oxen, I could not help but notice the way the beasts watched me, turning their heads as they did, straining against the heavy wooden yoke that bound them together just before their shoulders. I marveled at their size, that of a moose, and their calm dispositions. I told them "I appreciate your beauty and strength and I hope the two Awaunuy are good to you." In unison they lowered their massive heads in a bow. When I passed to their other side the youth with the axe stood and nervously shouted out while waving it in the air as I approached closer to he and his companion.

"Isaiah, leave him be!"

Realizing the one with the axe was becoming increasingly anxious with my presence which amused me to a degree, I stopped and stood before him, softly chanted a prayer for his spirit which seemed so troubled. Then I smiled at them both and raised my hand in the sign of peace and friendship we the People have always used before turning to begin my journey again. That poor boy, I thought, he saw me only as a nuisance and maybe even a threat.

As I walked away from the two, I began to think as I often have these last few years that soon it will be impossible to live alongside these Awaunuy. Unlike those who came first with their leader Whitfield to Mennunkatuck or the year before with Davenport and Eaton to Quinnipiac, their children and now grandchildren do not regard us as having the right to use and be in the lands of our ancestors. It was the intent of our sachems when they put their sign on the papers the Awaunuy always insisted they do, that we would all share in the gift of the Earth

Mother. It has become obvious over time the Awaunuy do not see the agreement as we do. To the Awaunuy, the land is a possession and they are strong in their desire to have and control it. This only reinforces for me the recent messages from the Spirits and Hobomock.

Not wanting to follow the Awaunuy made path to their village, I quickly returned eastward to the forest and tried to avoid where it had been destroyed. The day had grown warm and Father Sun was about to reach his high place in the sky as I entered the canopy of trees and around me were the sweet fragrant smells that come with the fresh growth of summer. I made my way through the grandmother trees, whispering softly to them as I did thanking them for the bounty they had always provided the People knowing their time before the axe would soon come. Our winged brothers sang in unison to my prayers and for a moment I knew that despite so many changes, this was still the world of our ancestors and to walk within it was a special gift from Keihtan.

I worked my way back to the river as I moved south and before long came out of the forest and into meadowland along the western bank that was interspersed with stands of trees and rocky outcrops. An eagle flew high above the trees and along the line of the river heading south and I saw in her flight and direction a good omen for she is the symbol of illumination of the spirit, healing, and creation. There is a reason for my going to the Awaunuy village; first the message of the dragonfly and now the eagle. I will trust in the Spirits and let them guide me to my purpose.

The further I walked, the more the landscape along the river changed. There were fewer trees and soon even the meadow gave way to the plowed and planted Awaunuy fields, many fenced with wooden rails or walls of stone that I climbed over as I went. No wonder the Awaunuy stick to their paths for it is hard to travel through the land when they block it as they do.

I came to a crest of a hill from which I could look down upon the Awaunuy village with its tall houses made of wood, arranged in clusters along lanes leading from a central open ground that was once the home of our village. Beyond, further south, were those of stone they had built when they first came with the help of some of our People. They had built them they said for protection from their King and the Dutchmannuck. I had heard at Mioonkhtuck many years ago that their King and later his son were angry at them. Further still was the sea which had always provided for the People. "So many years have passed since this was our home I thought. It lives in my memory now."

I decided to sit and wait to see what would come to me from the Spirits and found shade under a large oak tree that they had not yet cut and from where I could watch what was happening below me. No sooner had I sat than a raven flew towards me from below and landed in the branches above my head. "Hello friend" I said. "Do you bring me a message?" He did not answer but sat silently upon his perch intent on joining me in my watch. "I know you will tell or show me what I need to know when it is time." So together we watched the village below.

It was not long before my friend and I could see why we waited. An Awaunuy ship was entering the waters south of the village. I thought back to the first time as a boy I saw one, a floating island with trees and clouds some of the People had said the first time one appeared in the Dawnland. By my time on Earth Mother however, these ships had become well known for the Dutchmannuck came in ones of many sizes to Totoket to trade and often one sat for days there before the Awaunuy came. But this one was different. It was clearly not a trading ship and its sides held a row of openings from which I could see the large guns that were always frightening to us. As raven and I watched it arrive, we could see suddenly great activity in the village as men began running hurriedly and their spirit house bell began to sound. This ship must have been important I thought. I looked up to my feathered brother and said, "perhaps their king has come."

No sooner had I finished my words than raven left his perch and flew in a line straight towards the village and I decided to follow. "If only I could shape shift now and join him" I said to myself, "but now is not the time and I know the Awaunuy do not favor the red tailed hawk as they claim it kills their chickens." So I decided to walk to the village to see why I was called to go.

Descending the hill through open ground, I passed by the place where the Awaunuy had captured the water to have it turn a great wheel to grind their maize then found myself passing by the first of their houses. At first those I passed seemed empty but I knew from the sounds they were not. In one a baby cried and in another I heard an Awaunuy woman calling out. By the time I reached the third, a man came out of the door carrying his musket and stopped suddenly, surprised to see me. He stared for a moment before running ahead down the path between the houses that led to the central open ground of their village. I kept walking and came across others; men with muskets and women and children who were all hurrying towards the place in front of their spirit house where they gathered on their sabbath day. It appeared they did not notice me and I thought for a moment that maybe I had in fact become invisible to their eyes until one bumped into me and acted quite startled. "Give way ye heathen!" he shouted as he moved off to join the others who were putting themselves in the lines they used when preparing to fight. In front of them were their headmen and god-talker saying things that the others must have felt were important because they listened intently.

A crowd of women, older people, and children was gathering to either side and I decided to join one to see what had stirred them all into such activity. I looked to the top of their spirit house and recognized my feathered companion perched on the peak, as curious as I was. It was then that I could see William off to the other side, an Awaunuy I had come to know over these many years. He had come to Mennunkatuck as a young man with Whitfield and beginning when we were both younger had on occasion talked as he had learned some of our words and he often asked me about the People and our ways. At first suspicious, over time I had come to trust him as a friend. Despite the commotion of the moment, William noticed me as the crowd I had joined began to part around me and move away. Some of the women gathered their children protectively so as not to be near me. One looked fiercely at me and shouted loudly while motioning with her hands that I should be away.

"Ponaim!" William called out loud enough for me to hear despite the noise that filled the place where we all stood. In his broken tongue of the People he called for me to meet by a tree behind the villagers while I motioned that I understood. While he made his way through his people drums and flutes could be heard coming from the south where the ship had come and soon it was apparent that those who came were bringing warriors. When William reached me, a bit winded by his hurried pace, I asked him: "is it your King who comes?"

"Ponaim what brings you to Guilford on this day? Can you see there is some trouble starting and I do not want to see you caught in it."

"Is it your King?" I repeated. "If so I would like to speak with him of the troubles of the People. All we have are the sorrows brought to us these many years. Perhaps he will listen."

"Oh my friend, it is not King James but one of his sachems who comes to threatened us here in Connecticut for our reluctance to give up the freedoms we hold dear" William replied. "His plan is to force us to be one with the King's lands taken from the Dutch many years ago and we here in Guilford and all Connecticut refuse."

Just then a line of soldiers all dressed in red coats came to the open ground from the south, drums and flutes playing while their flags fluttered in the wind. On their shoulders were their muskets with long knives readily displayed for all in the village to see. "Now I understand William. They come to take from you what your people have taken from us."

The soldiers formed in two long lines across the south end of the open ground facing the villagers gathered at the opposite end. Two men, splendid in their colorful uniforms, stepped forward and shouted out to the village militia to be at rest for they meant no harm as they proceeded across the open ground towards them. "We come to speak with the magistrates of Guilford by order of Sir Edmund Andros, Governor of the King's Colony of New York for you now fall under his jurisdiction." William did not have time to explain to me what was said but it was obvious there was a great tension present. The god-talker along with three others, one being their headman named Leete, came forward from the crowd and approached the soldiers and after exchanging greetings walked together to the spirit house and went inside.

William turned to me and said, "we shall be most agreeable to consider their pronouncements then when they leave we will peacefully go about on our own as our brothers in New Haven and elsewhere have. In the end it is the will of God and not a King that will rule in this land."

"Manitou William, it has always been the will of the Spirits that in the end determine the fate of men. We the People understand this despite the dark shadows that have fallen across the Dawnland since you Awaunuy came. Will they take you all in the ship back across the sea?"

"No my friend, we are here to stay and I often regret much to the detriment of the Quinnipiac" William replied with a look of sadness. "From the beginning I had always hoped the Quinnipiac and we English could live together and share this beautiful country. I am ashamed that my people, not yours, have not allowed it to be."

Meanwhile, when most in the village were gathered about the door and windows of the spirit house, curious to see what was being said, some of the young attracted by my presence, came closer to William and me as we spoke. I did not know what they were saying but they approached cautiously then stared silently for a while. Eventually two of the older boys picked up some stones from the ground and motioned to others to do so as well. "It is the Devil's sorcerer himself" said one as his face became a mask of anger.

At that moment, William stepped forward. "Off with you, you rascals! He is a good man and one you should respect though his is a different way!" The boys stood for a moment then slowly turned away and as they did so dropped their stones. "I am sorry for their disrespect Ponaim" my friend said.

"It is not something that bothers me, for their taunts and stones are as mosquitoes" I replied. "They cannot harm me for the Spirits, especially Hobomock protect me always. Perhaps that is why they fear me."

"Yes my friend, that is the truth."

"I will leave you now William Dudley, for I know now why I was brought here and will make my way to Totoket."

"Walk with God my friend" was his reply.

"And you with Keihtan." As I turned to the west towards Totoket, the raven flew overhead and towards the late afternoon sun.

Chapter Thirteen

As I left the home of the ancestors, my thoughts drifted back to the time when the Awaunuy broke the power of the Pequot and thus opened all the Dawnland for their people to settle in it, including Mennunkatuck. Following closely after the death and heartache of two years of smallpox, the Awaunuy destroyed the Pequot and began to come to the lands of the People like a series of great, relentless waves brought by the raging sea in a storm that sweep all before it. All the people of the Dawnland were powerless to stop them as they took or made trades for our lands. We thought they would live peacefully alongside us, sharing in the bounty of the Dawnland for the benefit of all. We were wrong.

Mennunkatuck was virtually deserted the morning we heard the news. Many had taken refuge weeks before with our people at Mioonkhtuck, while others had fled north into the lands of the Tunxis and Wangunks. Some even fled to the villages of the Awaunuy clustered along Quinnihticut seeking safety from the fighting between the Pequot and the Awaunuy settlements. Since the summer before, the two had been at war. The People, under the leadership of Momauguin at Mioonkhtuck, remained neutral despite threats from Sassacus the Pequot sachem who demanded we join with them as their tributaries. The fighting, along with our fear of the Awaunuy whose recent arrival clustered around Pyquag on the Quinnihticut, had caused tremendous anxiety among all four Quinnipiac bands.

The Pequot had only recently lifted their siege of the small Awaunuy fort they called Saybrook. After a number of successful skirmishes and raids, they confidently declared they would soon rid the Dawnland once and for all of the white skinned vermin. It was they, the Pequot insisted, who had brought much suffering to all the people of the region, and who challenged their supremacy over the Quinnipiac, Niantic, and the Quinnihticut River Bands.

It was my sixteenth summer and the People now considered me an adult. This made me a potential warrior if it came to fighting, a prospect that both terrified and excited me. But by then I was traveling a different journey in this life, that of a powwow. My primary role was to become a healer in this physical realm, communicate with the world of the Spirits, and be a bridge between both. It was not a life of my choosing, but Keihtan the Creator had called me.

A runner from the Niantic had arrived exhausted mid-morning. He was clearly agitated as he shared word of a devastating attack by the Awaunuy against the Pequot, an ally of his people. Shaump-ishuh had welcomed the warrior with drink and food and implored him to sit. Nashump, and the few of us who had remained in our village sat too. Shaump-ishuh had proven many times by then to be a strong and wise leader of the People and the message brought by the Niantic, I know now, required all her skill. Because she was tall for a woman and power-fully built, the loss of her left eye further accentuated her appearance causing all who spoke with her to be riveted and hypnotized by her gaze. This she used to great advantage and this time was no exception.

"Come sit and refresh yourself before you tell us why you have come to us" the squaw sachem said. "It is rare these days for one of your people to come so hurriedly to Mennunkatuck. The tensions between our peoples have been strong since the Niantic have walked the path with the Pequot."

"I have been sent by my sachem with instruc-tions from Sassucus himself to alert you to what has fallen upon the Pequot at the village at Mistick," said the messenger as he eagerly lifted a gourd full of wa-ter to his mouth, then hesitated..

Shaumpishuh nodded permission to drink. He took three tremendous gulps while she motioned towards the Grandmother oak and its shade that would provide comfort from the growing heat of the summer day. I noticed Commossuck circle behind the Niantic and sniff the air like a bear as if to ascertain his truth before he spoke; his movements were purposeful and unhurried. When Shaumpishuh reached the shade, she motioned all to sit as she settled herself into comfort. As was our custom, Nashump was on her right, and the runner three feet before her. The rest of us clustered in an arc facing Shaumpishuh while Commossuck moved past the Niantic and with one more great sniff, took to his place by the squaw sachem's left. The messenger looked warily at him then quickly turned his attention to Shaumpishuh.

"My sachem has been instructed by Sassucus to tell you the fate of many of his people. Before the sun rose, their palisaded village was attacked by the Awaunuy from Pyquag, Uncas and the Mohegan, and some Narragansett." He hesitated with a nervous look that could be seen by those he faced.

Shaumpishuh peered at him intensely and the look from her eye only increased his nervousness while Commossuck began to softly growl at him, still having the bear in his spirit. "Please" assured the sunksquaw, "you have nothing to fear here for we are eager to hear what has happened to the people of Sassucus."

Regaining his composure the Niantic began. "Scouts tracked the Awaunuy from the moment they left their villages on the Quinnihticut in boats to drift down to their fort at the river's mouth. They were accompanied by Uncas and Mohegan warriors who were uncomfortable with the slow pace of the boats. Halfway down the river, they left the boats for the western shore and continued the journey to the Awaunuy fort on foot. Pequot scouts and a few of our warriors followed them the entire way from the opposite bank and while others remained outside the fort keeping a watchful eye."

Shaumpishuh nodded her understanding then asked if Sassacus was aware an attack was coming and knew of their numbers?

"Yes" answered the messenger, "they were joined by a number of men from the Bay settlements in the land of the Massachusett who were already at the fort. They left and were tracked along the coast as the entire party of Awaunuy and Mohegan went east in their boats to the land of the Narragansett. Sassacus moved some warriors to his palisaded villages at Mistick and Weinshauks, then sent others to monitor the shore and river near the villages so he could move quickly if threatened. He then gathered his council at Weinshauks to plan how to next confront the foe."

"If the Awaunuy sailed to the land of the Narragansett was that a deception?" asked the sunksquaw.

"It turned out to be, for along with Narragansett warriors they came overland in stealth instead of by water as had been expected. The Awaunuy have always proven themselves deliberate in their arrogance towards confronting our warriors. They came quietly in the night and fell on the village at Mistick well before Father Sun rose as all but a few slept. As the enemy surrounded the palisade, a barking dog roused the village, and those present fought bravely before being overwhelmed."

"Tell me of the village and the people?"

"What happened is hard to imagine. The Awaunuy and Mohegan surrounded the palisade" the Niantic replied, and as he spoke his eyes darted from the sachem, to Commossuck, and to the others he could see without turning. There was a burst of intensity in his manner when he continued. "There was no escape as the Awaunuy with their firearms and long knives blocked the two entrances and moved into the village itself—setting fire to the weetous and long houses as they went. Women, children, and the old were trapped inside and though some were killed by the hands of the Awaunuy most died in the flames of a great fire. Those who tried to flee the flames by breaching the palisade were killed by the men of Uncas gathered around the outside."

"And the Narragansett?"

"It is said they were awestruck and dismayed by the slaughter and many returned to their villages. Though an enemy of the Pequot, they found the Awaunuy way of war to be far worse than anything they could have imagined."

"Why did Sassacus not come to their aid?" asked Shaumpishuh.

"By the time the few who escaped reached him it was too late. The fight was over and the Awaunuy did not want to linger for what was sure to be swift retribution. They moved quickly with their wounded to try and meet up with their boats. I was told just as I was leaving that Sassacus had caught up with them and was seeking revenge. To what end I do not know."

There was a long period of silence as the magnitude of what had transpired began to sink in. I remember my sense of shock and worry for it was obvious that there would be more terrible mornings to come.

"Do you know how many at Mistick perished?" asked Shaumpishuh, her voice a bit hushed by the mere idea of what she was asking.

"This I do not know, only that it is said they are as numerous as the stars."

Shaumpishuh sat silently for a while as Commossuck began to softly chant and the rest of us tried to grasp what was to become a further shock to our new reality. This, coming after the two years of sickness that had killed more people of the Dawnland than now remained alive. It was another powerful omen that showed how our understanding of the world was being uprooted and torn asunder. My thoughts plunged through my mind like a fast-flowing stream cascading over rocks, and I found it hard to focus as if a spell had come over me. It was only broken when Shaumpishuh rose while declaring "Manitou! It is so. You will be fed and can stay the night if you would like" she said. "I thank you for telling us this."

"Thank you and am honored to accept your offer of food but will not linger for I want to be on my way back to my village across the Quinnihticut as soon as possible. I fear for my family and people for this is an uncertain and dangerous time."

As Shaumpishuh and Nashump began to walk away and the Niantic was being ushered to another shaded spot where he might be given food and water, Shaumpishuh paused and turned back towards him. "Is there more you have not spoken of friend? What of Sassacus? Was there a message for we of Mennunkatuck and the other Quinnipiac Bands?"

Taken by surprise, the runner turned quickly and as he did so, a feather dropped from his hair which was bound in a long braided top knot on an otherwise hairless head. It was an eagle feather, a sign of his position as a warrior and a man of renown among his people. He stooped to retrieve the feather before standing again, straightening his back, and summoning his sense of purpose and dignity that went with his position among the Niantic. "Sunksquaw, I was told that Sassacus will call on all those who owe allegiance to him and his people when the time comes. He knows that even if he annihilates those who have struck such a cruel blow, the struggle to rid the Dawnland of these demons has just begun."

Shaumpishuh advanced quickly towards the Niantic, her great size moving with the speed of a mother bear protecting her young. She stood before the messenger, glaring at him, trapping him in a moment of intensity that only she could create. "I shall relay all you have said to my brother at Mioonkhtuck and thank you for speaking of this. We the People have much to consider." She continued to stare at the messenger, but her countenance changed quickly and her face softened. "Please enjoy our hospitality and send our thanks to your sachem and sympathies to Sassacus." With that Shaumpishuh turned, her tunic of the finest deerskin painted with the sign of the thunderbird across her back ruffled softly as she moved. Her dignified, haughty bearing, a message the Niantic could not miss, was an unspoken signal that she spoke for her people and the ancestors who called Mennunkatuck home.

Even after all these years have passed, it is still impossible to imagine how within such a short period of time, everything in the world of the People changed. I remember the terror and confusion that came with word from the Niantic of what had happened to our seemingly invincible Pequot overlords. Their fortified village, impregnable behind its strong palisade of tree trunks, had been destroyed by the Awaunuy with the help of Uncas and his fellow Mohegan. "How could it be," I asked Commossuck that evening, "that such a proud and powerful people could have suffered such a horrible defeat in a way so hard to imagine?"

My mentor paused before answering. His long, gray hair was pulled back behind his head with three feathers of the raven. Their deep blackness formed a sharp contrast to his hair and matched his face, which was painted black with red streaks of lightning across each cheek. The shaman had painted it immediately after we had been told of the attack on the Pequot. This he did when seeking guidance from the Spirit World, especially the powerful Hobomock. Together with his piercing black eyes and ethereal mannerism, he took on an otherworld appearance.

"It was the Pequot's desire to dominate the trade in wampum, furs, and Dutchmannuck goods at the expense of all others in the Dawnland Ponaim, that sowed the seeds of their destruction. Their actions caused an increase in the unbalance of the natural world that started when the Dutchmannuck first came to our shores, then the Awaunuy with their smallpox. The actions of these people are of their world only and are increasingly destabilizing ours. The Pequot actions have made the situation worse and have made Hobomock and those of the Spirit World angry."

As he spoke, there was a rising sense of frustration mixed with anger in his voice as he stared into my eyes. "It is clear that by forcing all others to pay them tribute in wampum and fur to give them control of the trade with the Dutchmannuck, then challenging the Awaunuy, perhaps the Spirit World saw no choice but to bring about a rebalancing of the natural order. The Pequot had become too greedy in their quest for wealth and power." He paused for a moment while looking into the fire in the center of our weetou, then mused, "it puzzles me though that the Spirits would use the Awaunuy to punish them. Or was it not the doing at all of the Spirits?"

"I understand Commossuck, maybe that explains the way in which the Awaunuy destroyed the village at Mistick. Keihtan and the Spirits would not allow such a thing. The Awaunuy way of warfare is a manner unknown to the people of the Dawnland."

"Ponaim," the powwow replied as his voice turned to a greater earnestness. "What the Awaunuy did came from their world and not of ours. I fear it may have come from that black book they carry with them and refer to for all things. It may be the source of their power and in it are spells that turn them into people capable of such horrible violence." Pausing, he added, "remember how they unleashed the black robed sorcerer."

The powwow's demeanor suddenly changed as a wave of sadness gripped him with a strength that made me shudder. I could feel the energy and anger drain from him and pull mine with it. Crestfallen, my friend continued. "Such an act of ruthlessness on their part I fear has revealed what is now an even greater challenge to our world. The spirit energy the Awaunuy have brought from across the sea may possess a stronger and more powerful medicine that we must all confront or surely die as the Pequot have, just as so many of the People did during the years of sickness."

The two of us sat in silence for a long period of time. I occasionally played with the fire in the center of our weetou. By then, I remember, I had come to know the shaman and his ways and instinctively knew this was different. Ever since the arrival of the

Awaunuy and their settlements along the Quinnihticut only four years ago, Commossuck had struggled to find a way to renew and reestablish the balance within our universe. As time passed, he became
increasingly frustrated as he and the other shamans
of the Quinnipiac and Wangunk tried to protect us
from the chaos the terrifying and deadly diseases
caused by their coming to the Dawnland, threatening
the very existence of the People. But his reaction this
time was different. Commossuck seemed to sense
something. If he only knew what the future held; or
perhaps he did.

Chapter Fourteen

I walked along the wide path between Awaunuy houses on east side of the river and decided rather than wade across I would use the wooden path they had built so I could cross without getting into the water. I had to admit that with all their faults, these people did have a creative ability to make useful things. As I stood in the center of the wooden path and looked down into the water, I saw my image and remembered how this was once the only way to see oneself. Now it seems all the People have what the Awaunuy call a looking glass. I find them interesting and have used them as an opening to journey through into the Spirit World.

Once across I left the Awaunuy trail and walked through the meadow that followed the west bank of the river so as to move away from their farms and fences and then enter the woodland that would bring me to the forest and stony ridges that separated Mennunkatuck from Totoket. It was there that Commossuck had so often gone to find the will of Hobomock and where I have also gone countless times during my long life. It is still a place of spiritual power and one the Awaunuy have left relatively alone for its landscape of stony ridges and outcrops is not one they find useful. As I followed the ancient path of our ancestors that took me through marshland and woods, all around me were the sounds of the Earth Mother and her creatures and I felt a wonderful comfort there after being in the Awaunuy village. "Here our world still lives" I said to all who might hear me knowing I was where I should be.

I decided not to return to Totoket that day but to stay instead at the rock shelter near the lake that was nestled between the ridges; a place where I could rest, think, and pray for guidance. There I would find fresh water to drink, berries, and roots to eat, and time to be within the embrace of the Earth Mother and the other spirits of the natural world. I left the trail and climbed a series of knolls and ridges and came to the place of the Split Rock, an entrance to the Lower World through which we often thanked and sought guidance from Hobomock. It was here for many years the People from Mennunkatuck and Totoket would gather for a ceremonial dance in the autumn following the harvest to thank Hobomock, Keihtan, and the Earth Mother for sharing the bounty of this world before moving to our inland winter camps in the north. "How long has it been?" I asked as I reached out to touch the stone to let her know she had not been forgotten. "Perhaps I will bring the young from Totoket here to help them better understand our ways. So many are turning away."

A strong gloom came over me like a dark cloud as I thought about all that had been lost, not just all the People, we the Quinnipiac were very few in number now, but the world we had once lived each day was being transformed by the presence of the Awaunuy. I began to chant softly and sat by the opening to the Lower World, knowing I should stay for a while. I closed my eyes and continued chanting the Spirit Words Commossuck had taught me when I was just a boy and soon found myself move through the split in the rock and down into the womb of the Earth Mother. There I fell into a bright valley full of sunlight with a rushing stream running through it. On either side were verdant meadows full of grass and flowers that gently sloped upward until they met trees that continued the climb up the ridges. I knew instantly it was the valley I had seen in my vision the night of the solstice and I knew that Hobomock was again showing me where the People might journey to live as our ancestors had.

It was comforting to be in the valley and I did not want to leave but found myself being pulled upward against my will, but trusting in Hobomock, I let myself go. Floating upward I came to a place of darkness that felt heavy and cold and as my vision adjusted I knew where I was. It was Mioonkhtuck, but not of our time. Rather it was a time when it had been completely changed with large Awaunuy houses and many paths made of stone that were lined with poles that shined with white fire. In the distance two great beasts, one the color of red ochre and the other like a Dutchmannuck kettle of iron, came towards me. Both had bright white fire eyes and round spinning legs and their sound was loud and roaring but like nothing I had ever heard. As they passed by me I saw that their skin seemed to shine. "Strange Awaunuy spirit creatures" I said to myself with a bit of a shudder. As I looked around I could see there were no weetous, no trace of the People; just big Awaunuy houses with large openings of light, the beasts, and noises all around me that hurt my ears. In the darkness I could see tall towers across the water where the Awaunuy town New Haven had been that had many small fires high in the sky, some lined up in rows. The air was full of smells I did not know. I looked upward but could only see a few of the ancestors that had always covered the sky though the night was cloudless. Where had they gone I wondered? But Mother Moon was on the horizon above what I recognized was the tall ridge where Hobomock once lived. This was Mioonkhtuck, but not and I felt myself shivering not from cold, but from fear. "This is the future" I said. "The People must be gone for how could they live in such a place?"

I began to chant Sacred Sounds despite my surroundings and as I did I could feel the darkness replaced slowly by light and when I opened my eyes I was sitting against the split in the rock as evening shadows were beginning to surround me. I shivered with the thought of where I had been and what I had seen but understood what I was to share with the Council when the sachems and elders gathered. Together with this vision and the determination expressed by William that the Awaunuy were here to stay reinforced in me the power of the message from Hobomock. How will the Council and the People decide?

The evening air was still warm as I made my way from the Split Rock to the lake and the rock shelter. I could see when I arrived that none had been there since before the snow and I quickly set to work making a shelter by leaning saplings against the upper edge of the rock wall which I covered with pine boughs to provide some shelter. By the time I was done it was dark and I gathered some small sticks and branches and soon a fire was my companion. I took out the last of my dried rabbit and maize and ate contemplating all that had come to me these last few days.

I found great comfort in this place, the warmth and solid strength of the stone wall that towered behind and a little above me, the glow of the fire, and the sounds of the night; the blessings of Earth Mother and I felt fortunate and thankful to be alive. But why I began to ponder, why me all these years while so many were gone. I remembered Commossuck would always remind me that the Spirits choose we powwows for reasons we will never know. It is our place to do what we can for the good of the People. But it has been a lonely life as my thoughts drifted to Shambisqua, my dearest and oldest friend and then how she and her brothers, Nausup and Keyhow, were trying their best to help the People survive during these times of dark shadows. The Awaunuy are forever wanting more; more land, more everything. She and her brothers want only to preserve some places where the People can still live in dignity. That is getting harder and harder at Mioonkhtuck where the Awaunuy are pressuring the Grand Council to give up more of the land there. Nausup even speaks of some leaving Mioonkhtuck and Totoket and settling along the lake in the western part of the lands he has just given to the Guilford men to live in the old way. The Guilford Awaunuy say it will be allowed; we shall see.

Shambisqua had played an increasingly important role in the Grand Council at Mioonkhtuck as her mother and uncle Momauguin grew older. When her uncle, like her mother, travelled to the home of Kiehtan, she continued to work with his son Wyandot and often she sought my counsel in trying to decide what was best for the People. But the burden of the times weighs heavy on her and when she confides in me I always wonder if I am doing enough to help. Sometimes we have a chance to speak of our childhood together and how those happy days before the pox were part of a beautiful world full of life and possibilities. Then usually we sit for a while in silence as the memory, like a dream, slowly vanishes.

The call of a loon on the lake brought me back to the moment and my thoughts drifted instead to the plight of the People holding on at Mioonkhtuck. The Awaunuy who had come there to settle after the destruction of the Pequot were at first an honest but always determined group. Following their victory over the Pequot, the Awaunuy knew that there were none in the Dawnland who could stand in their way and prevent them from making our land their home. They also knew there were few of the People left at Mioonkhtuck after to the pox had killed so many. They arrived in their great ships intending to stay. From the beginning there were many more of them than all four surviving bands of the People. Having brought with them all their beasts and things they needed to build their town, from the moment they arrived they behaved as if everything around them was theirs for the taking.

Momauguin and the other sachems at first welcomed them as friends and protectors against the Mohawk and the encroachments of the Mohegan

Uncas and saw these Awaunuy as a source for all the tools and trade goods the People would have ready access to. In the paper they gave us, they said they would be happy to share the Dawnland with the People. It seemed to be a good situation.

The Awaunuy leaders, Davenport and Eaton were fair men and agreed to the arrangement that the People would continue to live on the eastern shore of the harbor and they on the other. This guaranteed that each would have their own place to have homes, grow crops, fish, and hunt while sharing the land that surrounded both villages. This also would not hinder the seasonal migration of those at Mioonkhtuck who chose to move into the northern lands in winter.

But it did not take long before tensions rose. Many of the Awaunuy did not respect the right of the People to share the land and began to act as if it was theirs alone. They began to tell Momauguin that there were places the People could not go and there were times when we could not enter their town such as on their sabbath which came every seventh day. They complained that the People should not enter their houses without invitation, a strange custom, and that our dogs should be kept away as well for they feared for their animals. Meanwhile, their swine destroyed our clam banks and their cattle ate our maize since they left them free to roam. Momauguin was continually being called to answer for some problem they said the People were causing. I did not like it there from the beginning and as the years have passed, I have found Mioonkhtuck an uncomfortable and difficult place to be.

There is little left now of our ancestral lands at Mioonkhtuck and many of the People have begun to drift away as increasingly it is difficult to grow enough food to feed those living there and hunting has all but disappeared. The Awaunuy have already taken the land that was once the home of Montowese and his band and have enclosed the People at Totoket on the neck of land where the summer village has always been. These last two villages are tiny islands surrounded by a sea of Awaunuy farms and towns.

Restless, I left the shelter and walked to the edge of the lake, lit by the light of Mother Moon. In the distance behind me an owl called, answered soon afterwards by another across the water. A warm wind blew softly from the home of Keihtan in the southwest and I thought about the day's events, Mequnhut and Apoawein, the Awaunuy boys in the trees, my visit to the Awaunuy town at Mennunkatuck, and the words of William. How strange it was to go to the place where our village once stood and see no sign of it except for the Grandmother Oak under which Shaumpishuh would hold council and through which Commossuck would speak to the Spirit World. The

Awaunuy must have understood its power for they built their spirit house in its shadow.

I decided to sit on a rock by the water's edge and thought about fishing here the day that Shaumpishuh had returned from Mioonkhtuck after meeting with the Awaunuy there to discuss first with Commossuck and then her council that a newly arrived group of Awaunuy wanted to build their village at Mennunkatuck. This was the year of my eighteenth snow and one year since Momauguin had agreed to let the Awaunuy settle near his village and two following the destruction of the Pequot. When I returned to our village late that afternoon with the fish I caught, Commossuck was sitting and talking under the Spirit Oak with Shaumpishuh and Nashump. When he saw me, the shaman called me over and motioned I should sit with them which I did. He said to the sunksquaw that I was now a man and a shaman in my own right and that my ears should also hear the words that were spoken. Shaumpishuh agreed and their talk resumed.

"But Commossuck, as I have already spoken, their headman Whitfield, would build his village here at Mennunkatuck and in return we shall receive much needed gifts for sharing our land with them" Shaumpishuh said with an air of frustration for it was clear the powwow was skeptical.

"They would also provide us with protection from the Mohegan since Uncas has come repeatedly to intimidate us claiming land between us and the Wangunk is now his" Nashump added. "He will do nothing however to bring about the wrath of his Awaunuy friends."

Commossuck looked sternly from one to the other, then closed his eyes and seemed to turn his attention inward. Seeing this, the sachem said "my friend, this is for the good of the People. Look at us, we are now just thirty three left, a little shadow of what once was. We shall continue to be free to live within these lands, hunt, fish, grow the sisters. The only difference is that our village here will be where the Whitfield people will put their village."

The powwow sat quietly, seemingly detached for a while before answering. "Sachem, I know your heart is good and you are thinking only of the welfare of us few who have survived these past years. But the Spirit World knows and has shown me that wherever the Awaunuy sit down, the People disappear. They die from disease or are forced to move away from the ground of their ancestors. I have seen it with my own eyes along the Quinnihticut where our brothers and sisters are suffering and being pushed away since they welcomed the Awaunuy. What makes you think these Awaunuy will be different?"

Listening to the words of both made me think of the first time I accompanied Commossuck to the Awaunuy town opposite Mioonkhtuck shortly after they had built their houses and had already begun to turn the Earth Mother with their plows to plant maize and a grass called wheat. Commossuck had wanted to see if he could understand what was the spirit energy behind why they did what they did. As for me, everything I saw and smelled was strange, new, and confusing. To see so many Awaunuy men, women, and children in one place was startling and I began to understand how many there must be on the other side of the water. I remember thinking that there are so many and they have so much, what will happen when more of them come? Sitting and listening to Shaumpishuh, Nashump, and Commossuck, I knew the answer.

One month later most of our village travelled to Mioonkhtuck and the next day met with the Awaunuy in their town in a great structure made of wood called a barn. It was made I learned later to store their beasts and harvest inside. Commossuck had not come but instead had gone to the place of Spirits. The shaman had told Shaumpishuh he was not comfortable with allowing the Awaunuy to live among us and would seek the guidance of the Spirit World. I have to admit I was interested in seeing the

Awaunuy and their village close up again and was glad when Commossuck suggested I should go.

We were warmly welcomed to their settlement they called Quinnipiac by a young god-talker who spoke our language much to our surprise. He said his name was Higginson which made a few of us laugh for it sounded funny to our ears since it was like the sound made by one who is sick. Besides Higginson, five other Awaunuy, most relatively young men, and Whitfield were there. I found Whitfield interesting in that he was older than the rest, his clothing was much finer than that of the others, and he had a very dignified manner about him. The other Awaunuy were very deferential and I could tell he was a great sachem among their people.

Qussuckquansh had accompanied us from Totoket and stood by Shaumpishuh's side as she negotiated with Whitfield through the efforts of Higginson. With the guidance of Qussuckquansh and Shaumpishuh, Whitfield made lines on a paper which were meant to show the places where the rivers, shore, and islands of Mennunkatuck were as well as where it was specifically that the Awaunuy would make their village. As part of the agreement, Shaumpishuh agreed that we Mennunkatuck would move to the eastern side of the Kuttawo River. It was also agreed that the People would not be restricted as to where we could hunt, trap, fish, or gather clams.

In return for sharing Mennunkatuck with them, Whitfield and his people gave us gifts of wampum, Awaunuy coats and shoes, looking glasses, hatchets, kettles, and other trade goods upon the insistence of Shaumpishuh. Afterwards, the Awaunuy looked quite pleased and though Shaumpishuh and Qussuckquansh seemed satisfied, the rest of us looked on silently for the truth was we did not quite understand what the agreement actually meant.

I remember Shambisqua, now a young woman, on leaving the barn looked apprehensive and the mood among the People was somber. The Awaunuy had brought out the gifts and laid them on some wool blankets on the ground before us and Shaumpishuh had gestured to the women present that they should gather them up. Shambisqua had been reluctant to do so much to the annoyance of her mother who made a gesture that she do her part. She did. Like Commossuck, she had told me that she did not agree with the decision to let the Awaunuy settle at Mennunkatuck but understood why her mother had agreed to it.

As all the members of our village began the walk back to Mennunkatuck, Shambisqua and I walked the trail together and as we did she had asked me as a shaman what I thought about what had taken place. I admitted to her that I found the Awaunuy village and ways strange and that the energy there was not the energy of our world. Because of that, I felt apprehensive for the People and that it was good at least that we would move away from the Whitfield people once they came to Mennunkatuck to the other side of the Kuttawo. I could feel the presence of the Awaunuy energy in Mioonkhtuck and it made me uncomfortable to the point where I knew living so close to them would in the end harm the People there. Already Shambisqua added, some of our men there had become accustomed to drinking the Awaunuy burning water and their behavior was unpredictable, sometimes violent, and usually foolish. "I know you tried it once" she had said to me. "What did you think?"

As we walked, I explained "the first mouthful burned my tongue and when I swallowed, it burned all the way into my stomach. Commossuck had asked me to try it so he could see what power was in it. At first I could not understand why a person would drink such a thing and told him so."

"But after?" she asked. "I remember you being very sick."

"It was not good" I responded. "After four more big swallows I had a warm but strange feeling as if the spirit of the liquid had taken over my body and mind. All I could think about is having more and as I did I became dizzy. Nothing made sense to me but at the same time everything around me seemed funny and made me laugh like a fool. I remember looking at Commossuck as he studied me and laughing; why I do not know."

"And then you were sick?"

"Yes, and after my head hurt. It was as if the spirits in the liquid were trying to break out and could not find a way. All I wanted to do was sleep. I remember Commossuck helping me to our weetou and in the morning we both decided that this liquid is not good, an evil that should be avoided for it takes over a person's body and mind."

Shambisqua shook her head in agreement and said, "we must remind the young men to avoid it because once the Awaunuy are in Mennunkatuck it will be easier to find." We continued along the path in silence.

Chapter Fifteen

That evening, upon our return to Mennunkatuck, it was obvious that most in the village were pensive about what was to come after witnessing the agreement between Shaumpishuh and the new group of Awaunuy. Having witnessed what their village was like, the People spoke quietly and expectantly about what the Whitfield town here in Mennunkatuck might be like while going about their evening routines in a heavy and methodical way. I was hoping that Commossuck might have returned so I could talk with him about what I had seen and what I sensed at the Awaunuy town but he had not and did not for three more days. That night in our weetou, alone with my thoughts, I was troubled and restless and could not sleep.

The move across the Kuttawo was planned to take place after our harvest was complete and our food stores were prepared for the winter. Previously, Commossuck and I had talked about one of us spending the winter with the group that stayed with Shaumpishuh whether at Mennunkatuck or elsewhere and the other to travel with those who planned to move to our winter grounds along the Upper Quinnipiac. We had discussed earlier that perhaps he would stay with those who remained with

Shaumpishuh and that I should move inland with those who chose that path.

I knew Shambisqua would stay with her parents which now we all knew would be the other side of the Kuttawo and that meant that following the harvest festival we would not see one another until winter's end. I remember being conflicted by that possibility and how I had been moved to speak with my dearest friend for I was painfully torn by two possible paths; one a strong affection for her and the other my commitment to a life as a powwow. I knew we both had a decision to make and with many suitors already, Shambisqua would soon be choosing her life partner. It was Shambisqua however, who came to me first the following morning as I was leaving the village to dig some medicine roots.

"Ponaim, may I walk with you and help gather the medicine? I have always enjoyed learning from you how those sisters can help us when we need them."

"I would be happy for your company Shambisqua" I replied. "I was going to seek you out later for I was hoping you and I could talk."

Taking hold of my hand, Shambisqua said " I wanted to talk as well. I felt a need on the path from Mioonkhtuck. Our silence told me we needed speak and I could sense your troubled heart as well as my own."

I remember feeling awkward as if I were still a little boy as we passed into a meadow, the home of some of the sisters I sought. I felt as warm as the morning air when Shambisqua took my hand again and looked into my eyes.

"Ponaim, we have always been the closest of friends and you know how I feel about you. That will never change, I want you to know that" she said with a look of deep affection. "But I know the shaman's path is your journey and as the oldest child of the sunksquaw mine has been chosen as well. We both know we must follow where they lead."

My heart pounding, I summoned the words I knew I had to say. "Shambisqua, what you say is true. I have been troubled by the fact that our close bond and love for each other might pull us away from our paths in life. As a shaman, I have come to understand through the Spirits that I must travel that path alone. To do otherwise would in the end be hurtful and unfair if I were to have a wife and family in this world as it is." I remember pausing and drawing up what courage I could before saying "besides, my friend, you must choose a suitable partner to assist you in the troubles that will certainly overwhelm the future of the People."

With tears in her eyes, Shambisqua nodded in agreement. "Ponaim, you will always be in my heart. We must always keep one another there and together do what we can to guide the People through the changes to come" she said as we embraced as only two who really knew and loved each other could.

Remembering that moment saddened me as I continued that evening to reflect on events that took place shortly after that morning when Shambisqua and I parted onto our life paths. Commossuck did return but in an agitated state and I could tell how deeply troubled he was by what he called the stream of occurrences. He explained to me that in his quest for insights and answers to all that had taken place since the arrival of the Awaunuy all the Spirits showed him was fog, shadows, and storm driven clouds. This vision he said, held so many ill omens that he was left feeling powerless and for the first time truly discouraged. I recall that he looked small in stature and old, like the life force was being sucked out of him. "Ponaim" I remember him saying, "perhaps Keihtan has decided it is time for what is left of the People to leave the home of the ancestors or even disappear for I cannot see beyond the shadows that lie across the Dawnland."

I would not say that my friend and mentor at that point had given up, but he was never quite the same. It seemed as if his spirit began to slowly leave him though he continued to work for the good of the People for the few years that he remained with us.

Commossuck could never reconcile that stream of occurrences caused by the new reality of the ever growing Awaunuy presence and how it was transforming the land of our ancestors and the lives of the ever dwindling numbers of the People. In the end I know he died of a broken heart.

Within days after Commossuck's return to Mennunkatuck an Awaunuy boat arrived in the water where the river opened to the sea and a group of Whitfield men came to our village. Their arrival caused quite a commotion for they carried their weapons as well as tools and their presence had been unexpected. The god-talker, Higginson was with them and he explained to Shaumpishuh and Nashump why they had come. Their intention was to begin building structures so that some of their people could move from Quinnipiac to Mennunkatuck before the snows. Shaumpishuh agreed and told them that soon she would be moving to the Kuttawo with some of the People while others would be going inland to the traditional wintering grounds. It was strange to suddenly have the Awaunuy here in Mennunkatuck and at first my fellow villagers stayed a bit of a distance from them as they began to busy themselves to the south of our weetous on the ground where we had recently harvested the Sisters. But within a short time some of the children began to follow them around, picking up their tools and examining everything including the clothes they were wearing to their increasing annoyance.

At first Commossuck did not acknowledge their presence but like everyone, he too became curious. Naked except for his breechcloth, painted half black and half red from head to toe, and with raven feathers in his loose, long, gray hair, he strove directly into their midst and as he did, shook his rattle made of turtle shell. The Awaunuy had been using a long line to measure parts of the ground and were putting sticks in the ground so his sudden presence startled them. Higginson approached Commossuck, saying something in our tongue to which the shaman replied with a loud, chanting exclamation while he shook his rattle above the god-talker's head. One of the Awaunuy nervously picked up a long metal knife, a sword, as if to threaten the powwow but another grabbed his arm to keep him from moving forward. For a tense few minutes, all were frozen except for Commossuck who's incantations grew louder and more animated. Higginson dropped to his knees and moved his hands in what I learned afterward was the spirit sign called a cross in the direction of Commossuck and the two locked eyes before the powwow abruptly turned and walked away while making a scowling sound.

I, along with Nashump and Wentubecum had followed the powwow as he had left the village for the fields suspicious of his intention and we had stood off a bit as he confronted Higginson. As he left, the shaman walked towards us and as he passed said nothing but the expression on his face was one of fierce dignity and pride. He later told me that his incantation was meant to make sure that these Awaunuy would not cause the People harm and that we find a way to share the home of our ancestors in peace and respect. That was his prayer and I told him I hoped it would be so.

The group of Awaunuy did not leave that day and in two more another boat came from Quinnipiac carrying more men and supplies. It was obvious they were here to stay. They began to build small structures Higginson explained for the winter which were curious in that they first dug a square hole in the Earth Mother as deep as a man's shoulder. Then with wood they brought from Quinnipiac, a top made of two sides that reached a point was made like I had seen in their other villages. These they covered with mats made of marsh reeds. They were very efficient and many of the People amused themselves by watching them. Within seven days they had built a number of these shelters and when the rest of their people came, we were told they would build one made of stone which fascinated me. I had seen the Awaunuy houses and fort at Saybrook, those on the Quinnihticut, and New Haven. They had all been made from wood. I have to confess it was interesting to watch them work as I wanted to better understand their ways and their spirit energy. Commossuck said he was not interested and did not venture again to where the Awaunuy were.

The process of building their house of stone drew the interest of the People and a number of the men of Mennunkatuck helped in the bringing of stones of various sizes to be used. The stones were brought from the rock ledges to the east of the place where the house was built and held together with a mixture of crushed shell, sand, clay, and water that became hard like the stone itself when dry. When asked why such a house was being built, the god-talker had explained they were afraid of the Dutch-mannuck coming and possibly the warriors of their King from across the water for they said he was angry with them. This was strange to us because the People are always able to leave a sachem they do not agree with and move to live under another. We were told the stone house would be a place to go and be safe if threatened or attacked and also it was the kind of house Whitfield and a few of the others were used to living in. This one was to be his house and the Awaunuy eventually built three more including one for the god-talker, Higginson.

When the leaves turned golden and began to fall, the People gathered together that year for our harvest ritual and dance under the Grandmother Oak instead of the Split Rock where it was usually held. It had been decided based upon the advice of Commossuck who had reminded us it would likely be the last time we might celebrate in the home of our ancestors and we all agreed. The festival as always, was held on the full moon with feasting and ritual dancing well into the night. Shaumpishuh had invited the Awaunuy to come and Whitfield, Higginson, and a few others came and joined in the feast and remained for the dancing for a short time before retiring to their shelters as they said they needed rest from their labor. It seemed that these Awaunuy did not enjoy the dancing and later I learned from observing their ways that their god frowned upon it. This I have felt was unfortunate for dance is a gift given to the People as a way to experience Manitou.

Thinking back on that night, I can see the faces of each of those who were there; a small group of survivors who had lived through great loss and heartache and who for that evening escaped into a ritual embrace of the past and the Manitou of a time and place that once was. It was as before the arrival to the Dawnland of the Awaunuy and we each danced, drummed, or sang for and of that yesterday, gone we all knew forever. In the morning, the Whitfield men woke to an empty village - the Mennunkatuck were gone.

It was a hard winter, the snow and cold were deep and food was scarce. I had travelled with five families to the inland wintering grounds where we were joined by others from Totoket and a few families from Mioonkhtuck. All had brought a supply of the Sisters as well as dried fish and clams but it quickly became apparent that there were few deer and other four legged brothers and sisters to hunt and as shaman, the People turned to me to conduct rituals that might bring their return. I can still recall the sense of urgency by the Wolf Moon (January) that plagued us as our food was divided for everyone in smaller amounts and sickness in the lungs and head began to strike many.

By then I was well practiced in the rituals needed to bring the deer, moose, or other large four leggeds to us and I conducted ceremonies with the men to appease the spirits of those we sought. We asked them to share their lives with the People and that we would honor them and thank them for the gift of their lives to save ours. The ritual dancing and fasting lasted two days and on the third Wentubecum and the others set out through the snow into the valley between the Quinnipiac and the lands of the Wangunk to the east. Two days later they returned with three deer, a moose, and five racoons. It was enough to feed everyone for at least another month and there was much rejoicing. I remember receiving many thanks from the People for my bringing about a successful hunt and I have to admit it gave me greater confidence in my role as a powwow because for the first time I was acting absolutely independent of Commossuck. Throughout that winter with the help of Hobomock and the Spirits I was able to help many overcome what the Awaunuy called the ague and influenza but as I had learned from Commossuck, some of the young and old, I could not help and they were called to the house of Keihtan.

During the Goose Moon (March) Montowese arrived from his camp further north on the Quinnipiac with a small group of hunters and they brought with them a large buck they had hunted along the way. There was much celebrating as old friends and relatives greeted one another and as usual he brought news of his father's people along the Quinnihticut. They were facing great pressure from the Awaunuy there who sought more and more of their land and many were leaving to join their relatives the Tunxis and Paugussett on the river to the west that comes from the uplands where the Mohican live. The sachem reported how the area was still full of game and that there were many fresh streams with abundant meadows. It was a place, he said, the People might go to live the life Keihtan had always wanted them to live away from the corrupting influence of the

Awaunuy. It was then I remember, I first began to harbor the thought that it might be best for the People to leave the land of our ancestors and move to a place away from the Awaunuy.

It was during that winter that I came into my own as a shaman, feeling confident in my ability and gaining the respect of the People. I also learned that my gifts and ability were directly tied to my respect of and appreciation for the world of the Spirits, a lesson I have never forgotten. By the time we broke camp during the Fish Moon (April) and began our journey back to the Kuttawo to join those who had moved there with Shaumpishuh, I was confident in my life path and thankful for the opportunity it would give me to help the People through the years to come. Two days before we were to leave the winter grounds, as a group we held a ritual celebration and feast which I proudly directed and afterwards we all spoke of our choices to come. Three families decided to move north to dwell with Montowese and four families decided to go to live at Totoket. The rest, six families chose to move to the Kuttawo and I with them. Wentubecum led us. None chose to return to Mioonkhtuck.

Our return to the Kuttawo and our people from Mennunkatuck was bittersweet. Although we were all happy and comforted to see one another, it was also odd for us who had been on the Upper

Quinnipiac to not return to our ancestral village. Shaumpishuh and Nashump welcomed us as did all the others but Commossuck I was told had left a week before and they did not know where he had gone. I had begun to worry about him that winter and his not being present on our arrival only magnified that concern. Shambisqua was there and we were happy to see one another as we embraced as true friends upon seeing one another yet we both recognized our relationship had changed. I remember her laughing and then saying how I now looked every bit the shaman which made me blush. My hair had grown longer and was left loose and I had taken to wearing a headdress of seven raven feathers for each of the years since I had lived with and learned from Commossuck as well as the sacred directions and Keihtan.

Shaumpishuh had indicated where we might build our weetous on a gentle hilltop where they had built theirs back in the autumn. It was a beautiful spot where the river opened up into marshes to the south with the sea beyond and I felt that though it was not the village of our ancestors, it was good ground and a place we might call home. It did not take long for everyone to join the others and settle into the routines of spring. The women and girls planted and the men and boys built fish weirs in anticipation of the return of our finned brothers and sisters. All seemed as it should be and I for a brief time began to believe all would. Yet behind those timeless routines was the knowledge that just beyond the forest on the opposite side of the Kuttawo was the Awaunuy village where Mennunkatuck had once been.

It did not take many days for me to realize that things were not as they first appeared to be. The trade in furs, which had been declining for many years, was all but gone denying the Quinnipiac of a much needed trade good needed to obtain the desired Awaunuy goods such as cloth and blankets, tools made of iron and brass, among many others. Most important to the hunters, were the Awaunuy muskets, lead balls, and gunpowder which the Awaunuy leaders had said the Quinnipiac should not have but were easily obtained. In order to obtain what was now needed, some of the men had taken to going almost daily to Mennunkatuck to do work for the Awaunuy and often came back with the fire water that the Awaunuy leaders had said was forbidden to Quinnipiac. It was beginning to cause the light of Manitou to disappear in those who felt they must have it.

I had gone to the weetou of Commossuck upon our arrival on the Kuttawo and had found that he had created a sleeping platform and space for me in anticipation of my return. After a number of days my friend and mentor did come back one afternoon when the sun was high and the fresh greens of the

Fish Moon were coming into blossom on the trees and plants of the surrounding woodlands. I knew his arrival would be soon because a Raven came that morning and called to me after circling our weetou three times and perching on a low branch of a nearby oak. I recall that Commossuck always sought a spot near an oak for his home because the oak was the mother tree and the tree of strength, and resolve. This practice I have always followed though at Totoket the only one left is twisted and care worn by the wind, a bit like me.

Upon seeing one another we embraced and quickly sat together under the oak to recount how we and those we had wintered with had faired. As I told him of the winter sickness and hunger on the Upper Quinnipiac and about the visit by Montowese he nodded in understanding and asked me of my efforts in regard to healing and the ceremony to call the four leggeds to feed the People. He clapped his hands in agreement for what I had done and told me that I was now certainly a powwow in the eyes of Keihtan and Hobomock. Then he told me of the struggles here on the Kuttawo during the winter and how difficult it became for many, not because of the lack of food, but the lack of heart. While my friend spoke, he looked drawn and forlorn, and I could see that just as he had those last days at Mennunkatuck, his spirit appeared to be draining. I asked how he was and for the first time ever, Commossuck said he was tired.

The powwow had spent many days at the great ritual rock shelter to the east of the Coginchaug Swamp, a place of ceremony and spiritual power for generations untold. Some said it was a place of Manitou that went back to the legend of the ice time. Commossuck had said he wanted to be away from a place that he saw as descending into the shadows and that there he could be with the ancestors and Spirits who had always been able to protect and lift the fortunes of the People. There, through many days and nights of dream walking, he had sought again the answer to the People's future. It was shadows and darkness again, my friend had said, but that he now had hope. He had stopped his story and looked intensely into my eyes before saying that in the darkness he had seen me standing with a stick of fire, and that as I did the darkness fell away around me wherever I turned. "Ponaim", he had told me, "you are the one to find the way."

Chapter Sixteen

Much of the time we spent east of the Kuttawo seems like a dream time as I reflect upon it. Under the leadership of Shaumpishuh the People did their best to forget the traumas brought upon them since the pox first appeared but most found it impossible to shake away the memories of those lost and a way of life that was fading away. Yet each day we all rose with Father Sun and went about the business of living; the time honored round of tasks that would sustain us for another year. There were the Sisters to plant and tend to, fish to catch, and hunting and trapping needed to provide both meat and hides to be made into clothing. But the presence of the growing Awaunuy village just to our west was always felt and its influence was a powerful reminder of change.

That first summer on the Kuttawo also brought a new source of problems for the Mennunkatuck. The Mohegan sachem Uncas sent his trusted council member Foxon and Weequash the Niantic sachem to speak with Shaumpishuh. They insisted that our village was in fact on land that belonged to Uncas by virtue of conquest of the Pequot and in order to remain tribute in the form of wampum and furs would need to be paid. Shaumpishuh strongly denied his claim to the land or tribute explaining that the land was part of the ancestral territory of the Quinnipiac and not that of the Pequot. Therefore, Shaumpishuh said, the claim of Uncas was not legitimate. For the next two years Uncas pressured and harassed us until under his continuing threat we finally abandoned the Kuttawo and joined our fellow Quinnipiac at Mioonkhtuck. Shortly after, Uncas sold the land along the Kuttawo to Whitfield and the Awaunuy at Mennunkatuck who required that he secure from the Quinnipiac a statement that he was in fact the sole owner and that he had met with them to obtain their agreement. This he claimed to have secured. Rather than resist, it was decided to abandon the village and move to Mioonkhtuck.

The trek from the Kuttawo to Mioonkhtuck was a depressingly sad time for the People as the realization that we had really abandoned our ancestral home weighed heavily on all our hearts and spirits. As we silently walked the path to Mioonkhtuck, we passed through the Awaunuy village which had once been our home. The people there stood and watched quietly as if they were witnessing the passing of phantom spirits. Neither we nor they said a word as each man, woman, and child among us carried themselves with dignity and pride, none more so than Shaumpishuh.

Commossuck was not among us, he had told me when the decision to leave the Kuttawo had been made that his time was coming to an end. The last morning there he had risen before Father Sun and had asked me to go with him to the shore. There he explained that he was being called to the world of the Spirits and that it was time for him to go.

"Ponaim, I have done all I can for the People in this world so perhaps I can do more in that of the Spirits" he said in a serene voice while an aura of peacefulness surrounded him. "You have become a man of virtue and integrity and as a gifted shaman. It falls to you now to guide the People with the help of Keihtan, Hobomock, and the Spirits. The People will listen to you for they know the Manitou that dwells within you."

I stood mute before him, my eyes filling with tears. After so many losses, I believed this one would be impossible to bear. I had always known this moment would come and had witnessed his spirit energy draining since the coming of the Awaunuy to Mennunkatuck. Yet the finality of the moment was a powerful blow.

"Where will you go?" I asked as I pulled myself together enough to ask.

"I will follow the Spirit Line to the home of Hobomock beyond the great river to the west in the land of the Mohawk. I have seen my death while there many times in dream walks and it is there I shall perform my last ritual and do my death dance. I will ask Hobomock one last time to help the People over-come the darkness and shadows that have descended upon them before I journey to dwell in the house of Keihtan."

Looking kindly into my eyes, he handed me his Otter skin bundle that held his sacred pipe. All I could do is silently accept his gift, at a complete loss for words as emotion welled up and enveloped my soul and spirit. My friend and mentor smiled at me and we embraced. Then Commossuck turned and be-gan his last journey, walking as he always did; his stride strong and his head held high. I watched him enter the tree line and disappear into the forest as I simply stood forlorn. For the first time since the death of my family, I felt absolutely alone.

While the Mennunkatuck were welcomed at Mioonkhtuck by Momauguin and set up their weetous to begin life again I found the close proxim-ity of the Awaunuy across the bay too stifling and disturbing so along with Wentubecum and a few oth-ers moved instead to Totoket where we were wel-comed by the ageing sachem Qussuckquansh. Alt-hough Totoket had been sold to the New Haven Awaunuy, their efforts to settle people there had not been successful and I like many others felt free to breathe away from their presence. It was my home village from then on but never replaced Mennunka-tuck in my heart or spirit.

Shaumpishuh and the others settled into life at Mioonkhtuck in the shadow of the growing Awaunuy town determined to hold onto the traditional home of the People and our way of life which, over time, became an increasing challenge. There were constant disputes over everything from fishing rights and hunting to basic use of the lands that was supposedly shared by both the People and the Awaunuy. The Awaunuy saw Quinnipiac lands surrounding their town as under their control and theirs to take and turn into places for their crops to grow, their cattle and pigs to forage, and the trees to cut. We on the other hand, saw the same forests, meadows, and streams as sacred places where we could hunt, fish, and gather in a traditional way which as the years passed became increasingly difficult. This was even though Momauguin, Montowese, and Shaumpishuh had been guaranteed that the People might hunt, fish, and gather clams on territory that they understood we were sharing with the Awaunuy. The actions and attitude of the Awaunuy as the years passed revealed that they did not share the same view.

As a powwow, I was immediately welcomed at Totoket and soon became busy helping those afflicted with sickness of the body and the spirit. Over time I gained more and more confidence in my abilities and every day thanked Commossuck and the

Spirits for allowing me to serve the needs of the People. By then the old Dutchmannuck fort had all but disappeared, but they did on occasion stop by to trade much to the annoyance of the Awaunuy in New Haven who saw their presence as a threat. They demanded that Qussuckquansh trade only with them but to no avail. But all that changed three years after moving from the Kuttawo with the arrival of a large party of Awaunuy from the town of Wethersfield on the Quinnihticut who set about building a settlement just up the river from our village.

Unlike Mennunkatuck, the People were not asked to leave which, because of the village location on a peninsula, was a bit removed from the Awaunuy town. Also, Qussuckquansh and Montowese had secured the right of the People to use the land that had been purchased when the Awaunuy first came to the Quinnipiac thus it came to be that we and the Awaunuy lived side by side as at Mioonkhtuck. The People at Totoket proved to be more experienced when it came to living near those from across the sea having first lived alongside the Dutchmannuck and their fort and then Molinar and his men. For better or worse, most had learned to compromise and tolerate their presence.

It was the second year after leaving the Kuttawo that Shambisqua committed herself to marriage, much to the relief and comfort of her parents who worried despite many suitors, that she was re-luctant to choose. She had been pursued for a year by a son of Uncas named Oweneco much to the concern of Shaumpishuh who saw in such a match an attempt by the Mohegan sachem to gain influence and even control over the Quinnipiac. Shambisqua did not ex-press interest in Oweneco who came across as arro-gant and persistent and I for one had confessed to her that I believed he was not a good match for her or the People. In the end it was Nawatokis, the son of the Paugassett sachem Nahuntoway who won Sham-bisqua's heart, a man of good character who like his bride, embraced traditional ways. He proved himself to be a good husband, father, and provider and for me a true friend.

Shambisqua and Nawatokis worked dili-gently for the good of the People and though they considered Mioonkhtuck their village, for many years they led a mixed group of families from there and Totoket inland to a winter camp along the Upper Quinnipiac and most years I went as well. Nawatokis was insistent that his children and eventually grand-children learn the old ways. Shambisqua gave birth to two sons and two daughters, one being the mother of Mequnhut. Sadly, like so many during those years, both sons died while still children and my friends' older daughter died just before she was to marry, all from disease brought by the Awaunuy. It was painful for me not to be able to save the children of Shambisqua and Nawatokis and it is a wound I carry in my heart to this day.

Nawatokis was killed during the great uprising of the People of the Dawnland led by Metacom the Pokanoket sachem. Nawatokis led Quinnipiac and Paugassett warriors in support of the Awaunuy in the assault against the Narragansett during the Great Swamp fight the winter of the last year of the war, a decision to do so I had counseled him against when he came to me for advice. Although he did not want to participate in the war against Metacom, he felt he must in order to prevent reprisals from the Awaunuy of New Haven and Connecticut who suspected the Quinnipiac and Paugassett of siding with Metacom. He told me he feared that the Awaunuy, in their suspicion of the Quinnipiac, might turn on the People if they did not join them in the fight. We all knew the Awaunuy brutally attacked those who opposed them and the survivors, including women and children were sold into slavery, often it was said to islands far away.

Fighting under the leadership of Uncas, some to this day suspect he may have been killed by him though there has never been proof. It was known that Uncas saw Nawatokis, like the other leaders of the Quinnipiac, as blocking his efforts to exert his control over them. It was always said he harbored ill will towards Shaumpishuh and her daughter for refusing Oweneco as well. Shambisqua suspected Uncas had a role in the death of her husband and ever since worked to resist any attempt by Uncas and his sons to control the People.

My thoughts were interrupted by the sound of a four footed sister patrolling along the edge of the water to my left and as I adjusted my eyes I saw that it was a skunk out searching for her evening meal. Watching her approach, I remained silent as she came closer. By the time I saw her she was certainly aware of me and not at all bothered by my presence. When she was within two arms lengths she stopped and looked up at me so I said, "it is a beautiful night is it not my friend?"

Sister skunk stood for a moment as our eyes met then seemed to move her head to agree with me before she passed behind me on her way, nose to the ground, following the scents that would lead to her meal. "Skunk medicine" I thought to myself, "another message to reaffirm what I already know I must bring to the council. Skunk medicine is powerful, one that not only garners respect, but is true to its purpose of moving forward without fear. The skunk follows its path with confidence and certainty knowing other creatures and men respect her power and pay attention when she is present. I must be as the skunk when I speak to the council and the People of my visions."

Gazing up at the ancestors one last time before returning to my shelter to sleep, I thanked them and the Spirit World for the gift of life and the beautiful night and pledged to them I would continue to work to preserve their memory no matter if it was here in the land of the ancestors or in a new home as shown by Hobomock. "Time will tell where the path will lead" I thought out loud as I entered the shelter and pulled the robe snuggly around me. "Tomorrow I return to Totoket".

The sky was beginning to brighten in the early morning just before dawn when I rose from my sleep feeling refreshed and ready to resume my trek to Totoket. I climbed a slight rise to the side of the rock shelter and then up a taller ridge behind it to a place I could watch Father Sun rise above the horizon to the east. The air was fresh and clean and the feathered brothers were just waking to begin their day, singing their morning songs of joy. I had brought my sage and sweetgrass to smudge in preparation for the emergence of Father Sun. As he began to rise above the horizon, sending rays of orange and crimson through the thin veil of clouds, I lit the herbs and offered the smoke to him and the Spirit World. Then I began the song so long ago taught to me by Com-mossuck:

> *"Father Sun, bringer of hope,*
> *welcoming this new day,*
> *as you rise above us*
> *and bring life to living beings,*
> *making things grow and bloom.*
> *Father Sun, I honor you*
> *and thank you for your gifts.*
> *You are the light of the day,*
> *and warmth for the earth,*
> *I celebrate you. Manitou!"*

Looking upon the Father as his light began to bathe and brighten everything around me, I waited on the ridge top until I could plainly see the canopy of trees that spread like a blanket before me. With my heart full of gratitude for this day, I faced each of the Four Directions to thank them; the East for wisdom and understanding, the South for life and destiny, the West for renewal, and the North for health. Then turning, I descended the ridge back to my shelter which I dismantled before leaving. I returned the branches and poles to the forest floor while thanking them for their gift of providing comfort for the night. Then picking up my bundle and robe, I started the last part of my walk back to Totoket.

My intent was to move quickly south to the edge of the sea and then follow the shoreline to

Totoket. As I made my way through and around the marshes and the trees of the forest that lined the shoreline, I could not help but appreciate the beauty of all that surrounded me. Around me were the tall grasses of the marshes interspersed with cattails, the twisted but sturdy trees shaped by winds from the sea, and the countless birds; red winged blackbirds, ducks, geese, and songbirds who were just beginning their day's journey as was I. I thanked them all for their company and soon found myself on the red sand of the beach. "From here I do not need to cross through the Awaunuy town up the river from our village but follow along the shore straight home instead. Branford, as the Awaunuy call their town, like Guilford and New Haven is spreading its farms further inland for it is land that they crave and we cannot stop them. Here on the shore, they do not care as much except for those who fish. They come often and some are starting to build places to stay. I guess it will not be long before these places too are swallowed up by them."

There was a soft breeze from the water and the sound of the waves mixed with the cries of the sea birds was comforting. The tide was leaving so I decided to pick up some oysters from the mud flat exposed by the retreating water and within a short time had six, each the size of my open hand. I thanked the creatures of Hobomock and sat on some rocks just above the line of seaweed left by the tide when it was high. With my Dutchmannuck knife, a gift many years ago from Nashump, I pried opened each oyster and thanked each for the nourishment they would give me. Just as I finished and was drinking some water from a bladder I had filled while at Quonnipaug, I was startled by the crashing sound of an Awaunuy gun being fired in the trees just beyond where I sat.

"Awaunuy hunters" I said out loud to the equally startled gulls and terns. "Perhaps we all should be away before they come closer."

But before I could leave two young Awaunuy men came out of the trees arguing as they did, one holding the musket while the other seemed to be scolding him. "We waited all night for that deer and you were not true to your shot Adam! Now he has fled and our time has been wasted" shouted the taller of the two. The one with the musket had a look of dejection and was about to speak when he saw me and froze in his steps. Seeing his companion stop, the other turned to see me sitting on the rocks.

"Look, it is Ponaim the sorcerer who sits before us," said Adam. "Perhaps he cast a spell upon me so my shot would miss."

"Not likely with the way you shoot," said the other sarcastically as the two walked towards me. "Let us see what brings him here."

I recognized the two; one was the grandson of the god talker Pierson who left many years ago with many other Awaunuy from Totoket to another place. At the time I was told he was upset that their town was to become one with Connecticut. Edward was the young man's name. The one with the gun was a Todd, a family that had come to Totoket from New Haven. Unlike many others their age, they were usually respectful of the People and even sometimes curious. I greeted them holding up my hand in a sign of friendship which they mimicked. To my surprise, Edward greeted me in the broken tongue of the People.

"It is a good way," said Edward in a serious and deliberate manner. "We hunt but not. I speak."

I nodded to him to show I understood and gestured to them by offering water. The one called Adam shook his head no while Edward reached out and accepted my offer. After he drank he said proudly, "I speak. I know from grandfather book made."

"You do well with our tongue grandson of Pierson" I replied, amused that he was trying so hard to speak. How much he understood what I said I do not know while the other looked puzzled and appeared to want to know what was being said. "I am on my way to Totoket and have stopped for oysters"

I continued as I pointed to the recently opened shells in the sand by my feet.

"It is that way" answered Edward pointing as well to the oysters. "We go" he said as he pointed to the woods behind them. He raised his hand in the sign of peace as did Adam when he saw his friend do so and the two smiled and turned to return to the trees.

"May the Spirits keep you safe" I said to the two as they moved into the trees, pleased that they had made a friendly attempt to talk unlike so many others who most often acted as if the People did not even exist. What would his grandfather have thought I wondered as I watched the two disappear into the forest. My thoughts drifted back to the time when Abraham Pierson and his group of Awaunuy came to Totoket.

When Pierson the god talker first arrived at Totoket from across the water it was obvious that he was one who in his heart was convinced that his world of Spirits was the path all people should follow, even the People. He set about making sure that the Awaunuy of the village were brought along that path and was uncompromising in his vision of how they should live. We were told that he was creating a kingdom for their god he called Yahweh. I came to understand that this was the same one of the other god talkers and the Awaunuy knew but he believed their path was not straight but crooked and twisted.

After one season Pierson began to visit our village with the purpose of convincing us to join his path to the Spirit World. He would wander among the weetous speaking in his Awaunuy tongue, gesturing the sign of their god-cross at all he came upon then holding up their black book of spells much to our amusement. Often he would stand for hours reading words from it. Some of the People made sport of him, especially the young men as they watched Pierson go about with a trail of children mimicking his gestures. Qussuckquansh tolerated his presence, most ignored him imagining him to be a phantom, and I for one studied him from a distance to see if I could learn something of his spirit energy. During that first year Pierson never approached me, obviously knowing that I was a shaman and I was told later he saw me as a servant of their Satan.

Qussuckquansh had asked me what I thought of his coming to the village and whether there was danger in it. I told him I found him interesting to study and by watching him I was able to learn more about what motivated the Awaunuy and better understand their spirit ways and could not see the danger in it. To make sure I had dream walked to the Lower and Upper Worlds to ask the Spirits if there was danger in his visits to our village. Unlike the Awaunuy at Mioonkhtuck and Mennunkatuck who were uninterested in talking to the People about this Yahweh, Pierson was obsessed with doing so.

One of our young men, Wayawousit, was at the time learning the Awaunuy tongue and he would follow Pierson during his visits and later tell me as much as he could make sense of what the god talker said. Most of it did not have any real meaning but there was a constant use of a word in Awaunuy tongue called salvation. This it appeared was significant to their Spirit World and a place they all wanted to go, a place it seemed like the house of Keihtan. Also there was a father god-spirit, a son god-spirit, and a true spirit; all three were important to them and were mentioned often. We came to understand that the father god-spirit was the one he called Yahweh. Eventually Pierson came to understand why Wayawousit so often followed him because one of the Awaunuy who was teaching him their way of talking told him he was trying to learn their tongue. Since the god talker came often to the village, the young man looked at it as a chance to practice. Pierson understood this to mean that Wayawousit wanted to know more about their Spirit World and salvation.

When asked by Pierson if he sought their salvation, Wayawousit explained that he did not, much to the god talker's disappointment. But Pierson then asked if he would teach him our way of talking and the young man told him he would consult others to see if it were something he should do. Wayawousit went to Qussuckquansh who decided a council should be held where the sachem could ask the advice of the elders and myself. Wayawousit explained that Pierson wanted to learn our way of talking so he could bring us his Yahweh and salvation. After we all took the pipe and spoke our thoughts on the matter, it was decided that Wayawousit should teach the god talker our tongue.

For many years Pierson struggled to learn our tongue whenever Wayawousit was able to have time to speak with him. Between those times the god talker would come to our village and try to speak what he had learned which usually made us all laugh. It was then that he even began to approach me nervously which I always found to be amusing since most of what he tried to say was unclear. One thing was obvious however, he did not want to ask me questions about our Spirit World but instead seemed to want me to leave Totoket and called me many names of what he said were demons and evil spirits. When he did this, I would usually shake my rattle at him or chant a protective Spirit Song which he disliked very much and he would quickly leave me.

According to Wayawousit, Pierson wanted to learn our tongue so he could put his black book into our words. That way we would better understand and find his salvation for in his thinking, if we did not then we were all doomed to go their place called hell where we would fall into a fire that burns forever and not the house of Keihtan when we die. Pierson had told Wayawousit that many of the people of the Dawnland elsewhere, especially among the Massachusett, had taken up their Spirit ways saying that its medicine was more powerful. After all, look at what had happened since the arrival of the Awaunuy? Perhaps their Spirit World would protect and save those who still lived he said. The People did not believe this.

After a number of years, Pierson did come to Qussuckquansh and asked if he could share his book with the People. The sachem told me that he thought it a wise decision to let each of the People hear his words and decide for themselves what they thought of it and the council agreed. I did not see harm in it and agreed as well, more curious than anything else. On a warm summer day, fourteen snows since the Awaunuy had come to Totoket, Pierson and five of his followers came proudly to our village to speak to a gathering of the People. I had covered my face and body in my white Spirit paint with the Thunderbird in red on my chest and back and wore a headdress made of raven feathers for the occasion. As the Awaunuy approached the People who sat or stood in the center of the village, I welcomed them with Spirit

Words and drumming which caused them to pause before Pierson said something to the others and they went to stand before the villagers while making their cross sign.

One of the Awaunuy came to stand before Pierson and held the open book as Pierson began to read. It was difficult to understand the words he spoke and a few of the People began to grow restless and begin to talk among themselves, commenting on their not understanding most of the words the god talker was saying. Eventually some began to laugh and others left to go about whatever tasks were at hand. Soon just a small group, mostly children sat before the Awaunuy as Pierson kept reading, apparently unmoved by the disappearance of those he had come to save. Even Qussuckquansh and the elders went away and thankfully clouds came on a strong wind from the home of Keihtan and with them rain, lightning, and thunder. I turned towards the wind and began to sing in praise of Keihtan and the Thunderbird as the Awaunuy hurried away in the rain and wind towards their town.

During the next few years Pierson continued to try to read and speak to the People about Yahweh and salvation and though most were usually polite, none were interested in what he had to say. To this day, unlike some others in the Dawnland, I do not know of any Quinnipiac who have taken up the Spirit World of the Awaunuy.

Chapter Seventeen

The day was becoming warmer as I followed the shoreline just above the waves as they ended their journey upon the sand and stones, each in turn replaced by another. The air was soft and the slight breeze brought with it the smell of salt mixed with the pungent, damp mud and sand left behind by the retreating tide. How wonderful are the gifts of the Earth Mother I thought as I reached the first of a number of streams I would have to forge before arriving at Totoket, removing my moccasins and deerskin leggings to do so. In the distance out on the water a small Awaunuy boat with its one triangle sail was moving with the wind towards the east and another closer to shore near one of the many small islands held men using nets to take our finned brothers and sisters. The Awaunuy, like the Dutchmannuck before them, scoop up large amounts in their nets, more than they can possibly eat, then dry them with salt. They put them in large, round wooden baskets and send them on larger ships across the ocean. Where I do not know. I assume where their home is.

By the middle of the afternoon I could see in the distance the peninsula that held our village and I began to wonder how what I had been given by Hobomock and his messengers would be received. So much has changed in all these years since my youth. Many of the People have begun to accept the ways of the Awaunuy, not necessarily because they want to, but they think they have to in order to survive. It is becoming more difficult every day to live in the traditional ways. That reason more than any other might make the decision to leave the home of our ancestors the choice to follow.

As I rounded a series of large boulders that Mashup had tumbled towards the sea I spotted two men of the People in the distance coming towards me. They were passing along the shore in front of a newly built Awaunuy house that sat on a slight bluff beyond the shore hen a large and fierce Awaunuy dog began to menace and threaten them. It was unlike the dogs of the People, but a type the Awaunuy had brought with them when they first arrived on our shores. They were trained to attack and kill not just four leggeds, but people, especially in a time of war. As the two shouted and waved their hands in the air to chase the dog away, I recognized their voices; my old friend Wentubecum and Mequnhut.

I watched in horror as suddenly the dog lunged at Wentubecum, knocking him to the ground as the old warrior struggled to free himself. Mequnhut drawing his knife, stabbed the beast in the neck killing it instantly, but not before it had torn the flesh of Wentubecum's hand, arm, and shoulder.

Meanwhile, three Awaunuy came running from near the house, yelling out as they did and one held a musket in his hands. It was clear they were upset over the killing of their dog and confronted Mequnhut who was trying to help Wentubecum to his feet.

"Ye heathen devil, you have killed my dog. He was trained to keep the likes of ye away for you would steal everything I have if you could" he said angrily and in a threatening manner that caused Mequnhut to stand ready to defend himself and Wentubecum who with his help had staggered to his feet.

Not understanding what the angry Awaunuy was saying but sensing his intent, Mequnhut quickly replied in our tongue. "The beast attacked us and has hurt Wentubecum. It might have killed him if I had not used my knife!"

One of the men, with dark skin, stepped between the two and spoke words to the angry man. "Be careful master, for you know that here in Branford when a Quinnie kills one of our animals we must not take retribution upon them but report it to the magistrates who will seek compensation from their sachem. This is a chance to gain more land. Just think, a dog for more land to claim as your own."

Staring fiercely at Mequnhut, then looking at the dark skinned man, the angry Awaunuy stated "you are a smart boy and it was a good day God gave me the wisdom to purchase you Cicero. Perhaps you are correct. I believe a good thrashing will teach these vermin a lesson, however. Especially this insolent young one. He needs to understand this is our land now."

It was at that moment I arrived, having hurried along the shore hoping to get there before a fight began. On seeing me, Mequnhut shouted out "uncle, this no place for you for these men seem intent to cause us harm and if I am forced to kill them we may all be hunted down to be killed or sold into slavery!"

"Satan be damned, it is the wicked sorcerer of Totoket, sent by the Devil himself. They must have magically called him to their aid." said the third man, the skinny Awaunuy who held the musket upon noticing me. "Be careful father, for he may cast a spell upon your soul and ours if you harm any of these Satan worshipers. Listen to Cicero. Let the magistrates settle with the sachem - a dog for land is a fair exchange."

"Perhaps you and the boy have a point" the angry one replied, still glaring at Mequnhut as he did. "Pick up the dog Cicero, we will leave these three to their fate as it is only a matter of time before they are sure to burn in Hell. Look at the one the dog bit. He is losing blood fast and already halfway to the eternal, fiery pit. That old Indian will be dead by evening" he said as he spit towards the feet of Wentubecum.

The dark man picked up the dog and the three backed slowly away before turning and walking up the bluff towards the house. As they did, Mequnhut scowled and exclaimed loud enough for them to hear "I could throw my knife and kill that man then kill the one who carries the musket with my tomahawk before they would even know what has happened to them. Only knowing it would bring the wrath of the Awaunuy upon Totoket makes me hesitate."

I turned my attention to Wentubecum who was bleeding badly from the wounds to his shoulder, arm, and his hand. He was struggling to remain standing and with the help of Mequnhut we helped him walk back along the beach towards Totoket until we reached some tall bushes and trees out of sight of the Awaunuy house where Wentubecum sat down on a fallen tree. "I must clean and bind those wounds friend before we go further. Mequnhut, could you gather some fresh kelp from the water and be sure to rinse as much sand as you can from it. I will make a wrap of them that can stem the bleeding and keep the wounds clean."

While Mequnhut ran quickly into the sea to gather the kelp, diving and resurfacing as he did so for he needed to go to the deeper water offshore to gather it, I used the fresh water from my bladder to rinse Wentubecum's wounds. The one on his shoulder was deeper and larger than the others which were more superficial so I tended to it first before cleaning the others. I then applied a powder made from ground wambona (starry solomon's seal), which I carried in my medicine pouch to help the blood clot. While I tended to him, Wentubecum began to tease me through his discomfort. "You old man, see what trouble you have caused" wincing as he spoke. "Mequnhut and I were on our way to search for you after you did not return to our village when he thought you might. He was worried as he knew you had gone to Mennunkatuck and that there had been trouble there with the Awaunuy king's soldiers."

"It is true, there was some trouble at Mennunkatuck with the arrival of soldiers sent by the Awaunuy king. I had hoped to speak with the king about the problems the People have faced these many years since his people have arrived but was disappointed to find out he was not with them. William told me he was still across the big water in his land there."

"Oh yes, your Awaunuy friend William" said Wentubecum.

Mequnhut arrived with the wet kelp and helped me use the long leaves to wrap the wounds while he began to scold me. "Uncle", he said with a tone of concern, "we were worried something had happened to you at Mennunkatuck. We had heard there was trouble there and that you might have been caught up in it. You do cause us all to worry, none more than my grandmother who had come to Totoket to see if you had returned from the solstice journey. When she became aware that your path took you to Mennunkatuck, she asked me to seek you out. The Awaunuy king's warriors had already been to New Haven and had been very threatening to the Awaunuy there. She said that it was only due to the words of a god talker there that they did not have a fight."

"I am sorry that I may have caused worry for you and your grandmother Mequnhut, but I walk with the Spirits and know harm from the Awaunuy cannot find me. I move as a phantom among them and they are wary of my presence if they notice me at all."

"They fear your gifts from the Spirit World Ponaim" said Wentubecum. "They have witnessed them many times and the smart ones like your friend William and some at Totoket know your heart and spirit are good and respect you for that."

"It may be so my friend and it is true I do not fear them," I replied. "It has always been what they have done to the Earth Mother, all who live on it, as well as the People and our way of life that causes me so much concern. Pausing for a moment, I continued. "I hope to speak with the Grand Council about all that I have seen."

Rising up and standing though a little shaky at first, Wentubecum said "Thank you for your healing gifts Ponaim, let us return to Totoket. I am able to walk. My Spirit Shield given to me by Hobomock and the Spirit World all those years ago along the Kuttawo has never left me despite the effort of that Awaunuy dog."

"You walk with Manitou as always Wentubecum," said Mequnhut as we left the grove of trees to follow the beach back to Totoket.

The people of Totoket were quietly going about their daily routines when we arrived. Seeing me and that Wentubecum was injured quickly created an atmosphere of excitement that replaced the calm. Wentubecum's grandniece immediately ran to him and asked how he had been injured while the old hunter replied that he had a run in with an Awaunuy dog and that Mequnhut had killed it. "I will be fine," he assured her, "Ponaim as always has used his gifts to help me heal. It will take more than a dog bite to send this old man to the house of Keihtan."

Shambisqua and her brother Keyhow, along with the Totoket sachem, Wampom, the son of Qussuckquansh, worked their way through the throng of villagers to greet us. "We are pleased for your return powwow" said the elderly sachem who was a wise and cautious leader like his father. "We knew from Mequnhut that you had gone to Mennunkatuck and with the tension surrounding all the Awaunuy towns, we were worried for your safety."

"None more than I Ponaim. You are too old for such wanderings by yourself" chided Shambisqua who did little to hide her relief at seeing her old friend safe.

Turning to Wentubecum, Wampom asked "what caused your injuries friend?"

Wentubecum explained the entire incident again as all eyes turned to Mequnhut with shouts of approval mixed with "Manitou!"

"Ponaim arrived just in time" added Mequnhut. "Otherwise there might have been more blood spilled other than that of the Awaunuy dog."

Wentubecum's grandniece took her uncle's hand and said "come uncle, let us get you out of the sun and some food and drink. Please Ponaim, come with us and sit in the shade to rest and eat. You must be hungry after a journey such as yours." I admitted I was tired and gratefully accepted her offer.

Early that evening, as a cool breeze came in off the water, Shambisqua came to see me and together we walked to the edge of the sandy, red cliff that overlooked the beach and the water beyond. "So many years Ponaim," the sunksquaw said as we sat watching Father Sun begin his descent to his place of sleep. "How many years have you made the journey along the Spirit Line to find meaning to the ways of this world my friend?"

"Too many to remember Shambisqua. But each has opened my eyes and spirit to the workings of the universe though at times the signs have been confusing, unclear, or not what I wanted to learn. Not this time however" I said with conviction as I looked straight into her eyes. "I have been given a series of messages and signs through both visions and the helpers of Hobomock and now understand the two paths the People must decide to follow."

Shambisqua looked at me intensely, something she always had done since we were children whenever she knew I had more to say. At that moment she was that young girl I have always loved; like me, her body may have aged, but her spirit and soul were still the same. I knew the question was coming.

"As shaman for the People, I understand you do not have to share what you have seen, but as your oldest and dearest friend I would hope you will" she stated emphatically.

Just then, two eagles drifted slowly above our heads before one darted down towards the sea and scooped up an eel in its talons. The other cut its circling short and swooped down following its mate, hoping to share in or steal its catch. "See Ponaim.

Why make me chase after you to try and pry just a morsel from you?" she exclaimed through a laugh.

Turning with a serious look that hid my amusement, I could only say "you must catch me first for the one with the eel is the one with the sustenance." We both laughed as we watched the one with the eel land on a tree branch just to the east of the village followed by its partner and together they gobbled the eel as only eagles can before sitting contently upon the branch.

Still smiling, Shambisqua said "there is your omen my friend because you know eagles seldom share. Do you not doubt the messengers of Keihtan?"

We talked well into the night.

I had asked Shambisqua to ask Wyandot, Wampom, and the other sachems to call a Grand Council at the Council Rock in Mioonkhtuck on the next full moon which was to arrive in three nights. I suggested that a ceremonial dance and feast appealing to the Spirit World be held the evening before to set the right conditions for the People to make the decisions that would show the path they would follow. Then after resting one day, I gathered up my medicine pouch, otter skin bundle, and robe and walked back along the shore past the Awaunuy house where the confrontation had taken place. From there I went to a place deep within the jumble of ridges and stones that dominated the area. It was a hidden place of spiritual power, a natural overhang and stone platform that was embedded within a cliff, that Commossuck had shown me that was a direct opening to the spirit energy of Hobomock and the Lower World where answers might be found.

I reached the platform by mid-day and once there sat to prepare to enter the Spirit World in order to gain further insights into the future of the People. For this journey, I called on red tailed hawk to guide me as I closed my eyes and began to chant the sacred sounds that would bring her to me. She came and together we descended into the Lower World and into a verdant green land that was a time vastly different than our own. Hawk had landed on a branch of a tree and as I asked her where we were she motioned to a weetou of a type I was not familiar with. It was small and conical in shape and covered with hides. The trees around us were cedars, spruce, and pines, low, and scrubby. The air was crisp and cool, like the start of winter, yet it was clear that it was spring or even summer with a carpet of grasses and wildflowers on the ground. This was a place I did not recognize but yet I felt the comfort of being home.

As I approached the weetou, a skin flap opened and a man dressed in furs came out and stood before me making a gesture of welcome as he smiled as if he knew me. He did not speak but I understood as he motioned that I should follow him. We worked our way through the scrubby growth of conifers and low bushes that surrounded his camp and up onto a ridge until I recognized where we were. It was the Split Rock where our people had always celebrated our harvest festival in the past and from which Commossuck and I had often dream walked. Gathered there were a group of around twenty men, women, and children, all dressed in furs like the man who welcomed me as if I was a long lost member of the family. They embraced me, patted me on the back, took hold of my hands, and spoke words of welcome though in a tongue I could not understand. Hawk had followed us and sat in a tree just to the west of the Rock and I was surprised she seemed invisible to the people there which, on reflection, made perfect sense for she was my animal guide and there for my guidance .

One of the men began to drum and everyone joined in a dance of celebration, circling the split rock and chanting sounds I did not recognize taking turns calling out, even the children. A woman elder with a wise and benevolent face came forward and took my hand and led me into the circle where I joined in the dance. I immediately felt free and exhilarated as I danced and understood that these were the ancestors of the People from a time before memory. They were welcoming me into their world. As I became more and more absorbed in the spirit energy of the dance I understood through that energy that the Dawnland would always be their home and ours as well, that despite the troubles that are plaguing the People, it would always remain that way, even if we sought refuge in another place. The Soul and Spirit of the People through the ancestors would remain in the Dawnland forever. We just needed to remember.

When the dance ended each member of the group came forward and we embraced, one at a time, even the smallest children. Then the ancestor who had brought me to the Split Rock approached me and while taking both my hands in his, looked into my eyes and seemed to bless and thank me without speaking. It was a powerful moment of shared destiny, brotherhood, and kinship. I stood with tears in my eyes as he walked away into the pines before hawk called to me and I was returned to the present.

Chapter Eighteen

While I was away, word was spread throughout Mioonkhtuck, Totoket, and to the scattered small camps of the People inland that I had asked that a Grand Council be held to share the message that I had received from Hobomock and the Spirit World. It seemed that the news had shaken many out of a sleepy lethargy in anticipation of what the message might be and when I returned to Totoket there was a level of excitement not felt for a long time. I was greeted by shouts of "Manitou" while earlier Mequnhut asked Wampom and Wyandot if he could have the honor of organizing the feast and dance the evening before the next day when the Grand Council was to be held. He and a group of young men dedicated to preserving the traditional ways had already returned from Mioonkhtuck making sure all was ready at the arbor they had built in the center of the village near the Council Rock that would hold the ritual fire.

"Uncle, Mequnhut said as we walked towards my weetou, "Apoawein and I along with other young men want to help in any way we can during the celebration this evening. All has been prepared for the feast and dance at Mioonkhtuck and it has made my spirit glad to see such excitement."

"Thank you Mequnhut, it is a good omen that you and the others have stepped forward to take charge. Our ways and traditions must not become memories" I replied as I patted him on the back. "You all are the future and your voices must be heard at the Council Rock tomorrow."

"The entire village is to leave when the sun is high for Mioonkhtuck. Would you honor me by traveling with me and Apoawein in our canoe?" he asked expectantly.

"No, I will rest for a while and later walk the shore path to Mioonkhtuck as is my way. I appreciate the offer grandson of Nawatokis. You remind me very much of your grandfather. He would be proud to know you have become the man you are" I said as I looked at him fondly.

"As you wish uncle. All will be ready when you arrive." We embraced and he quickly went off to join others loading a number of canoes with food and everything needed for the feast and dance.

After a meal and a short rest I gathered the things I would need for the ritual dance and the Grand Council; my medicine bundle, sacred pipe, paints, robe, and headdress, then set off towards Mioonkhtuck. It was late afternoon and Totoket was deserted except for the dogs left behind as all had left either by water or foot earlier. I wanted to be alone in my walk to the feast and found comfort in that since the death of Commossuck so many years ago, I have walked our Earth Mother alone. I knew in my heart and spirit this walk was to bring change since after the Council the People would choose which path to follow.

As I walked to the thin neck of land where Totoket was connected to the Awaunuy town, I moved quickly westward along its outskirts and through the edge of the marsh that separated it from the river and sea. Seagulls danced above me in the warm summer breeze and as I followed the path much of what surrounded me was little changed by the Awaunuy presence. "They stay away from the shore usually and use the trail further inland, which they have made wide enough for their carts. It is odd that so few of them prize the land just beyond the water but I was once told by William that many of them come from villages far from the shore and are unfamiliar with it. Some are even afraid after their journey here from across the sea."

Father Sun was close to sleep when I walked into Mioonkhtuck and once noticed was soon surrounded by well-wishers and expectant shouts of "Manitou!". It has always been an odd feeling for me when some of the People react to my presence in such a manner, calling attention to me in a way that makes me uncomfortable. As shaman, I serve the People and the Spirit World and to be greeted in a celebratory way makes me out to be more than who I am. "What would Commossuck think?" I mused. "But these are strange and unusual times."

Mequnhut soon rescued me and ushered me to his grandmother's weetou where I could rest before the feast began. I gratefully accepted his offer and once inside was surrounded by quiet. Shambisqua was not present, having gone to the arbor with her brothers Nausup and Keyhow to meet Wyandot and Wampom.

No sooner had I begun to get out my spirit paints in preparation for my role as the ritual leader, when there was a voice outside the door flap to the weetou. It was Wambusco, the young powwow who had recently come to live among the People at Mioonkhtuck. He was a Paugassett and had recently married Sebesqua the daughter of the elder Maug. I had welcomed him as a fellow shaman and though he had much to still learn, was an effective and eager healer and in time would be a fine powwow. He was also the grandnephew of Pawquash who had died many years before he was born. He often asked me to tell him of Pawquash and Commossuck and how they had battled the Black Robed Demon all those years ago.

"Ponaim may I enter?" he asked rather timidly. "I would like to speak before the feast and dance rituals begin."

"Of course my young friend, come in so we can talk" I replied.

Wambusco opened the flap and hesitated for an instant before entering. He was short but sturdily built with a kind, round face. He wore red spirit paint on the lower half of his face and torso with yellow stripes as well as a two pronged antler headdress in honor of his grand uncle and his Deer Clan lineage within the Paugassett people.

"I am glad to see you Wambusco and that you are well. I was hoping together we might conduct the rituals before the feast and at the start of the dancing. I do not often come to Mioonkhtuck as you know and appreciate what you are doing for the People here. As I have grown older it has become increasingly difficult to tend to those here and at Totoket."

"I would be greatly honored Ponaim" the young powwow replied, a smile on his face that would light up a weetou. "I was not going to speak of assisting at the rituals unless you did out of respect for you, your gifts, and all you have done for the People."

"We both do what we can Wambusco. Perhaps if you would perform the prayer ritual before the dancing and I would do the same for the feast or we can lead both together. But I think it would send a powerful signal to everyone, especially the young, if you took the lead for both the feast and the dance.

This night is in many ways marks the passing on of leadership to your generation. There are so few of us elders left and the future is yours, not ours" I said with a sincerity that I saw surprised him.

"I am humbled by what you have said Ponaim, but the People look to you this night. My time will come" replied the young powwow. "It will be a great honor to simply stand by your side."

As I thanked Wambusco for his gracious words and watched him leave the weetou, I could not help but feel a pang of worry mixed with anxiety. I knew that if the People choose to stay in the land of the ancestors, despite what I knew would be the best efforts of Wambusco, Mequnhut, and others, they will soon become overwhelmed by the great wave of Awaunuy that will come. I saw it in the dream walk in the Mioonkhtuck of a future tomorrow. I painted my face, arms, and torso, placed my raven feathered headdress on my head, picked up my medicine bundle, and went out into the fading light.

Our communal feast was ready just as I arrived at the arbor. Each family had brought cooked venison, fish, maize, squash, and the rest of the seasonal bounty given to us by the Earth Mother. There was laughter and excited talking wherever I looked and it reminded me of all the feasts and gatherings during happy times in the past. As I approached the arbor Wyandot called to me, motioning that I should join him and the other sachems and elders at the northern side of the circular arbor. "Ponaim" he said as I joined them, "we know the Manitou in you. When you feel it is time, would you do us the honor of lighting the sacred ceremonial fire?"

As I thanked the sachem, I was overcome by an odd feeling which, after so many years of acting as a ritual and ceremonial leader, suddenly made me feel as if this were my first time, or could it maybe be my last? Only the Spirit World knew. As I gazed at the smiling, excited faces I felt an incredibly powerful connection not just to each person, but to all those we had known and loved who had gone on to the house of Keihtan. "What a fortunate man I am I thought that I have had the privilege of being one of the People of the Dawnland." I nodded to Wyandot, thanked the sachems and elders, and lit the fire. On seeing the fire lit, the People fell silent in expectation of what I was to say.

"We are the People; we have lived here in the land of our ancestors since the time of the first Ones. I have had the honor of traveling to see them on a dream walk to their time and they welcomed me and through me all of you in a loving embrace and dance. Their message was clear and powerful. They know who you are and from whom you are from." Hesitating for a moment to collect my words, I continued.

"We now live at a time where the path before us has forked for all the Quinnipiac of Mioonkhtuck and Totoket. We are the survivors. We have no choice but to decide which of two paths to follow. Both are uncertain. Both paths hold unknown challenges. This we will speak of tomorrow at the Grand Council and hopefully with the help of our ancestors and the Spirit World, we, the People and each one of us will follow the path that is best."

When I stopped, everyone stood quietly absorbed in the words I had spoken. With all eyes locked on me in expectation, they waited for me to continue. I called to Wambusco and as he stepped forward, I continued. "We the People have always honored the Spirit World by celebrating in gratitude the many gifts they, the Earth Mother, and the ancestors have given us. It has always been our way and our gathering together to share in feasting and ritual dancing is the greatest expression of that. In this we all know they will hear our prayers of thanks, especially if our hearts are pure."

Meanwhile, Wambusco had circled his way around the fire and came to stand by my side and thanked me for calling him. He looked resplendent and dignified beyond his age in his paint and headdress as he looked out at the People who were waiting for him to speak. "There are no words I can say that would have more power or truth than those of the great and wise Ponaim. His council and gifts have sustained the People much longer than most of us here can remember. Even as a boy among the Paugassett I heard always of the great Ponaim. It is an honor and privilege to stand beside you."

With that every voice erupted into a celebratory chant of "hup, hup, hup…" which only ended when Wambusco raised his hands. "Brothers and sisters, let us all join in the feast as one people, committed to determine the future together. May the Spirit World and the ancestors guide and protect us!" Then, after another chorus of chants and shouts of celebration, Wambusco added "let us feast, dance, sing, and celebrate the gifts of Keihtan and the Earth Mother!"

We all sat and shared in the bounty brought to the feast; it was just like the old times before the coming of the Awaunuy. Through the laughter and joyful camaraderie of the moment I could not help but notice some of the little and subtle things that marked the transformation of the People and our way of life because of the influence of the Awaunuy. As I surveyed those gathered, I realized how few in number we now were. Here we were - all gathered from Totoket and Mioonkhtuck, and we were maybe one out of five or six in number compared to the time before the coming of the Awaunuy. We are disappearing.

There were other things as well. Over half those present were wearing Awaunuy clothing; some because they found them more comfortable than our traditional dress, but some because they had no choice. With the disappearance of the deer and the other four footed, we lacked the skins needed to make traditional clothing. And everywhere were the woolen blankets, pots, kettles, and tools of the Awaunuy. Food was changing as well. With less venison some of the meat at the feast was from Awaunuy cattle and hogs. Many at Mioonkhtuck had taken to raising the beasts in order to supply an adequate supply of meat for the winter. Besides the Three Sisters, we also ate the small round Awaunuy peas that made what was called porridge as well as bread from their tall grass called wheat. As each day passed, we were becoming more dependent on the Awaunuy for their goods that are transforming our way of life.

As the feast continued, a few of the younger men along with an elder the Awaunuy called Rum Tom, a name was he was flattered to call himself, began to pass the Awaunuy burning water called rum back and forth. Wyandot had forbidden it at the feast and dancing and when he saw them, he, along with Nausup, Wampom, Mequnhut, and Apoawein, went to them and asked them to stop. After a few tense moments, Rum Tom and three others agreed but two others did not. They said they were insulted and left angrily. Wyandot, speaking loud enough for all to hear said as long as he was sachem these drinks during ceremony would not be allowed. Most seemed to agree while some just shrugged their shoulders and the feast went on.

I had made my way to Shambisqua as the feast began and we sat together enjoying the moment, the food, and each other. She had been a bit late to the celebration having arrived just as Wambusco spoke and I asked her if she was not well since she had not been present from the moment I arrived at Mioonkhtuck.

"All is well my friend, though my bones often ache in the damp air" she said as she made a gesture as if to grasp her knee laughing as she did. "No Ponaim, I had gone to New Haven town to speak with the magistrates there. They were concerned about the gathering of all the People so suddenly and knowing it was not a time for one of our festivals were nervous about the reason. After these many years, it is sadly true they still fear and do not trust us even though we have never given them a reason not to. Sometimes I find these Awaunuy so exceedingly difficult" she said with a sigh of exasperation. "They did however demand that none other than Quinnipiac attend our feast, dancing, or Grand Council, calling them "outside Indians". They are afraid of an uprising I was told. I assured them that only we

Quinnipiac were gathering to discuss matters of importance."

While the feast was drawing to a close, preparations were made to begin the dancing which brought about a new surge of excitement. As those who were to drum gathered near the sacred fire, I rose up and gestured to Wambusco to join me. Together we lit our combination of sacred sweetgrass and sage and smudged the smoke over each drummer and drum. Then together, we led all gathered there in chanting the sacred sounds that would draw in the Spirits to help us dance and celebrate the beauty of this world and life itself. Once the drumming and singing began, the men gathered under the arbor around the sacred fire and began dancing in a circular manner, each imitating the movements of the power animal which was their spirit guide throughout life. The women moved in a circle in the opposite direction doing a dignified two-step dance.

As the evening wore on, participants would drop out of the dance for a rest while others would join again. The dancing, drumming, and singing did not come to an end until just before the rising of Father Sun. I enjoyed myself immensely, joining in with the others from time to time and feeling like a young man again as the drumming, singing, and dancing made me feel free and put me into a semi-trance that was good for my soul and spirit. As people began to melt away to find sleep in their weetous, I stayed to tend the fire along with Wambusco for it was important that it continue to burn until after the Grand Council later that day.

"I will tend the fire this morning Ponaim, please find some rest and when you wake you may take your turn if you wish. I am happy to watch over it since I do not think sleep will come to me."

"Thank you Wambusco, I will take your offer for it seems my body could use some rest." As I gathered up my medicine bag, Shambisqua approached from the arbor with my deerskin robe and otter skin bag holding my sacred pipe.

"I knew you would not come to the weetou so I will keep these for you" motioning to the items she carried. But take your deerskin robe and this one of the bear so you will not be chilled in the early morning air. Come and eat when you wake." She smiled at me in a knowing and loving way.

"Thank you Shambisqua, you have always been a true friend and companion these many years.

"Do not get sentimental Ponaim, you need sleep and rest before you stand before the People at the Council Rock." She smiled and turned to walk back to her weetou.

I watched her go thinking "if only our life paths had been different." As she disappeared among the weetous, I turned and walked to the edge of the sea and found a spot under a few trees to rest and wait for the arrival of Father Sun.

Chapter Nineteen

The morning was cool and clear for the season and I found it refreshing as I shook off sleep and looked out onto the water. Father Sun had just risen and a line of maroon clouds tinged with amber to the south along the horizon snuggled down close to the water promising a beautiful day. I gathered up my sleeping robes and walked back towards the village and up the slight hill to the arbor where Apoawein greeted me.

"It is a beautiful morning Ponaim. Mequnhut and I thought we would help tend the fire so that you and Wambusco might be able to get some rest" he said proudly. "It is the least we can do."

"Thank you Apoawein. I can tend to it now so that you may eat and prepare for the day."

"Actually, I just took over for Mequnhut who came earlier so that Wambusco might rest and eat. He left to make sure there was food for you this morning as if he did not think his grandmother would have had it ready for you." Smiling, Apoawein continued. "I was told to send you to her weetou."

"I will then," I said returning his smile.

As I walked through the village many were already stirring and when they saw me we greeted one another as is our custom. Babies were crying and fussing, children were beginning their day of play, and women were tending their cooking fires sending the aroma of maize cakes and fish mingling into the air. It did my heart good to see the morning of the People unfolding as it always has. When I drew closer to the weetou of Shambisqua, she was outside by her fire and I could see she was preparing a meal of venison, maize, and wild artichokes.

"Such a bother you are going through for a skinny old man Shambisqua" I teased as I approached. Are there not more important tasks for you to be tending to?"

"None more important than feeding an old powwow" she said with a laugh. Together we sat by the fire.

I was hungry and ate well and as I did Shambisqua and I began to talk about the situation facing the People, especially those here at Mioonkhtuck. From where we sat it was impossible not to see the Awaunuy town of New Haven across the harbor with its ever expanding growth and ships and boats of all varieties at the wharfs that lined their side of the water. As their population grew so did the pressure on Mioonkhtuck. Many were wanting to settle on our side of the harbor so the Awaunuy had agreed to build a fence along the northern boundary of Mioonkhtuck more to mark the extent of Quinnipiac land than to keep out their farmers who were clamoring for more access to it.

"Ponaim, we are now a small island in a sea of Awaunuy" Shambisqua said dejectedly. "Once we gave them permission to build their place on our land years ago for their ferry to cross the river they have been settling to our east in greater and greater numbers, filling up the land between us and the river that separates us from their town of Branford. We no longer have that land to hunt even though the paper we agreed to said we were to share it."

I agreed before saying "then came the agreement to let them build a fort where our own palisade had once been to place their big guns overlooking the harbor. They claimed it would also protect the People. But who would they protect us from? The Mohawk and Mohegan do not have ships and would never come so close to New Haven."

"I argued against letting them make a path through our land to the fort but the promise of aid from the Awaunuy if we allowed it was more powerful than the thought of the potential impact of such a thing" Shambisqua added. "Now those Awaunuy to the east of us use it regularly with their carts and horses and have made a second path from the fort to their farms, without our permission," she said in dismay.

We sat quietly for a while before I began again. "Shambisqua, what I find most troubling is how so many of our men have become slaves to the rum and other fire waters they get so easily. I know the Awaunuy claim they do not allow the sale or giving of it, but many of our men crave it and are often paid with it for work they do for them." I stared into the smoky fire as it began to burn down for a few thoughtful moments before continuing. "My friend, there is nothing the Awaunuy can do that causes more harm to the People. Those who are dependent on it become like crazed beasts as you know, arguing, fighting, and causing trouble not just here but in the Awaunuy town.

"I cannot even begin to count how many times we have had to pay in Awaunuy money to get our men released from the jailing place where they put them. As you know, they put them there when our men cause trouble in the town in their drunkenness" Shambisqua said. " If we do not have the money required to free them, then we pay by giving them another piece of our land. This breaks my heart Ponaim. We are trapped in a cycle of misery we cannot seem to escape."

"As we spoke recently at Totoket Shambisqua, perhaps there is. Remember the vision given to me by Hobomock. It will be up to the People to decide and I will speak of the two paths today at the Council Rock" I said with a slight tinge of hope.

"It may be so Ponaim, we shall see. But to give up the home of our ancestors may deliver a blow from which the People may never recover."

The Grand Council was to gather when Father Sun was high at the Council Rock, a great stone thrown down by Hobomock in his battle with the Stone Giants long ago and considered the heart of Quinnipiac territory. It was here where the annual three day harvest festival at Mioonkhtuck is held and where important decisions have been discussed by the People since the time of the ancestors. How they would decide on this day only the Spirits knew.

I decided I would not where my paints but appear at the council as a simple man of the People. I would bring a sacred pipe but not mine; that of Commossuck. It held tremendous spiritual energy and is a powerful symbol of our ceremonial and spiritual connection to the world of the Spirits. I knew that the sachems, elders and most gathered would recognize it and understand the significance and importance of its use. Those who were to speak would first, as was our custom, inhale the sacred tobacco smoke through it and thus be imbued with the spiritual power of the great powwow which would guide their words in truth.

I was restless after having eaten and my talk with Shambisqua so I went to the far southern end of our land to the shore, past the Awaunuy fort with its men sent to watch that we did not cause trouble. I wanted to sit, think, and pray. The day was warming and remained a gift from Keihtan and I found comfort in the smell of the salt water and the sounds of the sea. But my thoughts troubled me. I believed that some of the People would decide to move north, following the message from Hobomock to an unknown land to live in the ways of the ancestors. Others, I knew, would remain here at Mioonkhtuck and Totoket to hang on as best they could. I had seen what the future held for Mioonkhtuck yet sympathized with those who would remain knowing they could never leave their ancestral home. Too many had also become dependent on Awaunuy goods and would not want to give them up. I felt a deep sadness.

As mid-day approached, the People began to gather around the arbor, most at first on the shaded side but later arrivals had no choice but to endure the heat that was building from the Father from the south. The young men had built the circular arbor large enough to accommodate the sachems and elders who would sit in a circle around the ceremonial fire and still allow many others to find shade underneath. Pine boughs had been placed upon the cross supports to cover the top by Mequnhut, Apoawein, and the other young men that morning to provide shade leaving only a large opening in the center to allow the smoke from the fire to escape. During the feast and dance, the top had been left uncovered to the sky in order to let the ancestors look down upon us, joining in our ritual celebration of life.

According to tradition, once the People had gathered, the elders and sachems would arrive. As shamans, Wambusco and I would be the last. We walked to the arbor side by side as I insisted. It was important for everyone to understand that I was symbolically placing my trust in the young powwow as the future and as an equal, just as Commossuck had done with me. As we approached the arbor, I noticed once again how few in numbers the People had become; maybe 300 at most. This reminded me of how important the message of Hobomock was.

Wyandot and the other sachems and elders entered and stood in a circle around the fire with Wampom to his right and Shambisqua to his left. To her left were her brothers Nausup and Keyhow. When Wambusco and I entered the arbor, Shambisqua made a space for me between her and Wyandot and Wambusco as was tradition at the Grand Council, found a position directly opposite of me within the group of twenty elders. As Grand Sachem, Wyandot began the council.

"Ponaim, our great and wise shaman, has asked that this Grand Council meet so that he may share with us the profound messages he received from the Spirit World during the solstice when he followed the Spirit Line to look upon the face of Hobomock." The sachem paused for a moment before continuing. "The message is one of importance for the future of the People." With that, he turned to me.

I opened my otter skin bag and brought out the sacred pipe and I heard some of the People react upon seeing it, recognizing that it was the pipe of Commossuck. I filled it with sacred tobacco and lit it with a small stick which I put into the embers of the fire. Upon my lighting the pipe, everyone sat for it was customary that only the one with the pipe should stand and speak. I inhaled, held the smoke in my mouth for a moment, then exhaled sending the smoke skyward so the Spirits and our ancestors would know my words were true.

"My People, as Wyandot has said, I asked for the Grand Council to be held here next to the Council Rock, the heart of our land, so that I might share with you the visions and messages I have been given by Hobomock and the Spirits." I paused, then continued. "Like some gathered here, I have lived a long life and remember the time before the coming of the Awaunuy to the Dawnland. Needless to say, their arrival has brought great changes and disruption to our lives and world. As Commossuck often told me when I was just a boy, their presence has put our world out of balance. We have seen that the energy of their Spirit World from across the water is powerful and it has overwhelmed ours. We once believed it was hidden in their black book but know now that is only partly true. They are a clever people and create wondrous things that must surely come from a place of strong spirit. Many of our people find these goods and things attractive and they are completely transforming our way of life away from that of our ancestors."

Stopping to draw in smoke from the pipe, I looked at those gathered around the arbor, exhaled, then continued.

"The presence of the Awaunuy has been devastating to we, the People. All one has to do is look around. We are now so few in number while their numbers grow larger every day. William from our village at Mennunkatuck has said they are so numerous in their land across the water that it would be impossible to count them all. They are like grains of sand on the beach. We know this to be true; as their numbers grow, ours decline." I stopped before starting again. "Because of this, I sought an answer from Hobomock as to what path, we the People, should follow into the future. I was given an answer."

My words caused some to exclaim their agreement while others simply nodded their heads. Others remained silent their eyes fixed upon me.

"Dark shadows have engulfed the Dawnland, not just here, but wherever the Awaunuy have gone. So many others throughout the Dawnland have died, those who have resisted them are gone. Where are the Pequot? Where are those who rose up with Metacom? As each year passes, the shadows grow darker and it becomes more and more difficult to live the life that Keihtan has always wanted us to live. In my many dream walks, I saw the shadows and they have frightened me not for myself but for the People. Does this mean that we, the People are doomed? I'm afraid if we remain in the shadows then yes." I paused again, this time to a chorus of shouts and exclamations, many of grief and foreboding.

I could feel the energy of dismay and anger in the air as I purposely drew in more sacred smoke and slowly exhaled, making sure that everyone understood that my words were true.

"Yet my people, in each vision, even those of the darkest shadows, there has always been a glimmer of light on the shadow's edge, a clear message that there is hope, that there is a way around or through the shadows to the other side. That glimmer of light represents a return to the gift of life Keihtan has given the People and has been taught to us by our ancestors. This brings me to speak of the message from Hobomock."

"Hobomock had clearly shown me that there are two paths we the People might choose. One leads far to the north, away from the Awaunuy and a return to the traditional way of living as given to us by Kei-htan. I have seen and visited a northern valley and recognized many of you there. There were also people from other bands, some I did not know. They also embraced this message. All were living in harmony. The second path is to remain in this land of our ancestors and somehow try to maintain our way of life as best we can. I know many of you will make that choice. To leave this land means tearing ourselves away from the only home we have ever known and abandoning the spirits of the ancestors."

"But I must tell you I followed that path into the future and came to Mioonkhtuck at a time when there was no sign of the People, only an Awaunuy world that was frightening and full of strange sights and sounds. It was clear the People were gone." I stopped for a moment as there was a great deal of talking and shouting from the People while the sachems and elders sat in silence, transfixed by what I was saying. "To me the choices are clear. I have seen in the visions that each person and family must choose which path to follow." As I sat, I passed the pipe to Wyandot who motioned for it once he knew I had finished what I wanted to say.

The sachem breathed in smoke then released it. "Ponaim," he said, "I thank you for sharing this message. Your words have great Manitou and the messages given to you by Hobomock must be reflected upon by us all. On each path the visions show the People will walk into the shadows you have seen and therefore great uncertainty. Each of us must decide, as you have said, which is the right path to follow. As Grand Sachem, I want what is best for the People and will support the choice that each makes. However, I will remain here at Mioonkhtuck for I am old but more importantly, I have a responsibility to this place, those who stay, and the ancestors. My days are not long before I join them and I choose to do so here.

Nausup was next to take the pipe and once he had breathed in the sacred smoke and given it back to the Spirit World, he spoke. "Ponaim, I too thank you for bringing to us this message seen in your dream walks. You have always worked for the good of the People and know your heart is good. I agree that we are walking in shadows, I feel and see it every day when together with others we leave Mioonkhtuck or Totoket to hunt and must cross through the fields and pastures of the Awaunuy and travel farther and farther to find the four leggeds we depend on for food, clothing, and life itself. Yet though we are crowded and surrounded by Awaunuy wherever we go, there still are some places here in the land of our ancestors where we can live in the traditional way."

Nausup waited a moment to let his words speak to those gathered before adding, "As you all know, we recently gave the Awaunuy of Guilford the right to settle and use our lands to the north of their village. In the paper they agreed to not prohibit us from hunting and fishing there and I believe they are sincere. The land west of Quonnipaug is too hilly and rocky for their farms and though they have begun to cut some trees, there are still many places where we can set up our weetous and live as Keihtan has instructed. By doing so we do not abandon our ancestors. This may be a choice some of us should follow." Many seemed to agree with Nausup and there was a great deal of talking before he held up his hand to quiet them and seeing that Wampom wanted to speak, passed the pipe to him.

"People, we at Totoket have lived longer with those from across the sea than any. It saddens me to think that those of Montowese and the Upper Quinnipiac are gone, that Mennunkatuck is gone, and that most of our relatives and friends along the Quinnihticut are gone. Yet we at Totoket have been able to survive. Why? Because we learned to live first with the Dutchmannuck when they came to trade and cut the trees, and now with the Awaunuy in Branford town. This was the lesson taught to all the Quinnipiac by my father Qussuckquansh. He would often say to me son, where are the Pequot and others who defied the Awaunuy? Is that the path we the People should follow? He believed that only by finding a way to live with these strange and aggressive people would it be possible to survive. The idea of abandoning the land of our ancestors was something he did not see."

Many who heard his words reacted with shouts that agreed or disagreed and it was clear that just as there were two paths for the People to follow and there were two factions reacting to the words of each who spoke at the council. As I listened and watched, I could tell how divided the People were and in particular how some of the young men like Mequnhut, who sat behind the circle of elders were beginning to react.

Wampom continued. "People, I too see each day how living close to the Awaunuy is changing the way we live and think. I am proud that we have not given ourselves over to their god-talkers and their book as so many other survivors in the Dawnland have. But that may be something that is in the future. The pressure is great to not only accept their god, but to adopt their way of life. That is what I know in my heart the Awaunuy want. Is that what we want? Wampom paused amidst commotion caused by what he had asked.

"Like Wyandot, I am old and Totoket is my home. It is where my bones will lie. But I take to heart the words of Ponaim and the message he has brought to this council. Each of us must choose for I fear that in time those living in this dark shadow caused by the Awaunuy will eventually lose our way of life. For those of us who stay here at Mioonkhtuck and Totoket, we must understand that."

Maug, one of the elders of Mioonkhtuck motioned to Wampom that he would like to speak and the pipe was passed around the circle to him. He took the pipe and brought the sacred smoke into his mouth then exhaling, sent a plume into the branches that formed the roof. "I was just a boy when the Awaunuy came to our land. I remember being enthralled with all that they had and brought with them. To me everything about their world was magical and contained a spirit beyond anything the People had ever known. I was convinced that their ways were a better way and the more I saw the more I wanted to be of their world. As a young man, I even gave into their rum and became a problem for them when drunk as well as for our sachems. For that I am sorry. As you all know, I often try to help those of our young men who still follow that path to try and overcome it."

"I had to learn that their ways are very tempting and it is easy to fall into that trap. Once caught, it is hard to escape. We are like the four leggeds we trap in the winter. There is little chance for escape once you are snared. I for one understand that to remain here at Mioonkhtuck means the end of the People as we are today and in the past. Not because we will die from their diseases, but because all we have left to trade with them is our land. There is nothing else left. We once could trade venison and furs with the Awaunuy for what we thought we needed from them. Where are the four leggeds? They are gone. We are living a life that is increasingly dependent on those across the harbor and they see us increasingly as an irritation like the bite of a mosquito and nothing more. How soon will it be that we have no land left to trade?"

By then the arbor seemed to shake with the voice of every person reacting to what Maug had said. The roar was deafening and I was sure the sound echoed up into the Spirit World. Shambisqua motioned to Maug that she wanted the pipe and it was passed back along the circle to her.

When the pipe of Commossuck reached her, she took it in both hands and as she stood, Shambisqua offered it up to the Spirit World and the ancestors. The People fell silent for Shambisqua carried in her the Manitou of her mother, Shaumpishuh and her lineage going back into time forgotten. She drew in the sacred smoke then exhaled.

"My People, I too have lived a long life and remember the time before the coming of the Awaunuy. I also carry in my heart the loss of so many dear to me including my husband and all but one of my children since the Awaunuy brought the diseases and the many terrible changes to our Earth Mother. Those changes have often caused times of famine which before we had never known. I have witnessed the abandonment of my ancestral home at Mennunkatuck and the lands east of the Kuttawo. The Awaunuy desire for our land will never stop and Ponaim has shared with us the vision that in the future Mioonkhtuck will be no more. I'm sure it will be the same for Totoket."

"Each one of you must decide. Do you want to remain here and at Totoket and try to live alongside the Awaunuy? In that case you condemn you descendants to become as the Awaunuy are and our ways may be lost forever. Do you want to find refuge north as Ponaim's vision shows and live the way Keihtan has always wanted us to live? That will mean following the vision into the unknown and a land that is not ours or that of our ancestors. It is clear to me we each must choose a path." Shambisqua waited serenely as the impact of her words settled in.

"For those of you who do not want to abandon the lands of our ancestors there is one more part of the message Ponaim was given, not by Hobomock, but by the ancestors themselves. She looked at me and asked, "as shaman of the People, can you share that vision?"

As I took the pipe from Shambisqua, I looked into her eyes and saw again that young girl who so often helped and encouraged me to go beyond where I wanted and my heart leapt out to her in thanks. I accepted the pipe and breathed in the sacred smoke and exhaled slowly up to the ancestors asking them to be with me in this moment.

"People, it is true that I have been troubled by the idea of abandoning the land of our ancestors. That led me to a recent journey into the Lower World and the world of Spirits where I visited our ancestors, but not those of memory. They were our People from a time before our time, they were the first People. The land, plants, and animals as well as their lifeways were of a time our legends have always said was just after the ice world had gone. It was a beautiful but strange world to me and I was not sure that in fact I was here in the Dawnland until they brought me to the place of the sacred Split Rock between Totoket and Mennunkatuck." I waited a minute before drawing in the smoke and releasing it as my words caused all to murmur and some to shout out "Manitou!"

"I was embraced and welcomed by a man who wore furs I did not recognize and I could not understand his tongue yet I knew what he was saying.

He led me to the Split Rock which, when I saw it, I nearly wept for I knew this was our home too. Men, women, and children were gathered there and they all welcomed me as if they had known me forever; I was family to them and they were to me, this I knew to be certain. We danced, we sang, we celebrated life and I knew they were our ancestors. When it was time for me to go their message was clear and it brought me to a place of deep understanding. This they told me, would always be our home and that they would be our ancestors, no matter whether or not we lived within this land or not. Wherever we live, they will always be with us as long as we continue to honor them. We are the People and the important thing they said was to keep the traditional ways and view of the world. To lose that they told me, was to lose them."

What I said at first created a silence so soft that I could hear the fire crackle, the birds near the arbor sing, and the trees whisper as the wind blew softly up from the water. Not a person moved, not a person spoke. I stood silently holding the pipe of Commossuck feeling in it his presence and knowing that this was the answer he had always sought but never found. I thanked him as a tear fell from my eye.

After what seemed an eternity, Wyandot asked for the pipe then asked if there were others who would like to speak. Wentubecum motioned that he did and the pipe was passed to him.

"People, like those of us who have seen many snows, I know I will spend my final days here in the land of our ancestors. But I want to speak on behalf of those who are young and whose lives are still before them. You are the ones who will carry with you the ancestors and our way of life into the future. It is plain for us to see that here at Mioonkhtuck and Totoket within your lifetime or that of your children the Awaunuy will swallow what is left of our lands and thus the People. You will be forced to live among them as one of them but always not, for they do not see us as people equal to them. I know this. Like most of you here, I have experienced their contempt and ridicule more times than I can ever recall. I speak to you now; the path you choose will determine the future of all the Quinnipiac. It is a matter of survival. If I were younger, I would not hesitate to go to the north as Ponaim has seen and live as we were always supposed to live according to Keihtan and the Spirits."

The words of Wentubecum resonated with many of the young men and women and their cries and shouts of affirmation were loud and boisterous. The chorus continued until Wentubecum passed the pipe back to Wyandot. The sachem waited as quiet returned before speaking.

"Each of you must search your heart and decide which path you will follow and that we all need to understand that each path is a gift from the Spirit World. For each of us, there is no escape from either path; remain here in the land of the ancestors in the shadow of the Awaunuy or go north to live a traditional but uncertain life to follow the ways of the ancestors.

Chapter Twenty

The next morning, I woke before dawn, feeling both relieved and apprehensive for I knew my sharing of the visions and messages of Hobomock would mean the splintering of the Quinnipiac as a people. It was clear that those who were either too old to leave our ancestral land or too dependent on the Awaunuy and their goods would remain. I also understood that some simply could not leave the home of our ancestors. Others, those who sought to live in a traditional manner, including many of the young, would risk moving north to the unknown valley I had seen in my dream walks with the red-tailed hawk. How many would choose that path I did not know.

I had left the Council Rock shortly after the council had ended, not wanting to speak with others about what had been said. I saw my presence as a distraction since I knew many would seek me out to talk about their future choices. I had confided in Shambisqua that I would leave and told Wambusco and Mequnhut as well. All three understood and recognized that now that the two paths lay before the People, time was needed for all to determine which to follow.

Leaving Mioonkhtuck, I walked northward along our old path following the eastern side of the

Quinnipiac River until reaching the place of the former village of Montowese. The trail was lined with
Awaunuy farms and fields and as I walked I knew I
was seeing the future in the present. In the Awaunuy
village of North Haven, I did draw some attention to
myself just by my presence. A few of the older men
recognized me.

One called out "look, it is the old sorcerer"
while another warned a group of children "do not to
look at him for he will put a curse on you and steal
your soul." I did not understand what they said but I
had known the intent of those words before and continued on my way while two boys threw stones towards me as if to drive me away.

Leaving the village, I left the path and began
to cross some of the fields the Awaunuy had created
before finding myself along a ridge line where I
knew I could find peace away from signs of their
presence. I followed its base to the north until I came
to the Coginchaug and though there were signs of
Awaunuy had been there none were present. By then
it was dusk and I skirted the great swamp to the east
and into the hills that marked the boundary between
the traditional hunting grounds of the People and the
Wangunk before the time of the Awaunuy. In darkness, guided by Mother Moon, I found my destination, a place of powerful spiritual presence since time
began;   the   great   Coginchaug   Cave.   Like

Commossuck had before me, I had often sought refuge and guidance there. I made a fire and ate some of the food that Shambisqua had packed for me before I had left Mioonkhtuck. She knew why I was leaving and is the only one I told of my destination.

Tired from my journey, I put down my sleeping robe near the fire which was under the great overhanging rock which formed the canopy that had provided shelter for our ancestors going back to the time of the first People. In the distance in front of me, a wolf called and was answered by another quite close behind the rock shelter. This gave me comfort for I knew I was not alone and that the four legged brothers and sisters would keep watch in the night. The shelter was remote and of little interest to the Awaunuy in an area dominated by stone ledges and ridges, a place where all creatures could find safety from their increasing reach. I slept soundly.

In the morning I constructed a shelter by leaning poles against the wall of the overhang as the ancestors had close to where I had made the fire and covered them with deer hides Shambisqua had given me when I had told her where I was going.

"It is a place of great spiritual energy Ponaim. I know it will help you on your vision quest. But I worry because I get a sense it is one that you may not return from" she said with a sincere tone that she had

always used when voicing concern over my well-being.

"It is a vision quest and dream walk I have no choice but to make. Keihtan and Hobomock have called me and I must make this journey to see and understand the ultimate fate of the People" was my reply to my dearest friend as I took her hands in mine. "I do so with a heavy heart for I fear the worst. Maybe the shadows will not be overcome."

"Perhaps this old woman can come with you and tend the fire and watch over you while you seek the answers" Shambisqua proposed. "Besides Mi-oonkhtuck grows heavy on my spirit."

I thanked her and agreed that I would have liked nothing better than to have her company but this was something I had to do alone. So here I was.

Below the shelter in a narrow valley lying be-tween it and a tall, stony ridge directly across was a small spring fed stream where I brought my water bladder to fill with fresh water. I was to begin a two day fast and would have only water before the vision journey began. During that time I would chant sacred sounds and use my small handheld drum to alert the Spirit World of my coming and intention.

As I returned to the rock shelter, I thought about the stories Commossuck had told me about this place; how it was a powerful gateway into the Lower World and that it was in the past a place of ritual and ceremony, especially during times of trouble. That is why he said, it should only be used under those circumstances. I had accompanied him here only once although I knew he had been here other times. I had not come to the great shelter in many years, the last time was when I sought help in healing those at Totoket who were sick from the disease the Awaunuy call influenza. In that journey I had been given a mix of plants and roots as a remedy. It did help many.

For two days, I sat and chanted, sang, prayed, and drummed to let the Spirit World know that I was preparing for an important dream walk where they might allow me the vision to see the future for the People. I told them in my prayers that this question troubled my soul and that my spirit could not rest until I could understand. As Father Sun rose on the third day, bathing the rock shelter with light and warmth, I was ready to begin. I spread my sleeping robe on a high spot just outside the overhang, sat, and closed my eyes.

As I passed into a dream walk, I experienced the buzzing sound that announced the arrival of my guide, the red-tailed hawk and together we began the journey. I had asked the Spirits to show me the future of the People and we quickly flew through a bank of clouds before we came to a small village of maybe ten weetous nestled near a pond which I recognized was in the western part of the land Nausup had given to the Awaunuy of Guilford.

As we circled the village I suddenly found myself on the ground and standing by the edge of the pond. The village was behind me and as I turned to look towards it an elderly woman approached me with the kindest face and expression I have ever seen. Everything about her being expressed a welcoming love that I immediately understood. I was with the People, but this was not the present. She wore clothing of Awaunuy cloth and had a beautiful, embroidered blanket wrapped around her shoulders. Her hair was gray and pulled tightly back in the way of our women and she had a smile from ear to ear while her brown eyes sparkled.

"I was told you were coming by the Spirits but not when" she said in our tongue with a bit of glee in her voice. "My name is Hannah. Shambisqua and Shaumpishuh were my ancestors though many, many generations ago. I know you knew them both." Hannah waited a moment before continuing, noticing how her words had caused me to react in surprise.

"I am Ponaim, powwow of the People" I said, not knowing what else to say. "You are of the People; you speak our tongue. I believe I know this place but not the village."

"Oh, I know who you are Ponaim. Your name has been given to us in stories passed down from generation to generation. They tell of how you helped the People to choose the path and had worked all your life for their good. We know also that you were taught by the great shaman Commossuck. We still tell the stories to the young ones, though there are now only just a handful."

"Is this the village of Nausup?" I asked.

"Yes Ponaim, we have lived here now for over 100 snows. Nausup brought a few families from Mioonkhtuck and Totoket here, along with some Paugassett and Niantic. We have survived but as you can see, there are not many of us left and we live on the edge of what you called the Awaunuy. Those people call themselves Americans now, a separate people from the Awaunuy having fought a war to free themselves many years ago."

"So that is what happened. An Awaunuy in my time named William told me they wanted to live their own way and that their king was upset and an-gry" I replied which brought a smile to her face.

"Ponaim, the Spirits have directed me to tell you about the People and what has happened to us since you showed the paths that should be followed," said Hannah. I am afraid it is a story full of sadness." She paused. "We have been taught about your vi-sions and the shadows over Dawnland. Let us sit by the water and we can speak of the years since you shared those visions."

A bit overwhelmed by what Hannah had said, I began to grasp in this dream walk that I was in a place where a small remnant of the People had somehow managed to survive alongside a pond that had once been part of our Mennunkatuck lands.

"Hannah, thank you. In my heart I had always been worried that the Awaunuy world would in the end completely erase that of the People, even if they began to live in their way. Is that what happened?"

"That is part of the story powwow. I can tell you of the two paths you prophesied and the way in which each was travelled. Then there was this village on the pond, it became the third path for a small number" Hannah said.

"Are you a shaman?" I asked, unsure if she was a spirit or a person.

"Some call me that though since the Americans insist that such practices are inspired by their Devil I call myself a medicine woman. Because I use the plants from Earth Mother to heal even them, they do not bother me. Besides, most of our people go now to the Christian church on Sunday."

"What is a Sunday? Is it the seventh day when Awaunuy used to gather in their spirit house?" I asked. "The Awaunuy always tried to have the People walk that path but we did not do so even when others in the Dawnland did" I added with a touch of pride.

"Yes, they call it their holy day. They have convinced most of those still living in the Dawnland to worship their god and become Christians. That is what the spiritual belief brought here by your Awaunuy is called. It has made it easier to live in the shadows where we are not bothered by them. Although most have accepted their ways, there are still a few of us who try to maintain the old beliefs as best we can." Hannah looked at me with a sadness in her eyes before continuing.

"It is a hard time."

Neither of us spoke for a while as we looked out onto the pond. It was obvious that Hannah and these few with her were all that remained of the People here in the land of our ancestors. Wanting to know more, I asked "how many are in this village Hannah and where are they now?"

"There are twenty three Ponaim, they are here but you cannot see them and they cannot see you and I for we are in the Spirit World."

"Yes of course" was my reply. "Can you tell me of Mioonkhtuck? I had visited it well into the future and saw no sign of the People."

"The village at Mioonkhtuck is no more. The Awaunuy and then the Americans swallowed it up piece by piece. Some of us do return once a year to the Council Rock for a celebration but the American who owns the land is threatening to prevent us. He says that some of the men get drunk and cause trouble."

"So Hannah, there are others still living besides here?" I asked expectantly.

"Yes Ponaim, there are some scattered throughout the American towns. They live as the Americans do and try to blend in and not be noticed. Some have married non-Indians, even the Americans with black skin. After many generations, many of their children have no idea they have the blood of the People in them."

"Are there others?" I asked, afraid of the answer. "What of those who followed the path to the north I saw in my visions?"

"They did go to the north Ponaim, some fifty left soon after the Grand Council at which you shared the vision. They were led by some of the young men including a young shaman but I do not recall his name. It has been said that he was the last powwow and died during the Awaunuy war against the French."

"Did they find the valley in the north I saw in my journeys?" apprehensive yet needing to know the answer.

"We have always been told they did. According to legend, they stayed one year with the Tunxis before travelling north into the land of the Mahican. There they joined together with some of that tribe as well as others who came from throughout the Dawnland. They lived a traditional way just as in your vision."

"What happened Hannah? I sense in what you have said they are no longer."

"It has been passed down to us that eventually they were caught up in one of the wars between the Awaunuy, who we call English, and the French from Canada far to the north. The two were fighting for control of the land and used the Indian people to fight. It is said that the friends of the French, the Huron and Abenaki, attacked them and swept them away. They are no more though maybe some of their descendants live with those people but do not know they are Quinnipiac."

"What of Totoket? Does that village still exist?"

"They faced the same fate as those at Mioonkhtuck. They did manage to remain for a number of years but they too sold off their land piece by piece and eventually there was none left. By then most had moved on, some joined the Tunxis, some the Naugatuck, who eventually went to live as a new people called the Schaghticoke to the northwest in the mountains here in Connecticut.

I understood then that many of the surviving People had in fact been scattered just as Commossuck, Pawquash, and I had seen in the vision the night before the ceremony at Mashup's Rock. The sparks from the fire had blown upon the People and forced them to scatter in many directions. The vision had revealed the fate of the People after all. I believe Commossuck knew this was to happen but never gave up hope that it might not be true.

What Hannah also told me of the People giving up our beliefs to adopt those of the Awaunuy saddened me greatly. This struck me as particularly upsetting because to lose the world view and beliefs in the Spirit World of the ancestors took away from the People the very essence of who they were. Perhaps they found solace and comfort in the new way but this meant the People were no longer who we once were. It hurt me to acknowledge this.

"So many of our surviving people gave up our beliefs and adopted those of the Awaunuy" I stated in disbelief. "Once they did, many must have left the land of our ancestors."

"This is true" Hannah confirmed. "Many also joined the Christian Indian Movement and moved with others from the Dawnland first to the north to a place called Stockbridge and later to the lands of the Mohawk and Oneida. Years later they moved again to lands beyond the big lakes far to the west. There may be descendants there."

So much of what Hannah had told was certainly not what I wanted to hear yet the reality of her words could not be avoided and they broke my heart. In the end there was no escaping the dark shadows that fell across the Dawnland. First small pockets of the People survived but most were absorbed into larger groups of people who like them, sought to survive. Yet they lost their way of life and even the belief system that had allowed them to exist for countless generations. Perhaps, I wanted to believe, wherever the children of the Quinnipiac lived, there were still a number who clung to a sense of who they are and their history.

Hannah could see I was troubled and took my hand. "Ponaim, all life comes to an end yet is reborn again, maybe not in a way we understand, but it does. You have spent your entire life working for the good of the People despite tremendous odds. The English brought to this shore a way of life and numbers that in the end overwhelmed us and made our way of life impossible to continue. But there are enough survivors, though scattered, who may be able to keep our memory alive." She sighed. "As long as we are remembered, we will never disappear. For that matter nor will the memory of our ancestors."

"But what of your people here? Will they be able to continue?" I asked with a great deal of trepidation.

"I am afraid for us; it is a matter of time. The people of Guilford covet this pond and are already making plans to cut the trees and settle the land on the opposite shore. Like others of the People, we will be forced to live among other survivors, maybe the Mohegan, Pequot, or the Schaghticoke. They are made up of refugees from many broken bands including some Quinnipiac."

"In this way all is not lost" was my response. "In these groups the memory might continue."

I was shaken to my core at what I had learned. Yes, the People were overwhelmed by the shadows and a handful of survivors scattered to gather together with others. It turns out they were the glimmer of light I always saw in my visions, dwelling on the very edge of the darkness. I wept as Hannah held me. Then she was gone.

I found myself back at the rock shelter and opened my eyes. Standing before me was Shambisqua and she could tell from the look on my face that the future was troubling and grim.

"Ponaim," my friend said, "you have never been able to keep a secret from me. You must tell me what you have seen. When you are ready."

I wept again.

Glossary

People and Place Names
The following were recorded as residing in Guilford Ct (Mennunkatuck) in 1639 by the Whitfield Company or later by English in New Haven:

Shaumpishuh: *The female sachem or sunksquaw*
Nashump: *Husband of Shaumpishuh*
Shambisqua: *Daughter of Shaumpishuh and Nashump*
Nausup: *Son of Shaumpishuh and Nashump*
Kehow: *Son of Shaumpishuh and Nashump*

Actual Residents of Mennunkatuck:
Commossuck *(portrayed as shaman at Mennunkatuck)*
Meishunk *(portrayed as Mennunkatuck hunter)*
Mequnhut *(portrayed as son of Shambisqua)*
Ponaim *(portrayed as Quinnipiac shaman)*
Wantumbecum *(portrayed as Mennunkatuck hunter)*
Apoawein *(portrayed as friend of Mequnhut)*

Sachems of the Quinnipiac as recorded by the English:
Qussuckquansh: *sachem at Totoket*
Montowese: *sachem of the Upper Quinnipiac*

Momauguin: *chief sachem at Mioonkhtuck*
Wayhanatt: *son of Momauguin, chief sachem at Mioonkhtuck*
Wompom: *Son of Qussuckquansh, sachem at Totoket*

Other sachems and others:
Sassacus: *chief sachem of the Pequot*
Uncas: *chief sachem of the Mohegan*
Weequash: *sachem of the Eastern Niantic*
Sowheage: *sachem of the Wangunk*
Nahuntoway: *sachem of the Paugussett*
Sassious: *sachem of the Western Niantics*
Oweneco: *son of Uncas*
Nawatokis: *son of Nahuntoway (portrayed as husband of Shambisqua)*
Pawquash: *member of Montowese band (portrayed as Montowese Band shaman)*
Maug: *resident of Mioonkhtuck*
Wambusco: *resident of Mioonkhtuck (portrayed as shaman at Mioonkhtuck)*
Rum Tom: *resident of Mioonkhtuck*
Auquansh: *resident of Mennunkatuck (portrayed as older Totoket warrior)*
Tispaquin: *resident of Mennunkatuck (portrayed as shaman at Mioonkhtuck)*

Place Names in Connecticut:
Mennunkatuck: *Guilford*

Totoket: *Branford*
Mioonkhtuck: *East Haven/New Haven*
Upper Quinnipiac: *North Haven/Wallingford*
Mattabasec: *Middletown*
Pyqaug: *Wethersfield*
Sicaug: *Hartford*
Coginchaug: *Durham/Middlefield*
Mistick: *Mystic*

Rivers and Geographic Features:
Quinnihticut: *Connecticut River*
Quinnipiac: *Quinnipiac River*
Kuttawo: *East River (Guilford/Madison)*
Quonnipaug: *Lake Quonnipaug (Guilford)*
Face of Hobomock: *Bluff Head (Guilford)*
Spirit Line: *Hamonasset Line (Saybrook to Bluff Head)*

European Names:
Awaunuy: *Quinnipiac name for English, translates to "coat wearers"*
Dutchmannuck: *Algonkian (Narragansett) name for Dutch*

Other Words:
Wampum: *Beads made from whelk and clam shells strung together in belts*

James T. Powers

Weetou: *Circular shaped houses made of a saplin-
frame and covered with straw mats or bark*